ADVANCE READER PRAISE

Rio Cyborg is a fun book. A classic western story with science fiction flavor… it was entertaining and I am interested in reading the next one.

Rio Cyborg surprised me - the book is a very enjoyable read with relatable characters and a positive, uplifting plot. At about 230 pages of prose it took 3 days of casual reading to get through. Since I wasn't familiar with either author, I was also surprised at how well the book was written, with clear motivations, enough context and back-story to make things interesting, and a fulfilling ending.

Rio Cyborg reads more like a lighthearted Louis L'Amour western, with a bit of Firefly thrown in, than it does a science fiction novel. The SciFi provides some input as to why the various cyborg characters have the skills they do with cybernetic enhancements boosting strength and the senses. It also explains that they are considered inferior to unaugmented humans through discrimination and a lack of basic human rights (why many become outlaws I guess, scrabbling to survive) - these cyborgs were sent to planets to establish settlements and do much of the hard work prior to human settlers being shipped in as colonists. In general most of the cowhands and law enforcement characters are 'borg.

I delighted in the story and had fun in the reading.

It is a fun read that combines two genres for an interesting and novel story. It's NOT "O K Corral with Ray guns" but a genuine Western with advanced tech. The storyline plays well and is very realistic. I could easily see several well-known actors portraying Zestrum. Fun challenge: see how many western movie and series Character names you can spot.

The story is well-developed, following a renowned but soft-spoken cyborg colonization-engineer as he arrives in Copperbank after a job offer, neatly foils a highway robbery on his way in, gets quietly drawn into local struggles around water distribution and the rich rancher controlling most of it, meets the local boarding house proprietor, helps out the local Sheriff, and generally lays a foundation for what could be an entertaining series of sequels to follow. If the authors do continue the series, I'll very likely pick 'em up.

Rio Cyborg is a fun, quick-paced story with a bit of a sci-fi twist in a setting that I found mostly reads as western. There were times when reading that I nearly forgot the sci-fi components of the book's world and felt completely immersed in its western flavor, though the cyborg body modifications and anti-cyborg prejudice lent fresh material to action sequences, generated thematically useful conflict, and allowed the story to feel fresh even as it leaned into common western tropes for many of its key plot elements.

Most of the plot will not be greatly surprising to anyone with even a passing familiarity with westerns, but the authors satisfyingly tied up all of the key loose ends while leaving enough juicy threads dangling to leave me excited for the next two books in a planned trilogy… if you enjoy sci-fi or westerns, settle in for some pleasant and fun literary comfort food.

Rio Cyborg is a little sci-fi, a little old west. This is the first book of a trilogy and I am looking forward to reading the second and third book!

The characters are likable and well-rounded in description, at least the good guys are likeable. The bad guys are not so nice.

Rio Cyborg is a fun and easy read. If you like westerns, you will like this. There are little eggs of information that will hopefully expand the world in the future installments- such as a teletype from 1880 next to a 1920's typewriter. I would love to see how this world was devised and explore who/how this society was put together. I hope Baker and Willey give us more information.

Action...action.....action...can't wait for book 2....hopefully the Etcheverry's get what they deserve. Seems as though little Johnny has taken a turn for the better. And sounds like Zestrum and Jessica may have a future. Can' wait to find out what happens next. My dad watched a lot of westerns when I was a kid and before he died I watched a lot of the re-runs with him, he would have loved this book.

If a western and a sci fi story had a baby, with a diesel punk godfather lurking around ...

The plot of *Rio Cyborg* is basically the western; the setting is the science fiction. And the title is a clear allusion to the movie Rio Bravo, which contributes a lot of obvious elements to the plot ... like pretty much most of it. But it was a good movie and it's fun to see it reimagined.

Rio Cyborg is a very quick read, more like a pilot to what is obviously intended as a series. The cyborg protagonist is interesting with a somewhat mysterious background that this book doesn't really delve into. I initially expected a gunslinger character, but what little we've been shown so far doesn't go in that direction. That's a good thing, less cliché.

There's a town of colorful characters and the start of a romance. The world-building is intriguing, though minimal in this first book.

All in all, I'd say this is a rather light bit of summer fare that manages to be more engaging than I anticipated.

Interesting twist on the Western genre. The lead character is a cyborg on a colonized planet. He becomes involved in a local feud over water rights. Several secondary characters who hopefully will be built up in future books. His landlady at the boarding house whom he starts an affair with. Another cyborg living at the boarding house who has his eye on the local school teacher. And of course all of the protagonists.

Rio Cyborg reads as a light western with some oddities thrown in, it has its cowboys and cowborgs, gunfights and love interests. Many of the minor characters have names taken out of old western movies and tv shows, although that is as far as the similarity goes. The book is a light and enjoyable read.

BOOK 1 IN THE COPPERBANK TRILOGY

RIO CYBORG

BY

CAROL BAKER AND TERRY WILLEY

CineHunden

r25-1117

TABLE OF CONTENTS

CAST OF CHARACTERS

Zestrum (Tom) Doniphon – a cyborg mercenary, former engineer/landscaper for the Consortium, a good man with a bad reputation who seeks peace after Emancipation. He comes to Copperbank for a job offer as ranch hand and finds a water war instead.

THE LAW

Mitch Bodie – the Sheriff of Copperbank, an old friend of Zestrum. He considers his job token law enforcement, but maintains law and order the best he can. He's an older cyborg whose body and pride have sustained injury.

Deputy Ethan Edwards – a Vestal addicted cyborg attempting to hold onto his sanity and his job as deputy. Once a good man, now he struggles to be a man.

Deputy Puzzle – the old timer cyborg, he has a gammy leg but is feisty as hell. Good with a rifle, better with a verbal barb.

Louisiana Hannigan – a gunslinging cyborg, gambler, smartass but reliable. He worked security on the Eastern Seaboard, but his origins are mysterious.

THE ENTERTAINMENT

Doug McConnell – owner of the popular casino showroom bar, the Dual Majesty Saloon. He works closely with the Etcheverry clan but would like to work more closely with Angie.

Victoria Barkley – a beautiful cyborg songbird. She is the featured performer at the Dual Majesty, singer, dancer, and high-class saloon employee.

COLTON HOUSE

Jessica Colton – owner of the Colton House boardinghouse, Zestrum's landlady. She's a widow who's lost her entire family and figured she'd remain single. Zestrum's arrival might change her mind.

THE RANCHERS

Claude Etcheverry – a prosperous landowner who has dammed the river running through his property so he can charge exorbitant prices to townsfolk for water. He dominates the Badlands like a foul fog.

Chris Etcheverry – Claude's oldest son, 30. He likes to gamble, whore, and fight. He's constantly in trouble and bailed out by his family influence.

Angie Etcheverry – Claude's daughter, 25, de facto lady of the house. She carries on the tradition of putting the family interests above all else.

Gabriel Etcheverry – Claude's son, 20. A passive-aggressive bully dedicated to satisfying his own needs. More likely to set your house on fire than call you out to fair fight.

Johnny Etcheverry – Claude's hothead son, 14, who has always been a pain in the ass to everyone. He becomes fixated on Zestrum, which may get him killed.

Gerald Nowlin – a wealthy landowner of the Easterbrook Ranch. He is on the brink of all-out war to get back the water Claude has stolen from him.

Aaliyah Nowlin – Gerald's wife. An expert in raising Blanken Ox, she's frequently on the range with the ranch hands tending the cattle. She doesn't want war, but sometimes you have to take a stand.

Rachel Nowlin – their daughter, 26, a formidable partner managing the ranch. She oversees the chicken coops, selling eggs and roasters to markets and neighbors.

THE LOCALS

Doc Tim Hartman – Copperbank's physician who treats humans and cyborgs but is not proficient in all cyborg tech. He's a good general practitioner and a competent surgeon. He's tired of the dying.

Ephraim Judd, Esquire – the shrewd attorney representing the Etcheverry family. Land grabs, murder raps, and bribery are among his specialties.

Harris Black – the editor of *The Copperbank Sentinel*. Claude Etcheverry's advertising dollars keep him in business. He's always eager to get a juicy story even if the facts aren't 100 percent accurate.

CHAPTER 1 – THE HIGHWAYBOY

The shadows grasped at the endless strip of highway ahead of Zestrum as the sun sank low into the ridge of mountains behind him. He felt Shiloh twitch with apprehension as they rode through the gentle foothills in the sprawling Interior. The sky was darkening overhead but there was more to the dusk.

The road ahead was long and lonely. Not that he minded. He'd been alone for days since leaving the last town and heading toward the next. One more day to reach his destination.

Sometimes solitude was a blessing.

A faint boom activated his electromagnetic field perception and neuro-linked tactical vision augments. He looked the direction of the sound and saw colors. Not the colors of Earth, the colors of Blanken 9—the Iridescents that only appeared in the auroras on this planet.

Thunder rolled over the expanse from a long distance, but he knew what those colors were—lightning. In this odd atmosphere, lightning blazed in brilliant colors, not just blues and whites and greens, but reds and purples and browns and the spectrum beyond those hues.

Some said it was the high dust mineral content in the atmosphere that colored the air. Some believed it was caused by the purification of the planet when scientists tried to eliminate all the natural life and so many things were dusted that life became most unnatural.

Lightning like that meant a storm was brewing in the distant mountains to the north.

That downslope wind would be upon him in an hour. The reduced visibility and decreased air quality would make travel impossible. Being caught in the gale would at the least injure him and Shiloh, and at the worst kill them and leave him a pile of bones and rusting metal in the desert sand.

Already this journey was playing with a cold deck.

Scanning the surroundings, his augmented reality overlays indicated the nearby hills might be the place to ride out the storm. If a person could cram down into the nooks and crannies, the rock could protect him from the elements.

A cave would be even better. The early days of mining had left a lot of hollows in the mountainsides. While he possessed nano-lung adaptations to filter toxic environments, Shiloh did not. Walls of granite and stone would be safer shelter against particulates and electrocution.

He urged Shiloh toward the foothills, using enhanced optics to locate a suitable spot to spend the night.

This was one of those days where everything that *could* go wrong *did* go wrong. His instincts were telling him to cut and run, but he was curious.

The night was long and unpleasant.

***

The next morning Zestrum ate a minimal protein breakfast, extinguished the shadow fire, and cleaned up the temporary campsite, leaving no trace of his overnight stay. He led Shiloh out of the cave as the sun rose, revealing an aquamarine sky.

The long highway wound down the treacherous mountainside in steep grades and switchbacks. At the valley floor the road straightened and aimed due east through a barren landscape. Two hours later, eucalyptus trees appeared on the verges, signs of civilization. Many settlements in the Interior planted trees along the road to indicate trade markets and valuable water ahead.

A vague image in the distance caught his enhanced vision. Zestrum would have thought the covered wagon had merely broken down in the middle of the road if not for the man aiming a gun at a couple in the road.

He sighed. *Humans.*

Often he forgot he was more human than machine. Of course, most humans considered him more machine than human—once they figured out there were improvements under that dark hair and rugged good looks.

With his enhanced auditory modifications, he heard the conversation from half a mile away as he approached the wagon on horseback.

"Give me that box," said a male voice—a young voice.

"Put down the gun."

"Toss it down."

"It'll break."

"Toss it down!"

He heard a wooden box striking the dirt highway and something breaking. A quiet sob.

"Take it and go."

"What else you got in the wagon?"

"Nothing of value. All the money's in the box."

"Move back. Put your hands up."

Zestrum steered his horse through the shadows of the eucalyptus trees lining the highway. The trees were a nice windbreak; a splash of green in an otherwise beige landscape; and a cool respite from the fierce Blanken 9 sun, more penetrating than the sunlight of Earth. His horse Shiloh was shod with muffle iron, so his hoof beats faded noiselessly into the quiet morning.

A quick enhanced scan of the area revealed a horse tied in the shade of the trees off the shoulder of the highway. No doubt the thief's getaway plan.

Zestrum halted behind the wagon and dropped to the ground, hearing the rummaging within the canvas cover as the thief tossed things around, shattering more property.

The couple stood in the middle of the road, watching helplessly as the bandit grew increasingly violent with their belongings. The man wore simple jeans, shirt, and hat. The woman wore a faded green dress and straw bonnet. Homesteaders, from the looks of them.

First the man, then the woman, noticed Zestrum. Zestrum placed a finger to his lips to order silence, then gestured them away from the wagon. They quickly retreated to the line of eucalyptus trees on the other side of the highway.

Zestrum crept to the front of the wagon and gauged the interloper's next move. Footsteps stomped around in the bed, then toward the front. A minute later the thief climbed over the bench, his back toward Zestrum, his attention fixed on the couple in the shade. Seeing they'd moved, he faltered, then stood his full height to glare at them.

He was a kid, not more than 14, dressed in expensive dusty denim jeans, linen shirt, and leather vest. He had an expensive hat, too, and a Ginwalt pistol in his gun belt. More firepower than a 14-year-old needed.

"That's it? That's all you got?" The kid pointed at the wrecked box in the road.

The box was polished mahogany trimmed in pearl, carved with intricate designs, the kind of chest a woman stored her precious mementoes in.

"That's all the money," said the man.

The kid hopped down and pulled the gun. "Looks like I'll have to search you. You first, mister, then the lady."

The woman clung to the man, terrified.

The man wrapped the woman protectively in his arms. "You got no call to do that."

"You settlers always hide your money where you think nobody will look." The kid strode boldly toward them, brandishing the fancy gun.

He was halfway across the highway when Zestrum caught up to him from behind. Zestrum pushed him forward and the kid flopped face-first into the road, losing the weapon. Zestrum kicked the gun out of reach and planted his boot in the kid's back, pinning him to the ground.

"Hey!" was all he got out before Zestrum levered his weight to shove the brat's face into the dirt so he sputtered and gasped for breath.

The man and woman watched the takedown with a combination of fear and gratitude.

"You folks might want to move along," Zestrum said.

The woman darted to the wagon and climbed onto the bench.

The man stowed the broken box in the boot, sat beside the woman, and snatched up the reins. "Thanks, mister." In the next minute, the team of horses was moving at a rapid clip.

Zestrum immobilized the squirming cursing delinquent until the wagon was well underway. He considered his options.

The kid was obviously experienced at robbing folks—he showed no remorse in confronting the couple; he forced them to damage their own property in his demand for valuables; and he threatened violence to terrorize them. Typical punk.

He was a teenager, but some teenagers were hard-core felons. This one was well-dressed, so he either came from money or was successful at thieving.

In any case, he needed a lesson in humility.

"You treated those folks poorly. I'm not talking about the robbin', I'm talking about your manners." Zestrum pressed on his back until he was flailing. "Don't move." He lifted his foot and the kid scrambled to get up. He kicked his ass, flattening him on the ground again. "Don't move."

The kid lay still, fuming. "You're gonna be sorry!"

"Only if I have to give you another lesson." Zestrum whistled and Shiloh trotted to him. He uncoiled a length of rope from the saddle and proceeded to tie the kid's ankles together.

"Hey!" Again the kid scrambled to rise.

Zestrum lifted his bound feet, knocking him onto his chest and forearms. A series of catastrophic curses tumbled out of the kid's mouth.

Zestrum shook his head. "Bad manners and a foul mouth. This is just the kinda thing that gets you tied up and left somewhere."

He tightened the knots, then flipped the kid onto his back and swiftly tied the other end of the rope around his wrists. The kid attempted to sock him and earned an elbow to the chin. Dazed, the kid watched in horror as Zestrum tied his wrists to his knees with about a dozen elaborate knots.

Zestrum fetched the horse tied under the trees and led him over. He noticed the fine black leather saddle and bridle with beautiful hand-carved tooling and silver decoration.

"What are you doing with my horse?"

"What do you think I'm doing with your horse?" Zestrum found a nice length of rope on the saddle and used that to secure more knots around the kid's knees and ankles.

"What are you doing? Let me go!" On and on. It was amusing more than anything else. Demanding to be released like he had any power in this situation.

"My pa is going to *kill* you! *Kill* you!"

Zestrum tethered the kid's horse to Shiloh with a lead rope.

The kid stopped struggling, watching with open rage. "You can't take my horse! That's a felony!"

"So's robbin' people, but here we are."

He glowered and struggled against the ropes, flopping onto his side and churning up dust.

"That'll tighten the knots." Zestrum scooped up the Ginwalt and tucked it into his saddlebag.

"That's my gun!"

"That makes two felonies for me and one for you. You're falling behind." Zestrum mounted his horse.

"Do you know who I am?"

"Don't wanna know." He clicked his tongue and Shiloh started down the highway with the kid's horse in tow. With his enhanced hearing, he enjoyed the curses for a good ten minutes before the shrieking voice faded in the bright sunlight.

* * *

Six miles on he came upon his destination, the town of Copperbank. As with most settlements in the Badlands, there was a large cemetery on the outskirts of the incorporated city, a church on a hill, and then the city proper. This municipality was laid out in a nice grid pattern, straight streets, five blocks wide, six long, with businesses and residences mixed throughout.

The highway connected directly to Main Street, the major thoroughfare through the center of town. There was the general store and a saloon opposite each other. On the next block the sheriff's office was between the barber and the post office. On the following block stood the courthouse and other government offices. In the Civic Square a big round clock kept time.

Outside the post office, Zestrum tied the horses to the hitching post. He removed the lead rope from the kid's horse and tucked the confiscated gun in the saddlebag. Once the kid untangled the ropes from his wrists—an easy job—he'd have to untangle the complicated knots around his knees and ankles—a much more challenging chore. He might be at it half the day. Then he'd have to walk to town.

That thought made Zestrum smile.

Inside the post office, he waited his turn to speak to the postmaster about a message left for him from one Claude Etcheverry.

"What's the name?" said the postmaster.

"Zestrum Doniphon."

The postmaster's eyes widened in recognition as he involuntarily took a step back. He checked his wall of box slots. He plucked out an envelope and handed it over. "Mr. Zestrum Doniphon."

"Thanks."

"Any message in return?"

"I'll deliver it myself. Is there a hotel round here you recommend?"

"There's the Gem on Fourth Street. The Sapphire on Regent. The Opal on Seventh. Then there's Colton House on Regent and Sixth. It's a little nicer."

"A *lot* nicer," said the woman in line awaiting service. "The Widow Colton is a good housekeeper. Runs a clean house."

Zestrum tipped his hat to her. "Thanks, ma'am. I do like a clean house." And to the postmaster. "Thanks." He crossed the lobby, opened the envelope, and read the note. Instructions where to meet with the man who wanted to hire him.

Better to get that done now.

He stepped into the street and approached Shiloh. From outside he could hear the postmaster whisper to the woman: "That's *the* Zestrum Doniphon."

"Mister!"

His mods activated, his hand automatically seeking his weapon until he identified the man who'd been driving the wagon on the highway. He relaxed his hand.

The man hurried to him and stopped at a respectful distance. "I saw you pass by and I come to thank you again. My wife—she was damn scared—and I won't lie, I was too."

"It was no trouble."

"That kid popped out from nowhere and scared the hell out of us. We're damn lucky you came along. And damn grateful."

"I'm glad I could help out."

"You gotta let us repay you somehow." He pulled paper money from his pocket.

Zestrum shook his head. "Once a man stopped and helped me. I'm just paying it forward. Someday you'll help somebody."

The man pocketed the money. "I'm mighty obliged. What's your name, sir?" He reached out a hand.

"Doniphon." He shook the man's hand.

"Thanks, Mr. Doniphon. I'm Will Benjamin. And I won't forget what you done for us."

"Take care." Although he was thinking, *Most folks don't have much of a memory.* Zestrum mounted up and steered Shiloh to the north.

* * *

Zestrum rode the seven miles to the Etcheverry ranch, noting the industry going on throughout the property. Farming, fishing in the reservoir above the dam in the river, and cattle in grassy meadows. Lush grass and flowers.

And around a hundred Blanken Ox in a security field.

Blanken Ox were one of the few native species that were exempted from the planetary sterilization program. They were larger than the biggest earth ox and their meat was savory. They had to be pastured behind electrified steel bars as the males could walk right through barbed wire and when provoked, walk through the wall of a house.

One of the things that provoked them was pasturing them behind electrified steel fences.

And that was just the males. The females were even angrier and tougher.

At the homestead there were a dozen cowborgs, some cleaning the place, some working the cattle, a few standing around looking hostile. All armed to the teeth and watching him with suspicion. One in particular looked familiar, someone Zestrum encountered on the coast at the start of the landscaping years ago.

Half of these hired folk wore apparel more suitable for gunplay than ranch work. Their weapons looked more appropriate for enforcers than wranglers. There was the occasional military issue Variable Cartridge Pacifier (VCP), a particularly nasty weapon that was illegal outside of combat.

That was a bad bode for peaceful employment on this range.

One of the women was built for speed, which was not as much fun as it sounds. Her mods improved her reaction time and quickness. She'd tire quickly, but for a few minutes she could be the deadliest borg in the group.

Zestrum hoped she didn't have Deadeye. And that he'd never have to square off against her.

Zestrum dismounted and declined to tie up Shiloh. The horse was smart enough not to wander.

One of the cowborgs was staring at him. "Hey, are you. . .?"

"Probably not."

The cowborg turned to another hand and whispered. "That's *the* Zestrum Doniphon!"

A woman wearing buckskin trousers, a linen blouse, and a cowboy hat noticed him. She looked like she could chop up a man with her eyes. "Can I help you, mister?"

He held up the invitation. "I'm here to see Claude Etcheverry."

"And you are?"

"Zestrum Doniphon."

Her expression changed from mistrust to hospitality. "Welcome to the Etcheverry Ranch, Mr. Doniphon. My father tells me you're the kind of man we need around here."

"Looks like you've got plenty of folks like me already." He glanced round at the cowborgs, then looked at her.

She smirked. "We can always use a better one. I'm Angie Etcheverry." She extended a hand and shook firmly.

Her self-confidence impressed him. His keen eye judged she wasn't much over 25, but she was de facto lady of the house.

"Come in." She ushered him into a fine ranch house and directed him to a large salon. She provided a glass of cold water, then went to fetch the patriarch.

Zestrum noticed a bunch of framed photographs on the mantel, obviously family pictures of the patriarch, his daughter, his sons—and the hothead kid from the highway. *Damn.*

"Mr. Doniphon?"

He turned as the rancher entered the room.

"Claude Etcheverry." He was a barrel-chested man, middle-aged, tough as nails, and accustomed to getting his way. They shook hands. Claude was appraising Zestrum from the get-go. "Thanks for coming all the way out here to talk."

"Well, it's not every day a man is offered such good pay for ranch work."

Claude weighed Zestrum equating himself with a human. "Or a cyborg."

He acknowledged that with a cynical smile. At least the prejudice was on the table. He indicated the photos. "This your family?"

"Yes. My boys. My daughter. My wife. My parents." He pointed out the pictures.

"I think I've met one of your boys." Zestrum gestured at the kid.

"Johnny? Where was that?"

"Mr. Etcheverry, we might as well get this over with before I waste your time. On the road into town I came upon your boy robbin' some folks."

Etcheverry frowned at the unwelcome news. "What did you do?"

"I tied him up some, took his horse and gun, and left him."

Etcheverry took a breath. "What'd you do with his horse and gun?"

"They're waiting for him at the post office. After he walks to town."

"I see."

"I figured the boy needed a lesson in manners. If you don't want to hire me after tellin' you this, that's fine, I wouldn't want to work for you anyway."

After a beat, Etcheverry broke out laughing. "Sit down."

They sat, Etcheverry in a large armchair, Zestrum on the couch.

"The reason I contacted you is I'm looking for some strong borgs to work for me."

"Looked like you found some."

"I need more. And someone of your reputation. . . well, I'd like to have you on board."

Zestrum wasn't sure he liked carrying that kind of reputation. People seemed to think he went looking for trouble.

"The ranch is five hundred acres. We're developing property, expanding operations. That's gonna take hard work. A lot of hard work. Can't have too many men. We've been here 32 years and expect to stay."

"You arrived pre-Colonization?"

"Let's say I like having a head start on establishing commerce in a new place." He smiled. "I came with my father when he came over. He put everything he had into this stake. I intend to make it flourish. Now that the railway's running, the possibilities are as wide open as the Interior."

"What exactly is the work?"

"Ranch work, mostly. Repairs around the place. Mending fences, wrangling cattle, breaking horses, the usual. And perimeter defense."

That caught his ear. "For five hundred acres?"

"That's why I need men."

"Looks like an army."

"I need 'em. Protecting the ranch. The family. The operation. I'm not gonna sugarcoat the situation. We've had some incidents. People encroaching on our property. Stealing our water. Shooting our men. Part of the reason I'm hiring on cyborgs is because they're durable and sustainable."

"Expendable."

Etcheverry pursed his lips. "Well. That's the nature of any risky business venture, isn't it? I can promise a decent decommission and commensurate retaliation." He leaned forward. "I always even the score with those who cross me."

"My policy as well."

Etcheverry's harsh gaze did not waver. "I think we understand each other." He opened a desk drawer and extracted a form. "I believe it's best to get things in writing." He offered the form. "It's a simple agreement, outlining duties, pay, and rewards."

"Rewards?" Zestrum took the paper and glanced at the fine print.

"All my men receive bonuses when the ranch profits. And rewards for loyal service." He watched as the cyborg perused the contract, in no hurry to accept the offer. "I realize you may want to review terms before you sign on."

"I do." He looked at Etcheverry. "I'll have to think about it."

"Of course." He handed over a red coin. "In the meantime, have one on me at the saloon."

Zestrum studied the red coin. "What's this?"

"I do business with Doug McConnell, the man who owns the Dual Majesty in town. I get a discount on services. Take a room. Take a lady. This coin will give you a free night. For both."

Zestrum considered the incentive. *That* had never been part of a job offer before.

Etcheverry smiled gregariously. "Just a sample of rewards available to my employees. Get back to me in two or three days. And until then. . . enjoy!"

CHAPTER 2 – OLD FRIENDS, NEW FRIENDS

Zestrum left Shiloh at the hitching post outside Colton House, a square two-story building with a cool shady front porch six steps up from the wooden sidewalk. There was a nice span of lawn on either side. Windows at ground level peeked out from a basement. He unhooked the satchel from the saddle.

At a public hotel, he would have simply walked in but this was a private residence converted to a bed and board. He knocked on the frame of the outer screen door.

The inner wooden door opened and he found himself looking through the screen at a curvy woman with her brunette hair tied down under a bandana. She wore a green checked dress and sturdy boots.

Zestrum pulled off his hat.

Her eyes scanned him head to toe to face, then she ran a hand over her bound hair—for her, an automatic reaction to a tall handsome man. "Can I help you?"

"Are you Ms. Colton, proprietor of Colton House?"

"I am. And you are?" She assessed him with keen perception.

His clothes were not new, but not threadbare or stained, just dusty from the road. His hair looked to have been combed but was damp and awry from wearing a hat all day in the sun.

"Zestrum Doniphon. I'm looking for a room to rent. Postmaster recommended your place."

"Won't you come inside?" She pushed aside the screen door and he entered the house.

Inside, the air was cooler, with a flow-through breeze from the windows at the front and sides of the house. A staircase in the main entry led upstairs. There was a big front parlor at the left and a smaller parlor on the right, more doors further down, with one wide door at the end of the hall leading into the back of the house.

He stood acclimating to the interior light.

He must have passed her assessment because she said, "I have a room available. How long will you be staying?"

"A week."

The prospect of a week's rent appealed to her. Her eyes wandered over him, taking in his physique and level of trail grime. She had remarkable gray eyes. "I can provide accommodations for a week."

"Are meals included?"

"Breakfast and dinner. Lunch is on your own. Most folks aren't here through the day." She started to take his satchel but he indicated with a look that he would carry it. His chivalry impressed her favorably.

She led him up the stairs and down a narrow corridor past five doors on each side. "The bathroom is here." She pointed at a door with a "Washroom" sign, then continued to the end of the hall. She stepped inside a bedroom with a window overlooking the street.

He set the satchel on the little table and perused the room. Small, but neat and clean, and a bed with a real mattress, a luxury he hadn't had in a while.

"The room has a basin for washing, but the bathroom has a sink and a tub. There are towels in the cabinet." She pointed at the cabinet under the basin.

"That would be welcome, ma'am." He knew he smelled of road and days of travel.

"Breakfast is at seven am. Dinner at six pm. The dining room is right behind the front parlor."

"What do I owe you for the week ahead?"

"One hundred five."

He extracted bills from his wallet and handed over payment.

She tucked the money into a pocket and studied him. "Anything else I can do for you, Mr. Doniphon?"

He smiled pleasantly. "Right now a warm bath and a soft bed are kinda preoccupying most of my thinkin'."

For a moment she stood still, her gaze intent on his, then she departed and shut the door.

He quickly searched the room to satisfy himself that there were no surveillance equipment or traps. A force of habit and matter of survival. He unrolled his bedroll on the bed and placed his few toiletries on the sink in the tiny adjoining washroom.

He decided to clean up before casing the town to find out what was what. He wanted to know all the players before he agreed to take the job.

* * *

First place to go was the sheriff's office, to check what the wanted posters said. The combination sheriff's office and jailhouse was on Main Street. Around the businesses were shops and private homes.

On the porch outside the entrance, he scanned the posters nailed to the front wall. There were human and cyborg criminals, wanted for burglary, rustling, assault, and homicide.

Cyborgs were supposed to be better than that. *Human helpers,* the Consortium always insisted in their promotional materials, *designed to assist Colonization in a new world.*

And after the Colonization, they were cut loose to fend on their own.

He entered the office to inspect the posters on the inside wall. At a desk, a man in dusty rawhide clothes slumped face down on the blotter, asleep. Zestrum smelled whiskey. He was irritated to find law enforcement inebriated so early in the day.

Then again, each man faced his demons in his own way.

More posters showed more criminals—many robberies and burglaries. There was a lot of crime around here. Expected in the Badlands. There must have been more than this drunken deputy to assist the sheriff. If not. . . no wonder there was so much crime around here.

He deliberately banged a chair to wake the deputy—to no effect. He smirked. He glanced past the interior door and saw four large, barred cells, all empty. So nobody in custody. Zestrum circled the outer office, curious. Three desks, a locked rack of rifles, a locked trunk of ammo. No windows, only the front door with a peephole cover, and a door to a closet at the side.

The front door slammed open, making him tense for conflict—until he recognized the hothead he left stranded on the road.

Johnny Etcheverry was filthy, overheated, streaked with muck from his long walk, and hopping mad. His anger magnified when he saw Zestrum. "What the hell are *you* doing here?"

Zestrum considered whether to continue the smackdown he started on the road. "Didn't we already have this discussion about manners, boy?"

Johnny fumed. "When my pa finds out what you did, you'll be sorry you messed with me!" He slammed a fist on the desk beside the deputy's head. "Wake up, Edwards! I need to file a complaint!"

The deputy didn't rouse.

Johnny hauled back to kick the man—until Zestrum took a menacing step toward him. He cowered, intimidated. He puffed up when the cyborg didn't move again. "You stole my horse!"

"Left him tied up outside the post office."

He blustered at that. "You stole my gun."

"Left it in the saddlebag."

Deprived of his allegations of theft, he snorted. "You beat me up."

"If I'd have beat you up, you wouldn't be awake yet."

His face registered worry, then he covered with anger. "You touch me again, you'll be damn sorry, borg!"

The door opened and Sheriff Mitch Bodie arrived.

Johnny instantly turned on him. "This borg ambushed me on the road! I want to prefer charges."

Bodie closed the door and looked at Zestrum. "Doniphon."

"Bodie." Zestrum touched the brim of his hat. He was surprised to see his old friend and wondered if he was as worn out on the inside as he appeared on the outside.

Johnny gaped at them. "You *know* him?"

"From way back." Bodie hung his hat on a hook behind the desk. His clothes were grubby and frayed. He was older and thicker than last time Zestrum had seen him, and he was slightly stooped at the shoulders.

Johnny wheeled on him. "This borg robbed me in the middle of the day on the public highway. I want him arrested."

Bodie nailed him with a steely eye. "What were you doing when he robbed you?"

Johnny faltered on that simple question. "Errands."

"Tell him about the couple you were robbing at gunpoint," Zestrum said. "I saw their wagon down by the general store. They probably swore out a complaint on you by now."

The kid's eyes widened with anxiety.

Bodie regarded Johnny with speculation. "You were out harassing folks again?"

Johnny sneered. "I was running errands for my pa. Pa's business." He pointed at Zestrum. "This *assborg* stole my horse and my gun. That's a crime. Arrest him!"

"I don't take orders from you, boy." Bodie sounded weary. "And I saw your horse outside the post office five minutes ago. Why don't you fetch him and get on home?"

"Pa isn't going to like how you disregarded me."

"Then your pa can come in and swear out a complaint on your behalf. Now get out of here before I arrest you for making false claims and committing highway robbery."

"You can't talk to me like that."

"Run along and finish your errands." Bodie mustered the glower of a warrior cyborg.

Johnny scoffed openly and slammed the door on his way out.

Bodie looked at Zestrum. "Looks like you made an enemy."

"And in less than half a day." Zestrum grinned and shook hands with the sheriff. "Nice to see a friend."

"Nice to see you, too, Doniphon. You better watch your back." He jerked a thumb toward the departed kid. "He's a little shit. His Pa's even worse. What happened?"

"He was terrorizing a couple driving a wagon toward town. Threatening the woman with bodily harm. I persuaded him to leave them be."

He bestowed a mordant look. "Still trying to correct the humans?"

"Somebody's got to keep them in line." He gestured at the office. "Looks like that's you in this territory."

He sighed heavily, glanced at the intoxicated deputy, then shuffled papers out from under the man's hand. "They put me here because I've outlived my usefulness. Token law enforcement."

Zestrum sat in a chair. "Tell me more."

Bodie knew this was no idle question. "You know the Etcheverry clan?"

"We've met."

"Claude Etcheverry owns five hundred acres of land. He fancies himself king of his kingdom. Anybody gets in his way gets removed."

"Who's in his way right now?"

"There's six families got sizeable spreads. The most vocal is Gerald Nowlin. Things were pretty quiet till last year when Etcheverry dammed up the river and cut off most of the water."

"I thought there were laws against that."

"There are. Don't mean Etcheverry cares."

"How does the town exist without water?"

"He sells water to the city 'cause he likes the benefits of a nearby town. But everybody else gets gouged."

"So he's hoping to starve out the competition."

"That's about it. Man's got five hundred acres and he wants more. Can you imagine one man tending that much land?"

"He had a dozen hands at his house. How many others are out doing perimeter defense?"

Bodie regarded him with proficiency. "You talked to him already?"

"Earlier today. He made the job sound reasonable enough. Ranch work with security and rewards."

"You came to Copperbank for the job?"

"He invited me, but the offer sounded off. He bestowed two days to consider."

"You walked into a range war, Doniphon. Be careful who you side with."

"I'd rather not side with anybody."

He jutted his thumb toward the door. "That runt is just a sample of what his other kids are like. Be damn careful if you turn him down."

Zestrum scowled. "Well. I came because the pay was so good. But there's always a catch, isn't there?"

"Just about always."

He lowered his chin. "So you know, I paid in advance for a week at Colton House."

"And after that week?"

He shrugged. "Don't know. Maybe I'll look up some of those fellas on the posters out front."

"As long as they don't get you first."

"I said maybe. I never have enjoyed bounty hunting."

"So you might be looking for a job."

He heard an underlying note in the old man's voice. "I might be."

Bodie glanced again at his deputy. "I could have an opening. If you were interested."

"I might be."

"Work's hard. But to make up for it, the pay's lousy."

He smiled. "Old joke."

"I'm an old borg. Perks are tiny. Nothing like a red coin at the Majesty."

"Well, I'm set for the week. After that, I am open to suggestion."

The sleeping man stirred, sat up, and blinked. "Bodie." He squinted at Zestrum. "Who are you?"

"This is an old friend of mine," Bodie said. "Tom Doniphon."

"Zestrum." He offered a hand to the deputy.

"Edwards." He tried to make his grip firm. "Deputy Ethan Edwards." He peered at Bodie with bloodshot eyes. "Am I still a deputy, Bodie?"

"You are," said Bodie. "Why don't you do rounds?"

"Sure thing, boss." Edwards staggered to his feet, found his hat, and departed on shaky legs.

Bodie watched him go with regret. "He was a good man once. Before the whiskey and the Vestal."

Vestal was the drug of choice for most cyborgs seeking euphoria or amnesia. Zestrum figured the deputy had his reasons for using. "How reliable is he now? That's what counts."

"He does desk work while I'm out."

"Who else is on board?"

"Puzzle. He works evenings while I have dinner. He's a testy old codger, but reliable. Good with a rifle."

"Sounds like you could use fresh blood."

"Could I ever. Man, if you're in the market for work, I could use you."

"Give me a day or two to ease out of the deal with Etcheverry."

"Sure thing. That's gotta be done delicately."

"Delicate is my middle name."

CHAPTER 3 – PRETTY LITTLE BIRD

Zestrum cleaned up proper for his initial night on the town. A quick shower with soap and water, a thorough shave, fresh clothes. He should at least present to the locals as a clean-cut well-dressed individual. Folks should know up front he was capable of presenting well. In case he stayed on.

Down the way, next street over on Main, the Dual Majesty Saloon dominated the end of the block, a wide building with swinging double doors at the corner and picture windows on either side stenciled with the name of the establishment. A huge sign above advertised the name in carved wood, just in case anyone missed the windows. A balcony ran along the second floor, with windows at each room. The third floor was indented, with a wider balcony and smaller windows.

From the outside the place looked prosperous and inviting. Inside even more so; the rooms had red wallpaper and shiny hardwood flooring. On one side of the wide space was a casino and a staircase rising to upper floors; on the other side round tables and chairs, a bar along the west wall.

An arched doorway at the end of the bar led into a showroom. The poster on the wall beside the doorway publicized the entertainment, Victoria Barkley, with a painting of the performer. She was a stunner, but new paint often hid old performers.

In the corner, a woman played ragtime piano. She was good, maybe augmented good.

The place was tangled with customers at the bar, at the card tables, at the casino games. Hardened men and women from outlying ranches, in town for the night. Businesspeople and errant spouses out for a good time. Traders and salesclerks seeking a respite from repetitive chores. Human and cyborg both, so they weren't segregated. The proprietor was willing to take anybody's money.

The bartender was a beefy cyborg with the distinctive markings of the Sore Serenity clan over his left eye. He was polishing glasses with a cloth as Zestrum eased to the bar.

"Bourbon," Zestrum said.

The bartender set up the drink and Zestrum put down a coin. From the bar he had a nice view of the entire first floor and its inhabitants.

Among the clientele were at least eight lovely ladies dressed in various stages of petticoats and corsets. Some clients preferred a brazen experienced companion; others preferred an innocent-looking flower. The women working here were playing assigned roles to maximize profits.

There were also three pretty young men in smart suits mingling among the patrons with the same purpose. The proprietor catered to all strata of society.

Zestrum recognized several hands he'd seen at the Etcheverry Ranch. And now the name of that familiar cyborg came to mind: Matt Dillon. He'd worked the explosives on the coast, blasting the tunnels to facilitate the railway. Dillon had been a troublemaker, constantly getting into fights. And he liked fire a little too much.

Movement on the stairs on the far side of the casino caught Zestrum's eye and he watched two ladies escort a satisfied customer down from the second floor. The customer went to the roulette wheel and rubbed his hands on the ass of each lady for luck.

Zestrum surveyed the card tables in the bar. A circle of onlookers surrounded one table with a large stack of chips in the center. Two men held cards, engaged in a battle of nerves. Zestrum recognized Chris Etcheverry from the photos at the Etcheverry ranch. The other man he didn't know.

That man set a document on the pile, calling the bet. Chris revealed his hand and smiled, reaching to collect the pot.

The man dropped his cards and Chris's face fell. The crowd cheered and jeered. Chris stomped to the bar and demanded a drink. The winner collected his winnings into his hat to redeem at the cashier.

Zestrum could practically see the scuffle when the loser ambushed the winner in a dark alley later tonight.

Music commenced, a bouncy tune from the showroom adjoining the bar. The sound was like a lure; folks hurried into the showroom. Curious, Zestrum followed them through the doorway past the captivating poster. The round tables filled with customers.

The front row of tables was cordoned off with a red velvet rope guarded by a bouncer who had rolled up the sleeves of his white shirt to make visible the marks of the Moonshadow Clan, a warrior class of cyborg.

The bouncer was one of a select few Zestrum appraised as someone he wasn't sure he could take in a fight. The cyborg's stance indicated he handled trouble well—feet shoulder-width apart, knees slightly bent, straight back, body relaxed, his heavy frame balanced and ready to move in any direction. There was a heavy baton hooked to his belt.

Zestrum stood at the back wall where he had a view of the entire space.

The crowd was loud and rowdy, competing with the little band in the orchestra pit in front of the curtained stage. Lights dimmed and the audience quieted. The curtains parted on a dark stage. A spotlight illuminated the backside of a woman wearing a short skirt and pink corset. Her honey blonde hair was piled on her head in soft curls. The music lowered to a vamp tempo.

The woman peeked over her shoulder. "How is everybody tonight?"

The men howled greetings. The music picked up and the woman turned, revealing her scant costume and glamorous loveliness, and began singing.

Whatcha doing tonight?
Whatcha doing in here?

Whatcha doing so close?
You're so far but so near.

Take a load off your boots.
Take the fork to the right.
Take a look at the stage.
Oh I need you tonight.

Sometimes you walk into a place
and right away you know.
You see someone across the room
and you can never let him go.

Whatcha doing tonight?
What's the chance that you're free?
Can'tcha make it for two?
Why don't you do it with me?

Sometimes a single look can haunt you
for the rest of your life.
You see someone and know someone's
gotta become a wife.

Whatcha doing tonight?
You turn me to debris.
Whatcha doing forever?
Why don't you spend it with me?

Whatcha doing tonight?
What's the chance that you're free?
Can'tcha make it for two?
Why don't you do it with me?

With every lyric, every gesture, the crowd went loco. The woman had a beautiful voice; she was programmed with the songbird function. An expensive enhancement, especially for such a backwater place. Singers of this caliber were employed in big cities with big city audiences. McConnell must have had big city money to afford one.

The patrons were properly entertained.

The singer strutted to the edge of the stage at the last line of the song and struck a pose. Applause shook the rafters. She acknowledged the crowd, scanning the room, and her eyes came upon Zestrum. Her head canted and her smile turned genuine. He touched his hat in response. The smile blossomed.

He had to admit she was a magnificent creature, better than the painted poster.

She spun and marched to the center of the stage, turned, and six dancers joined her, three from each wing. The band struck up another song and they sang and danced through the number.

> *Put your boots on the floor, dear,*
> *at the bottom of my bed*
> *Put your hat on the bedpost when*
> *you want to rest your head.*
> *I want you when you're riding high*
> *and when you're crawlin' low*
>
> *When your pocket's empty and*
> *when you've got cash to show.*
> *When you're dirty, I do laundry and*
> *I put it in my drawer*
> *There's nothing that you can't ask of me,*
> *I'll always do some more.*
>
> *I'd take you anytime*
> *I'd take you anywhere*
> *You can't leave my love behind*
> *I've still got your underwear!*

The bawdy piece riled the crowd into a frenzy. Zestrum sensed the energy and violence inherent in the inebriated spectators. A mob like that might do anything.

After the show, the crowd migrated into the front rooms primed to gamble and drink.

Zestrum waited until the showroom emptied before strolling into that arena. The bar was crammed with men calling for drinks, the gaming tables were busy with gamblers, and the saloon ladies and gents were choosing clients for the next hour.

He noticed, in the corner, Ethan Edwards, speaking with a shady looking character. Edwards passed some cash and received a small packet in return. Buying Vestal in the saloon? The deputy should know better.

A lovely brunette approached Zestrum. "Haven't seen you here before." She had the demeanor of an experienced woman looking for a protector.

"I've never been here before."

"New in town? Let me show you around." She curled her arm around his bicep and led him through the room. "My name is Kaya. What's yours?"

"Doniphon."

"Mr. Doniphon. Welcome to the Dual Majesty. Best saloon in town. Best show. Best games. You look like a poker man. Are you a poker man?"

"I've played a few hands."

She ran her fingers down his arm and clasped his hand, admiring him. "Such big hands! I like a man who works with his hands." She led him into the casino. "We have every game you'd care to play. What's your pleasure?"

"Tonight I'm just taking in the show. But I'll be back."

"How long you staying?"

"No firm plans."

She smiled. "Care to join in one of the games down here? Or would you like to see the games upstairs?"

He had that red coin in his pocket. But this woman—lovely as she was—was not his type. "How about roulette?"

She steered him to the table and stood beside him while he observed the game in progress. Men who looked like they couldn't afford the cost were betting on a game that depended on luck. Some were betting too much and losing—and getting aggressive.

And the table had a double-zero wheel. A worse proposition than the single zero wheel.

The croupier spun the wheel and rolled the ivory-colored ball the opposite direction. The ball lost momentum, dropped past the deflectors, and fell into a pocket. The outcome pleased no one standing at the table. The banter sounded heated and there was too much liquor in the air.

Zestrum moved on to the blackjack table. His companion clung to his side, pressing against him, reminding him she was available. While he could use a spell of pleasure, he preferred a woman who was real.

Then the songbird waltzed into the casino, dressed in a red velvet dress cut low to accent her figure. Here and there she greeted folks by name, blew on a pair of dice at the craps table, tousled a customer's sparse hair, and wandered through the room chatting up patrons.

He couldn't help staring. She had the aura of class in a classless milieu. As out of place as a rose among foxtails.

She must have felt the weight of his eyes because she looked at him and a faint smile appeared. Chatting with folks along the way, she steadily crossed to the blackjack table.

The brunette's hand tightened on his arm.

"Introduce me," said the songbird, speaking to Kaya but her gaze firmly on him.

"The gentleman's name is Mr. Doniphon."

"Zestrum." He reached out and the songbird clasped his hand. And held on.

"Victoria." Her smile was like fresh water on a parched soul.

Kaya shifted on her feet and cocked her head, aware she'd become superfluous. "I guess you've chosen your game for tonight." She produced a plastic smile and wafted into the crowd to hunt more obliging clientele.

"I caught your act," he said.

"Did you?" Victoria's fingers curled more securely around his hand and she closed the distance between them. "Did you like my songs?"

"I did. You could sing in Ambassador Hall."

Her nose crinkled. "Less competition out here." She lowered her voice. "I'm the best singer within three hundred miles. Keeps me employed."

He decided not to mention a combination casino/showroom/bordello in the Badlands was several steps beneath a prestigious venue like Ambassador Hall on the coast. "But is it worthwhile?"

"It is if you need to disappear." Her soft laugh tinkled. "I make a good living." She changed subjects. "What are you doing in Copperbank? Business or pleasure?"

"Business."

"Ahh. What kind of business?"

"I'm contemplating a job offer."

Her delicate eyebrows arched in inquiry. "Doing what?"

"Ranch work."

"With which ranch?"

"Etcheverry."

Her nonchalance flickered a moment as she registered the name. "Why, that's not too far away. You could. . . visit every night if you wanted."

"If I wanted."

She renewed her smile. "We'd be neighbors." She pressed the back of his hand against the slopes of her chest above the bodice. "Wouldn't that be exciting?"

He felt her heartbeat, rapid and steady. He started to speak when violence erupted at the roulette table. Two men swung at each other in quick succession and ten seconds later six or seven men were punching one another.

Victoria frowned and recoiled. Zestrum wrapped an arm around her and directed her toward the stairs. On the casino floor the flash fight spread and degenerated into a huge melee of fists and booted feet and crashing furniture.

Zestrum shepherded Victoria to the second floor into a long corridor of doors on either side. A third of the way down the hall, he stopped.

"Which room is yours?"

She pointed at a door ten feet on. He opened the door. She hurried inside and turned to face him, her face flushed, her body eager.

He stood in the doorway, hands on either side of the door frame. "I'll say goodnight."

She looked crestfallen. "Goodnight?"

"The mess downstairs has me a bit preoccupied and a beautiful woman like you deserves my full attention."

She stepped closer to him. "You should comfort my anxiety."

He advanced into the room and she backed up, pleased he was coming in. When he reached the edge of the door, he grasped the doorknob, reversed into the corridor, and shut the door.

CHAPTER 4 – ACCIDENTAL DEATH

On the landing, Zestrum surveyed the scene. The fight had escalated to encompass the entire casino and bar. The house ladies and gents had collected along a wall near the showroom, keeping clear of flying debris.

The bartender and four cyborg bouncers protected their domain, flattening unruly humans and cyborgs to break up the scuffle.

The man who instigated the mess was attacking the man he'd picked the fight with, a slugfest that knocked aside others as they battled from the casino into the barroom.

Zestrum noticed a well-dressed man standing halfway down the stairs observing the altercation with cold calculation. He looked annoyed more than anything else. Was he the proprietor? Zestrum disliked him on sight.

Someone yelped. The cry acted like a douse of water on fire. Men paused in beating each other, attention riveted on something in the barroom, out of Zestrum's sight.

The well-dressed man descended the stairs and the crowd parted, according him respect that suggested he was feared. He continued into the barroom and spectators moved aside.

Zestrum followed in his wake, curious.

A man lay on the floor, a knife in his chest, losing blood. Zestrum recognized a fatal wound. He also realized this was the man who bested Chris Etcheverry earlier in the evening. Did Chris take advantage of the fight to save himself a trip to the alley?

The well-dressed man stood near the victim as the bartender checked him.

The bartender confirmed the kill. "Don't look good, Mr. McConnell."

"Call Doc Hartman," said McConnell.

A couple of men rushed out. Whether they'd fetch the doctor or hightail it home was anyone's guess.

"Folks, it looks like we've had a little problem," announced McConnell as if there had been a run on whiskey instead of a homicide. "I'm afraid we'll have to close down for the evening."

A general racket of discontent rumbled throughout the saloon. Movement near the showroom caught Zestrum's eye, and he saw Edwards peering over the shoulders of the men in front of him at the dead man on the floor.

The swinging doors flapped as Sheriff Bodie arrived. Patrons opened a path to the fallen man. Bodie scanned the room, taking in who was where. Edwards stumbled forward, and Bodie noted his presence. He gestured at the door and Edwards scurried to guard the entrance.

"Sheriff," said the saloon owner.

"McConnell," said Bodie. "What happened?"

"Anderson got stabbed."

"That's apparent. Who did it?"

"Can't rightly say."

Bodie eyed McConnell. Zestrum watched the incident play out.

The doors swung into Edwards, making him spin around and grasp the gun at his side.

The man entering held a medical bag. "Somebody called for me?"

"Here, Doc," said Bodie.

Edwards stepped aside. The doctor knelt beside the injured man and conducted a brief exam while the entire assembly watched in silence. Doc Hartman pressed a stethoscope to the man's chest, checked his pulse at the wrist, then stowed the stethoscope in the bag and stood.

"He's dead," he announced.

Bodie pulled out a handkerchief and extracted the knife, holding it up by the handle so all could see. "Who does this belong to?"

Nobody volunteered.

Bodie examined the wooden handle. "Looks like the Bar X brand." He zeroed in on Etcheverry. "This yours, Chris?"

Chris folded his arms across his wide chest, sniffing with disdain. "Nope."

Zestrum could only admire the bold lie. There had to be witnesses to the crime.

"Did anybody see what happened?" Bodie surveyed the room.

Folks shifted further from the crime scene, murmuring negatives.

Doc Hartman scowled. "Take him to the mortuary."

Three bouncers followed his orders. Edwards stepped aside long enough to let them pass, then blocked the doorway.

"I'm going to need to take statements from all the witnesses," Bodie announced.

A general din of groans.

"Can't this wait till tomorrow?" said McConnell.

"Gotta do it now while memories are fresh."

McConnell's face registered disagreement with the directive. Then he smiled and pretended to cave. "Sure, Sheriff. Folks, line up and we'll get this done right quick." He gestured and the patrons formed a rough line. "I can tell you what I saw. A fight broke out and a lot of folks were swinging chairs and weapons. Not sure how Anderson stumbled into the knife, but I'm pretty sure it was an accident."

Bodie's eyes narrowed. "An accident?"

"From what I saw. People were shoving and pushing each other. Things were so disruptive, it's hard to say who hit who or even who started it." McConnell looked at the faces around him. "Isn't that so, folks?"

The customers agreed.

"We'll take statements," Bodie said. "Starting with you." He pointed at Chris.

Edwards guarded the door, allowing each person to leave after he or she made a statement. Zestrum waited at the periphery as the saloon slowly emptied. The house ladies and gents filed to the staircase as they finished their official statements.

Bodie listened like a man hearing familiar bedtime stories.

McConnell remained nearby, observing, intimidating the witnesses. Zestrum disliked the proprietor even more.

Zestrum stepped up last.

Bodie gave him a keen look. "Doniphon. You see anything?"

McConnell noted that the sheriff knew him.

"I didn't see who did it," said Zestrum. "I did see Etcheverry lose a poker hand to him earlier."

"Etcheverry don't like losing." The sheriff wrote notes in his book.

"Men win and lose all night long," said McConnell, casting doubt. "You're a stranger here, aren't you?"

Zestrum's dislike for the saloon owner intensified another degree. "I am. Don't mean I didn't see what I saw."

Bodie continued. "Where were you when Anderson got stabbed?"

"Top of the stairs."

McConnell noted that, too—and probably the absence of the lovely songbird Victoria.

Bodie looked at the saloon owner. "I think, in light of the incident tonight, you'd best close the casino while we investigate."

"For the night, sure."

"Until we finish the investigation."

McConnell frowned, displeased. "This can't be right, Sheriff. Chris Etcheverry hasn't a mean bone in his body. We all know the Etcheverry family. They're a fine, upstanding clan."

"We all know the Etcheverry family," Bodie repeated in a flat tone. Apparently, the clan wasn't as well *liked* as it was *known*.

McConnell bristled. "I run a clean establishment, Sheriff. Everybody knows that, too. Fair games, fair chances. I've always cooperated with the law."

"You have, McConnell, but for the time being, shutter the casino till we straighten this out."

"That's half my business."

"Fight originated at the roulette table. It's technically a crime scene. Cordon it off." He watched as McConnell formulated more argument. "Or I can shut down the whole saloon."

McConnell's eyes flared rage, but he shifted into easy obsequiousness. "I'll close the casino until you lift the order, Sheriff." He smiled but the eyes weren't friendly.

"I appreciate your cooperation." Bodie glanced at the staff. "I appreciate your cooperation, too, ladies and gents. If you remember anything else might help the case, let me know right away."

A general murmur of agreement from the employees under the watchful eye of their boss.

Bodie looked at McConnell. "Lock up for tonight. You can reopen the bar and showroom tomorrow."

"As you say, Sheriff." McConnell bestowed another false smile. He addressed his staff. "That's end of shift, people. Bright and early tomorrow." He lifted a hand and the staff scattered to right chairs and clean tables.

Bodie strode out the door. Edwards glared at McConnell, then walked out. Zestrum followed. McConnell shut the inner barricade doors as staff shuttered the picture windows.

Out in the deserted street, Bodie spoke with the other two. "Edwards, take this to the office and put it in storage." He handed over the knife and Edwards hustled toward the sheriff's office. Bodie looked at Zestrum.

"You think Etcheverry did it?" asked Zestrum.

"Without a doubt."

"The knife is evidence."

"He'll claim someone stole it from him. Or he lost it and someone found it. Always has a dozen witnesses to his favor."

"There'll be fingerprints."

Bodie scowled. "Judge Roberts is a friend of Claude Etcheverry."

"So the trial would be a waste of time?"

"Yep. The only way to convict the man would be to hand him and the evidence over to the marshal for trial in Steelreach, and that's two hundred miles from here. I'd have to hold him in jail for three days till the tumbleweed wagon picked him up."

"Three days ain't so long."

"It is with Etcheverrys and their army of ranch hands banging on my door."

Zestrum recalled the sullen cyborgs he'd seen on the man's property. "What if someone delivered the man to the marshal instead?"

"The marshal's on the circuit right now, which means it's a crapshoot getting in touch with him. Most towns don't even have telegraph yet. He should be here in a couple weeks."

Zestrum acknowledged that. "Sounds like they got you over a barrel."

"Not the first time. We got a lot of barrels here." The sheriff sighed heavily and gazed up and down the empty street, darker now with the lights of the saloon extinguished. "Authorities knew what they was doing when they sent me here. 'Do a little justice—but leave the big justice alone.'"

Zestrum nodded. "It's the human way."

CHAPTER 5 – A CLOSE CALL

Zestrum lay on the bed in his rented room, awake at 6 am as the sun rose. He wanted to assist Bodie if possible. Perhaps working for the Etcheverry clan would provide a chance to gather evidence. Perhaps it would get him killed.

How much did he want to risk involvement with these folks?

He needed money, but he had enough for a few more weeks. He needed more information before declining the job offer.

He heard noise at his open window. A creaking roof plank. Staying perfectly still, he scoped out the window and saw a shadow at the edge. Someone was there—stalking him. The barrel of a Ginwalt poked through the window.

In one fluid motion Zestrum rolled off the bed, grabbed the barrel, and yanked the stalker into the room.

Johnny Etcheverry sprawled on the floor. He scrambled to his knees and froze when Zestrum pointed the weapon at him. The hotshot raised his hands, blood draining from his cheeks.

"You wanted to see me about something?" Zestrum said.

Johnny glowered. "You took my gun."

"Before you shot me."

"Ain't a *real* crime to shoot a borg, you tin-pot half-breed."

The boy's smartass mouth was too much. Zestrum slapped his face with his open hand, then pocketed the gun. Johnny fell to the floor, stunned. Zestrum hauled on his boots, put on his hat, then seized the kid as he got on his knees again. One quick jerk and Zestrum had the kid on his feet. He hustled him out the door and down the stairs.

In the entry, Ms. Colton saw them and paused, a tray in her hands. She cocked an eyebrow. "Will you be wanting breakfast, Mr. Doniphon?"

"Yes, ma'am. Just taking care of some business first." He shoved Johnny through the front door and down the dusty street to the sheriff's office.

*　*　*

Townsfolk noticed as Zestrum dragged Johnny along by the scruff. At the sheriff's office, Zestrum tossed the kid through the doorway. Johnny banged into a desk. Zestrum shut the door and looked at the startled deputy at the desk, an older man he hadn't met before.

"What's this?" said the older man.

"This brat just tried to shoot me." Zestrum set the Ginwalt on the desk and stood between Johnny and the exit.

"He's making that up!" Johnny charged, assertive now that he wasn't alone with the cyborg. "He jumped me in the alley and stole my gun."

The old man squinted at the kid. "What was you doing in the alley at six in the morning?"

Johnny's jaw tensed. "Errands for my pa." He pointed at Zestrum. "He punched me! That's assault with intent to. . . to commit bodily harm."

The old man's face brightened as he looked at Zestrum. "Did you bodily harm him?"

"I slapped him," said Zestrum.

"That's assault!" Johnny screeched. "Assault on a minor!"

The old man studied Zestrum. "Who are you?"

"Zestrum Doniphon."

The old man's face lit up. "*The* Zestrum Doniphon?"

That reputation again. "Probably." He gestured at the kid. "Yesterday I came upon him harassing a couple driving a wagon on the highway. This morning he came after me with a gun."

The old man glared at the kid. "That's attempted murder, boy."

Johnny sneered. "You ain't going to do anything to me, old scrapheap."

For a moment the old man didn't move. Then he hobbled around the desk and seized the kid's arm.

"Hey!"

The old man yanked him through the inner doorway toward the holding cells. He was favoring his left leg, but steady on his feet. An older cyborg who'd seen action in his colorful past. He pushed Johnny into the nearest cell and clanged shut the door.

Johnny grasped the bars and shook the door. "You can't hold me! I done nothing wrong!"

"Tell it to the sheriff." The old man returned to the office and shut the inner door, muffling the kid's curses. He smiled at Zestrum. "Nice to meet you, Mr. Doniphon." He offered a shaky hand.

Zestrum shook his hand. The old cyborg was one of the early recruits, squat and sturdy, but a bit hunched from age and wear.

"I'm Puzzle." The old man peered at him. "You're not as tall as I thought you'd be."

"How tall did you think I was?"

"From the stories, twenty feet high and bulletproof." He cackled a loud laugh and Zestrum found himself smiling despite the circumstances. Puzzle returned to the desk and slapped a form on the blotter. "Swear out a complaint?"

"Is it going to go anywhere?"

"Probably not, but I collect 'em." He leaned in conspiratorially. "Got a thick file on that one." He jabbed a thumb toward the cell.

Zestrum chuckled, took the pen the man offered, and began filling out the form.

"How long you here for?"

"I'm paid up at Colton House for a week."

"Oh. Short time, eh?"

"No definite plans."

"What brung you here?"

"Job offer."

The old man's expression darkened. "Etcheverry?"

"How did you know?"

"He's hiring every loose cyborg he can find into his personal militia." He became suspicious. "You a mercenary?"

"Self-employed."

There came pounding from the other side of the inside wall separating the office from the cells.

Puzzle glanced at the wooden wall, then looked at Zestrum and smiled. "It's steel reinforced inside. All the walls are."

Zestrum chuckled and finished the form. "How long can you hold him?"

"Till his pa hears. Once they figure out he's missing from the ranch, they'll send someone. Course that could take days." Again he became confidential. "They'll make trouble for ya."

"His pa wants me to work for him. I'll see how it goes."

Puzzle pointed at him. "You be damn careful what you do with that crazy human. He ain't honest. His whole family is criminal."

"I kind of figured that out."

Puzzle skimmed the form and smiled at the allegations.

The front door opened. Bodie paused, shut the door, and hung up his hat. "Morning."

"Morning," said Zestrum.

"Morning, sheriff." Puzzle held up the form. "Look what I got here."

Bodie approached the desk. "Who's it for?"

"Johnny Etcheverry. That damn fool kid tried to shoot him." Puzzle jabbed a thumb at Zestrum.

Bodie looked at Zestrum. "Seems you've attracted his interest."

Zestrum snorted. "I don't want to have to kill him to get him off my back."

"Wouldn't bother me none, but his pa." Bodie shook his head in dismay. "His pa just paid those new homesteaders to circumvent their complaint on him."

"Dad pays so the kid don't. Without consequences, he'll never be more than a dumb kid."

"Money comes cheap to Etcheverry."

That accounted for the kid's fine clothes and expensive weapon: his father was buying his way through life. Zestrum declined further comment. His own father was just as bad.

"This is *the* Zestrum Doniphon," said Puzzle with a flourish.

"We know each other," Bodie said.

Puzzle's eyes widened to moons. "Really? You ain't never told me that. Where from?"

"It was a long time ago," Zestrum said.

"Ages," Bodie agreed.

"So you ain't gunna tell me," Puzzle griped. "Nobody tells me nothing I wanna know."

"Some later time," said Zestrum. "I have breakfast waiting for me at the hotel."

"Jessica makes a good meal," Bodie said.

"She sure does," said Puzzle. "She's a right nice lady, too."

Damn nice. Zestrum headed for the door. "See you later."

Puzzle beamed at the complaint in his hand. "Gonna frame this one."

CHAPTER 6 – A SHORT STAY

Other boardinghouse tenants were at the table when Zestrum entered the dining room. They gave him wary looks as he skirted around them to an empty chair.

Ms. Colton—Jessica; he could call her by her first name in his mind—filled his cup with coffee. "Get your business taken care of, Mr. Doniphon?"

"Remains to be seen. Thank you, ma'am."

Watching his reactions to each platter of food, she scooped scrambled eggs, biscuits, gravy, and sausages onto his plate. "Plenty of seconds if you like."

"Thank you." He sampled the fare. Quite good.

"You ain't from around here," said a man wearing a black suit.

Zestrum saw them all waiting for his response. "No, I ain't."

"Where you from?" asked the man in the ill-fitting brown jacket and trousers.

"West coast." He declined to elaborate. The biscuits and gravy were exceptional.

"What's your line of work?" asked the man in black.

"Landscaper." It was what the cyborgs called the work: diverting water, clearing fields, leveling terrain, paving roads, constructing pre-fab homes and basic office buildings. Preparing the land for human habitation. Humans like the ones sitting at this table interrogating him. Even though that wasn't his job anymore, he always said it was to shut them up. He'd put in his twenty years; he owed no one explanations.

"Rough work," said the man in brown. "You here to start engineering the Badlands?" He snickered, then a couple of the others chuckled.

The government had long ago abandoned the idea of landscaping the interior of the continent. Far too much wild territory and construction would displace folks like Claude Etcheverry. That made the prospect untenable.

"I'm here for the cookin'," Zestrum said.

"Ms. Colton is a great cook," said the woman wearing a blue crinoline. She looked too refined for this company. Spoke with good enunciation. Had clean fingernails. A banker? A teacher?

"Best reason to board here," said the man in brown, inviting other tenants to laugh at his little joke.

"More coffee, Mr. Bainbridge?" Jessica had the pot in hand at the man's left. Zestrum again noticed her remarkable gray eyes.

"Believe I will, thanks." Bainbridge watched her fill his cup and added five spoonfuls of sugar.

The woman in blue rose from her chair. "Wonderful breakfast, Ms. Colton."

"See you this evening, Ms. Nolan." Jessica began collecting dirty dishes.

Ms. Nolan left the dining room. Others made their departures. Zestrum noticed a copy of the local newspaper, *The Copperbank Sentinel,* on the table, opened to an editorial about road improvements necessary for commerce and trade, demanding the Consortium fund the work.

On the opposite page was a large splashy ad for Etcheverry Dairy and Beef. A smiling man pointed at a bold type slogan: "When you think dairy, think Etcheverry!"

He flipped to the front page where a big bold headline declared, "Death at the Majesty!" There was a long story about the accidental death of Blake Anderson during the evening. Many of the quotes came from McConnell and steered blame far from Chris Etcheverry. Other witnesses corroborated McConnell's version of events, indicating his patrons wanted to stay in his good graces.

Zestrum folded over the paper to avoid thinking about murder, dairy, or the Consortium. Alone at the table, he was free to enjoy his meal in peace.

"Mr. Doniphon?"

He *thought* he was free to enjoy his meal in peace.

In the doorway, Claude Etcheverry held his hat in his hand. He nodded politely to the landlady. "Ms. Colton."

"Mr. Etcheverry." Her smile was tight, as if she barely tolerated his presence in her house. A personal animosity or a longstanding feud?

"Just need a word with Mr. Doniphon."

The rich land baron was asking permission to enter the room. After a moment, Jessica acquiesced and went into the kitchen.

Etcheverry stood on the opposite side of the table. "Ms. Colton sets a good table."

"She does."

"I came to see you about a personal matter. Seems my boy has been incarcerated at your complaint."

"That's true."

Etcheverry's frozen expression hinted he had expected an apology. "Perhaps you could enlighten me on the charge."

"This morning he was at my window aiming a gun at me. I disarmed him and took him to the sheriff as prescribed by law."

Did Etcheverry know Zestrum could easily have killed the boy and buried the body somewhere in the desert without detection? Cyborgs were nothing if not efficient.

The land baron shifted weight on his feet. "Well, that's a problem. I need him to run errands for the ranch, and if he's in jail, he can't run them. Is there a possibility you might see your way to dropping the charges?"

"Well, that depends on your boy."

"On him?" He scoffed. "Seems you're the one preferred the charges."

"I did, but only after he provoked me. You see, this is the third time we've met, and this time he saw fit to aim his pistol at me. As you can imagine, that's not something I take lightly."

"Of course not." He became reasonable. "Perhaps I could compensate you for your inconvenience in some way. Say, a week's worth of red coin."

"That puts a cheap price on my life, Mr. Etcheverry."

"All men's lives are priceless, Mr. Doniphon, including that of my boy."

Zestrum leaned his elbows on the table, aware he couldn't win this negotiation. Many humans considered cyborgs less than human, and Etcheverry was one of them. "Well, maybe you can do something more effective for me in return."

"Name it."

"Warn your boy off bothering me. Sooner or later he's going to draw on me and, well, you offered me that job for a reason."

"Indeed." His expression hardened as he realized his son was walking a thin line. "I'll have a stern talk with him and tell him to leave you be. I'll make sure he knows he needs to behave."

"Then I'll withdraw the charges as long as he holds to that."

The man's head canted, his eyebrows knitting. "I appreciate that, Mr. Doniphon. And I will wait for your decision on that job. Good morning."

"Morning."

Etcheverry departed the house and the front door closed.

Zestrum scowled. That impulsive brat wasn't going to listen to his pa, no matter the threat. Sooner or later. . .

Yeah, sooner or later.

* * *

Zestrum walked into the sheriff's office. Puzzle was sweeping the floor. Bodie was writing a report on the murder last night. His notes were on the desk.

"That didn't take long," Bodie said.

"I must have been the first errand of his day." Zestrum sighed. "Looks like I'm dropping the charges."

Bodie gestured to Puzzle, who scowled and got the key, then opened the inner door and limped to the cells. Bodie and Zestrum held silence.

Johnny sauntered into the office and made a big show of straightening his clothes, giving the older men the stink eye. He glared expectantly at Puzzle.

"Do I gotta?" Puzzle asked his boss. Bodie nodded. Another scowl. Puzzle opened a drawer and set the kid's Ginwalt and bullets on the desk, unwilling to hand them over in person.

Johnny waited, expecting more deference than that, then realized he'd have to fetch his gear himself. He shuffled sideways, attempting to maintain his dignity, and scooped up the six bullets and the pistol. He ostentatiously fondled the weapon, spinning it and quickly dropping it into his holster, drawing it, and aiming it at Zestrum's forehead.

Click.

Zestrum didn't blink. Instead, before Johnny could blink, the cyborg grabbed the gun with his left hand and deposited it back in the holster.

"If it had bullets, you'd be dead. That's your second warning. Next time you'll not walk away." Zestrum took a sudden step forward.

Johnny flinched, yanked open the door, and dashed outside.

Zestrum and Bodie exchanged a look and both smiled.

Puzzle outright laughed and closed the door. "Seein' that was worth letting him out!"

"Since you're here." Bodie offered Zestrum a paper. "Verify your statement and sign it if you will."

Zestrum scanned the paper—his statement from last night. "Had any significant clues?" He signed.

"Nope."

"You seen today's paper?" Puzzle said.

"Yep," said Bodie.

Puzzle shook his head. "Harris licked McConnell's boots in that story. No wonder the whole thing was bullshit. He even talk to you?"

"Nope."

"He couldn't show both sides if he were twins."

"He knows which side butters his bread." Bodie accepted the paper back in hand, then gave Zestrum a warning look. "Be careful out there, Doniphon. That kid don't listen to anyone, not even his pa."

"That's what I figured. Good luck on the investigation." He stepped out onto the porch and surveyed the street.

Outside the mercantile on the next block down Main Street, Johnny was talking with Claude Etcheverry while his brothers Chris and Gabriel loaded supplies into the family buckboard. The discussion became heated as Johnny swelled with indignation, defending his actions. Claude smacked him across the face, ending the argument, and ordered him to get his horse.

Sullen, smarting, Johnny shambled toward the hitching post where his horse was tied.

CHAPTER 7 – OPTIONS

The wind blew hot outside of town and not much grew. What was once alive was all but exterminated by the sterilization. The Consortium had nearly wiped the slate clean before the cyborgs arrived. Few lifeforms survived that weren't handpicked for reintroduction to the planet.

Zestrum stood off to the side at the cemetery observing the funeral of the murdered Blake Anderson. The widow, drowned in black garb, was flanked by six kids and two sets of elderly parents. Bodie, Edwards, and Puzzle were among the dozens of mourners.

The pastor kept it short. "Blake Anderson here wasn't a perfect man, but he was a good man. That in itself should get him into heaven. He never killed nobody and nobody ever had any good reason to kill him. Yet here we are. I know God forgives all sin when you ask, but I hate to admit I hope his killer never gets the chance. I like to think I'm a forgiving man, but I surely do want him to go to hell. Bless Blake Anderson and watch over his family. Amen."

He closed his holy book.

The widow placed a rose on the simple wooden casket. The pastor spoke to her. Folks offered condolences. A man in a pinstriped suit held up a camera and took pictures.

Bodie slipped off his hat. "I'm sorry about your loss, Ms. Anderson."

She was stoic, rigid with self-control. "Thank you, Sheriff Bodie. And what are you doing about this?" She pointed at the coffin.

"I'm working the investigation, ma'am."

"We all know who did it," she declared sharply. "Why isn't he in jail?"

"There's a legal process I'm obligated to follow, ma'am."

She scoffed loudly, and one of her small boys huddled at her side. She cupped his shoulder with a hand. "This town isn't safe anymore, Sheriff Bodie. None of us is safe."

An elderly man intervened. "This isn't the appropriate time, Martha."

She lifted her chin, fighting emotion. "It never is. That's what we say every day to keep the peace. The only peace we'll ever have is in the grave." Ms. Anderson marched out of the cemetery followed by her children.

Zestrum saw Bodie's despondency at his powerlessness. Edwards' fury at the situation. Puzzle's empathy for the family.

The mourners trundled away. Two gravediggers lowered the coffin into the hole. The man in the pinstriped suit swooped in on the sheriff with questions about the killing. Edwards pushed him aside with a big hand. Bodie, Edwards, and Puzzle headed toward town.

The pinstriped man hustled after the widow. Ms. Andersons's oldest son fended him off with a rude gesture. The pinstriped man lifted his camera to take pictures.

Zestrum strolled through the older section of the cemetery, scanning names on the tombstones and markers. He came to a section enclosed by a wrought iron fence with the name "Colton" on the gate.

Five tombstones stood in the plot: Marcus Beauchamp, age 70; Ellen Beauchamp, age 75; Kenneth Colton, age 35; Winthrop Colton, infant; and Charles Colton, age 2. Kenneth had passed away five years ago, the two children before that. Fresh flowers adorned each vase.

Zestrum removed his hat and paid respects without words.

* * *

At noon Zestrum patronized Slade's Café for lunch. The menu on the blackboard on the wall promised "homemade food." The waiter/owner served passable chicken and dumplings, but it was not as good as Jessica's breakfast.

The thought of the delicate landlady pouring his coffee and filling his plate brought a smile to his face. She might be bestowing attention on him as she would any new boarder, but it was nice to think maybe she liked him as something more than a tenant.

The waiter at Slade's kept imparting the suspicious eye, as if he expected Zestrum to declare the fare inedible and throw dishes. The food was bland, not necessarily bad. The coffee was drinkable. Zestrum sat gazing out the window into the busy street, finishing his coffee.

"Tom Doniphon?"

Apparently, he would never finish a meal without interruption in Copperbank. He regarded the man standing by his table. "Not anymore. Call me Zestrum."

"Zestrum Doniphon. My name is Gerald Nowlin." He offered a hand. Three other men stood behind him, feigning casual interest. Bodyguards, no question.

Zestrum shook hands briefly. "And your friends?"

"My top wranglers, Gene, Randy, and Travis. I hear you're looking for employment."

Who was spreading this news around town? Surely not Etcheverry; he wouldn't want competition. "Could be."

"I own the Easterbrook Ranch, east of here. I'm in the market for good men." He lowered his chin, bestowing a significant look. "I hear you're a good man."

"I try."

A not entirely savory smile spread across the man's face. "Are you interested in work? I will make it worth your while. More than some. . . red coin." He sneered the last two words as if they were poison.

"What's the job?"

"Ranch hand."

"That can encompass just about anything."

"The duties are flexible. Right now I'm running cattle, farming, and fishing. Someone with your expertise in engineering would be invaluable."

Zestrum wondered how he knew about the "expertise in engineering." He left landscaping behind four years ago, but his skills remained sharp. And he was fit enough for hard labor if he chose that course.

Nowlin saw him considering options. "Come on out to my place and take a look. Can't do no harm. It's a nice trip out. And I'll even provide you a good dinner." He cast a disdainful look at the plate on the table.

The café owner, watching from across the room, sniffed in offense.

"Sure." Zestrum reached for his hat. "Let me pay the tab first."

"Taken care of." Nowlin lifted his eyebrows, allowing no argument. "You're my guest for the rest of the day."

CHAPTER 8 – THE LURE OF WATER

They crested the rise and the Easterbrook Ranch came into view. The main house was built on a hill not far from the edge of a riverbed crackled with parched earth. In all directions lay bare scrubland choked with dying weeds and cacti. The trees along the riverbank were gnarled and dying in the heat. Nothing lived long in the Badlands when the water stopped running.

Nowlin halted his horse on the rise overlooking the devastated countryside. "I think you can see why we need help around here."

Zestrum nodded. Etcheverry was starving them out. "It's a problem."

Nowlin grunted. "It's a *big* problem. And the law ain't no help round here. Come on." He led the way down the hillside and across the bridge over the desiccated river.

A young borg watered the horses with buckets. Zestrum noted the boy struggled with balance where he should have handled the weight of the bucket with ease. Then he noticed the black eye—tissue infected with Hashrise.

Hashrise was a risk of implants after surgery, quick to spread and hard to treat. If the sensitivity affected an eye, it could destroy depth perception and cause vertigo. If the sensitivity infested an arm or leg, it could impact mobility and strength.

The Consortium discouraged anyone from talking about failed implant surgeries. Bad PR.

Stricken cyborgs were considered unemployable by the Consortium, who wanted healthy employees to perform hard labor with minimal problems. Someone with sensitivity impairments would struggle to do manual labor—if they could find a job.

Hiring this borg was a point in favor of Nowlin.

Nowlin and Zestrum stepped inside the house. The large rustic living area had open beams and a big fireplace. A door led to the kitchen on one side and stairs rose up to the second floor on the other.

Nowlin invited Zestrum to sit on the oversized couch and a woman delivered iced drinks. After the long ride, the fresh water was welcome.

Zestrum stood to take the glass. "Thank you, ma'am."

The woman gave him a sweet smile. "You're welcome."

"This is Zestrum Doniphon," Nowlin said. "My daughter, Rachel."

Zestrum nodded to her. "Nice to meet you, Ms. Nowlin."

"Nice to meet you, Mr. Doniphon. Oh please, sit. Mama wanted to be here to greet you, but there was some trouble with the Blanken Ox." She watched as he sat on the couch, then looked to her father for direction.

"Aaliyah's our ox expert," said Nowlin. "She treats those beasts like children." He looked to Rachel.

At his subtle nod, she left to let them talk in private.

"The big problem stems from a lack of water," Nowlin said. "The lack of water stems from Etcheverry damming the river on his property. I've talked with him, reasonable like. I've talked with the law, reasonable like. I've even filed a proper lawsuit in court, reasonable like. But the time has come to cease being reasonable."

"You filed in court here or in Steelreach?"

"Both. But court takes a long time here. Etcheverry's lawyer can stall for years. And then if I win, he can just ignore the decision."

"So you plan to take action."

"I do. Now, I'm not advocating riots and murder. I'm only looking for a permanent solution to the problem."

"What is your tactic?"

"Well, we need water. First thing I thought is: remove the dam. I have experts to do that. But Etcheverry has a fleet of boys ready to repair whatever we remove, so that is a temporary fix.

Second thing I thought is: run water direct from the source up in the mountains. That takes someone with engineering expertise to bring to fruition."

"Who owns the land in the mountains?"

"That is government land, owned and operated by the state. There ain't no state regulators here, otherwise my lawsuit might've had some traction.. However, I intend to acquire a strip of land between my ranch here and the lake."

Zestrum knew the Consortium-backed government was always willing to sell land to humans for development. Profit was their entire motivation.

"What I plan to do is build a canal and bring the water here through my own land, with my own construction materials, using my own employees." His eyes narrowed on Zestrum. "You have the experience to do the job."

Moving rivers was feasible with a team of highly trained cyborgs, but with a band of random borgs scraped together with hooligan money? "It's been a long time since I managed a crew."

"But you have the knowledge and the management skills to succeed. I have strong men in my employ, raring to go. None of them have the training for large-scale engineering. When I heard your name, I knew you were the man for the job."

That damn reputation again. "I'd have to scout the landscape, see the terrain, calculate the materials."

"Sure, sure. I'll put you up for the length of time necessary for your evaluation."

As if he'd summoned her, Rachel reappeared and set a tray of tiny sandwiches on the oval table in front of the couch.

"You can take as many of the boys with you as you see fit for the assessment," Nowlin continued. "I want a proper done evaluation so I can calculate the costs and procure whatever I need."

Zestrum lifted a sandwich and studied the meat between the bread slices. "You must also have heard that I'm currently considering a position with another rancher." He glanced at Nowlin.

The man selected a sandwich. "I heard. But my offer is better. More money, more leisure. And once the job is complete, I will guarantee you a piece of land at the end of the line."

His ears pricked up. Few cyborgs owned land. Humans wouldn't sell to cyborgs, so they were forever renting with no possibility of keeping their own place. Owning land would mean permanence, proprietorship, roots. He would no longer need to roam to new places, searching for work. He could farm, raise cattle, chickens, whatever he chose.

And have a companion.

Nowlin saw he'd generated interest. "I can offer you a room in the dorm tonight, to save you a ride back to town. You can stay till you make your decision. Be my guest. And if you choose not to work with me, no hard feelings."

No hard feelings. Right. *Meant no human ever.* Zestrum tasted the sandwich. Fine beef and homemade wheat bread.

Rachel stood by, watching the men.

"This is good," Zestrum said.

"My daughter sets an excellent table." Nowlin was on his second sandwich.

"We have the best beef in the territory," Rachel said proudly. "And I like to cook a good meal."

Zestrum admired self-sufficiency. "You have a map of the property?"

"I do." He signaled and his daughter brought a rolled paper from the desk. Nowlin unrolled the map and pointed out the area highlighted with a red line. "This right here. As you can see, the terrain is challenging. But I believe it can be done."

"Challenging is an understatement."

"That's why I need an expert engineer."

Possibilities materialized in his mind. "I'll consider your offer, Mr. Nowlin, but I must decline your generous room and board for the time being. I paid for a week at Colton House and I like to get my money's worth."

The rancher looked perturbed but tried to conceal his irritation. He'd expected Zestrum to jump at the offer. "Your choice, Mr. Doniphon."

"Can you lend me the map?"

Nowlin's attitude improved. "Sure thing." He rolled up the map and handed it over. Then he indicated the tray. "Help yourself, and rest long as you like before you set off again."

"Thank you, Mr. Nowlin. I'll sit a spell and then be on my way." He smiled to prove he was not ungrateful or intimidated. Negotiating with humans was never less than an ordeal. But the beef was good.

CHAPTER 9 – CHRIS CROSSED

The entertainment was the draw, really; the idea of seeing the lovely songbird on stage brought him in against his better judgment.

The Dual Majesty Saloon was as lively on a Wednesday night as any Saturday; plenty of local cowborgs, businesspeople, and shopkeepers seeking a good time. The casino tables were draped and yellow tape cordoned off all but a narrow path to the staircase, but the round tables in the barroom were occupied by card players.

Chris Etcheverry lounged in a chair with his back to the wall at a table with five other players. One—a cyborg wearing a bold red leather vest, crisp blue shirt, snug jeans, and red leather boots—seemed especially arrogant as he caressed his cards and tossed chips into the center pile. Zestrum recognized the model, a fighter designed to subdue hostiles during initial landscaping. He carried a high-powered weapon in his holster.

Zestrum hoped the red borg didn't have "Deadeye." And that he'd never have to square off against him.

Zestrum approached the bar where Deputy Edwards cradled a glass of whiskey. Edwards nodded greeting. Zestrum returned the nod as he sidled up beside him and ordered from the bartender. When he had his bourbon, he surveyed the room.

Edwards was watching Etcheverry's table.

"Who's the borg in red?" Zestrum asked.

"Don't know. Some guy came in with the wagon train this afternoon."

Zestrum noted the deputy's intense interest in the newcomer. "See something odd about him?"

Edwards touched his thumb to his nose and scrunched his face. "He ain't done nothing, but he ain't *not* done nothing, either."

Zestrum's gut said the same thing. He watched the red borg, too.

The game progressed with betting and dealing, the pots growing larger. One man bailed out, then another and another, leaving the pot between Chris and the newcomer. The audience around them watched the play with fascination. Two saloon ladies stood near the red borg, attracted to his stack of chips.

The final play of the game. The red borg stared across the table at Chris, showing absolutely nothing the way a well-trained warrior would. Chris raised the stakes and the borg called. They showed cards—and the borg won. The borg smirked and leaned forward to rake in the pot.

Chris fumed—then said it. "That wasn't a fair hand."

The borg froze in gathering his prize. "I don't think I heard you proper, mister."

"I said that wasn't a fair hand. You swapped cards."

"I'll attribute your poor gamesmanship to poor eyesight." He resumed raking over the chips.

Chris slapped a palm on the tabletop, startling the bystanders. "I said you swapped cards." He signaled to the three burly cyborg henchmen behind him. "Search him."

The borg didn't take his eyes off Etcheverry. "I ain't inclined to be searched, mister."

"If you want to walk out of here intact, you'll submit."

The henchmen closed in on the borg.

Edwards gestured toward the table, murmuring to Zestrum. "See what I mean?"

"No man likes being called a cheat," Zestrum said.

Edwards pushed off from the bar and came alongside the table where the henchmen surrounded the red borg. "How's the game going, gentlemen?"

"This unenhanced male seems to think he has the right to search me," the red borg said.

Chris didn't lift his gaze from the cyborg. "This tin-pot half-breed cheated. Search him."

"I wasn't planning on getting friendly with any rough hands tonight. If I change my mind, I'll let you know."

Chris looked at Edwards. "Maybe you should search him, Deputy." Off the cyborg's frown, he added, "A deputy's got a right to search whoever he sees fit."

"Only with probable cause," Edwards said. "Don't look like he's done anything except beat you at cards."

Zestrum saw Edwards' hand quaking from the tremens. Zestrum's opinion of the deputy's capability was sinking almost as quickly as his opinion of Chris Etcheverry.

"Maybe you should be careful what you put in the pot." Edwards motioned at the red cyborg. "Collect your winnings."

Chris lurched to his feet. "I say he's a cheat! You're gonna be searched one way or the other."

Bystanders gasped and backed away, frightened but not sufficiently to leave the saloon. Zestrum scowled, angry that bad-tempered humans were ruining another night. He'd hoped to see the songbird in the showroom.

The first thug seized the red cyborg, pulling him to his feet; the other two shifted to surround him. Edwards moved in to intervene, but the second thug knocked him to the floor, pulling his weapon to keep him at bay. The third thug reached to begin the search.

The cyborg acted with lightning speed. His right foot came up, kicking the table, forcing Etcheverry back. As his foot came back, he drove his heel into the knee of the thug holding him, causing the thug to yowl and release him. A fist into the second thug's jaw floored him.

By now Chris was reaching for his gun. The borg, off balance, with his right fist full of the second thug's face, drew and fired with his left hand before Etcheverry pulled the trigger.

Chris slammed into the wall behind him as the bullet struck his shoulder. The bullet he'd meant for the red borg went wild into the crowd. A man said *Ooof!* and dropped like a sack of potatoes.

Edwards fumbled to draw his weapon and get to his feet, each process hindering the other.

The cyborg knocked down the startled third thug and held a bead on Chris, who slumped against the wall, clutching his wounded shoulder, his face a mask of astonishment.

"No means no," said the red borg.

Two men knelt beside the bystander. "Get Doc Hartman," yelled one of them.

By now Edwards managed to get to his feet and yank out his pistol. "Everybody stay where they are!" He looked at the man heading to get the doctor. "Except you." Edwards waggled his gun to urge him on.

The man darted out.

Edwards trained his gun on the thug recovering on the floor. "You three, over there." He pointed with his weapon toward the wall where their boss leaned, gritting his teeth, suppressing moans.

The thugs looked at their boss before complying.

"You," Edwards indicated the red borg, "put down your weapon."

Reluctantly the cyborg laid his Rickenhower on the table beside his winnings. The Rickenhower was a borg's gun. If a human fired it, the recoil would at best spoil his aim and at worst break his thumb. It also worked well with Deadeye.

At another jiggle of Edwards' gun, the cyborg raised his hands in the air.

"Now," said Edwards, "we're all taking a walk over to the jail to straighten this out."

"He broke my arm!" Chris's arm was hanging at his side at a sickening angle.

"You'll get treatment at the jail. Let's go." He jiggled the gun toward the doorway.

Zestrum wondered if Edwards' gun could do more than point.

"You got no cause to hold me," Chris groaned out through his teeth. "I was defending myself."

"You drew first." Edwards indicated the crowd with his gun. "And all these witnesses saw you do it."

Chris glowered at the crowd with warning not to contradict his assertion.

"He's dead," announced the man beside the fallen bystander.

Edwards' expression darkened. "That's manslaughter at best."

"Self-defense," said Chris.

"He wasn't even in the game."

"He's got a gun."

"Everybody in here has a gun." Edwards muttered under his breath, "Something we probably should remedy." He raised his voice. "Let's go." He motioned at the doorway again.

Chris shoved away from the wall with sullen defiance. "I want my lawyer."

"I'm sure one of your hired boys will fetch him." Edwards kept distance from the red cyborg, Chris, and the three thugs as they exited the barroom.

Zestrum followed, along with most of the spectators. In the street the crowd spread out, attracting attention from passersby. The news soaked through the crowd like the plague. The doctor marched along the wooden sidewalk into the saloon.

Doug McConnell and several bystanders appeared on the saloon porch, observing the arrest. McConnell issued instructions to a young borg who raced toward the livery.

Edwards maneuvered his prisoners down to the next block into the sheriff's office.

Puzzle was sweeping the floor with a broom. "What's up, Edwards?"

"Book these guys," Edwards said, gun quaking in his hand. He nodded at Zestrum, welcoming him into the room as support.

Zestrum guarded the front door. Puzzle stripped the thugs of armaments, stacking them on the desk. A curious combination of firearms and knives and a stick of dynamite.

Chris plonked into a chair. "I've been shot!"

"Ain't mortal," said Puzzle. He inventoried the thugs' ID papers. "Will Penny. Tom Horn. Rowdy Yates."

Edwards prodded the thugs toward the jail cells. They shuffled unwillingly through the inner door.

Puzzle peered at the red cyborg. "Don't know your name."

"Louisiana," said the cyborg.

"Welcome to Copperbank." Puzzle started to search him but Louisiana's glare deterred him. "You got any more weapons, Louisiana?"

Slowly he reached into his clothing and produced two small pistols and three knives. He placed them on the desk.

Puzzle admired the pieces. "Nice craftsmanship. And a Rickenhower! Hell, my cyborg parts can't even handle that anymore." He frowned at the cyborg. "Into the back with ya."

Louisiana scowled with indignation. "I'm the wronged party here."

"Tell it to the sheriff when he gets here." He waved toward the cells.

Maddened, Louisiana sauntered into the inner room. Edwards locked the men into cells, the three thugs in one, Louisiana in another.

A knock on the door. Zestrum confirmed who it was and let the doctor into the office.

Doc Hartman went to Chris. "Good evening, Mr. Etcheverry."

"No it ain't," Chris complained. He indicated the wound and glared in the direction of Louisiana in the cell. "That asshole shot me."

"Ain't mortal," Puzzle insisted, cataloging the weapons on a form.

"Let's take a look, shall we?" The doctor assisted in removing Etcheverry's vest and shirt to inspect the wound. "That's quite a hole."

Chris scowled. "No shit, Doc."

"The bullet's still in there." The doctor leaned back on his heels. "It's an impact round."

Puzzle grinned. "Oooo, that there's gunna hurt."

"What's an impact round?" Chris sounded worried.

"Not surprised you've not heard of them," said Doc. "They're less lethal."

Puzzle was less happy about that.

"They flatten out when they hit, so they don't go so deep, but do put you on your ass." Doc picked up his bag. "We'll have to get that out."

"Then get it the hell out," Chris said.

"Perhaps you'd like to lie down for the procedure."

"Cot's in the cell," Edwards said.

Chris glared, then snatched up his vest and shirt and strode into the inner room. Edwards directed him into a cell and the doctor followed.

Edwards stood in the doorway, observing as Puzzle sorted through the confiscated armaments while keeping an eye on the prisoner.

"I don't need a damn audience!" boomed Chris.

"Gotta make sure you receive adequate medical care," Edwards replied, wincing as he watched the doctor slice into the man's shoulder to retrieve the bullet. But he did give a slight smile.

Zestrum didn't have to see the surgery to know what the doctor was doing. He'd witnessed extractions plenty of times. Although if it wasn't an impact round, it would have come out the other side.

Another knock and he checked to see who was outside the door. On the sidewalk stood a man wearing a tailored business suit and, beside him, Johnny Etcheverry. Zestrum noted the curious onlookers milling in the street.

The tailored man presented a business card. "Ephraim Judd, Esquire." When Zestrum didn't register the name, the man added helpfully, "I represent the Etcheverry family in legal matters."

Zestrum allowed Judd inside but blocked Johnny. "Why don't you go home and let your pa know your brother's in jail."

Johnny's face screwed up in disdain. "He'll be out in an hour."

"Why don't you go home," Zestrum repeated, the command deep in his voice.

Intimidated, Johnny sneered and trod toward his horse tied to the post down the road. Zestrum shut the door. Judd showed his card to Edwards.

"Yeah, I know who you are," Edwards said irritably. "After Doc's done."

The attorney pocketed the card and observed Zestrum with a mild smile plastered on his face. A higher class of thug, Zestrum reckoned, with book learning to keep his clients out of prison.

"Ow! What the fuck?!"

Zestrum enjoyed the sounds of Etcheverry's discomfort. Some men deserved it.

"It's going to get worse." The doctor was curt. "I gotta put your shoulder back in."

"Wait—" Whatever Chris was going to say next was blocked out by his scream.

"There, there. All done."

"Damn right you're all done. Get out of here."

"I'll be back tomorrow morning to check on you."

"Get out!"

Doc Hartman toddled out and spoke with Edwards. "I'll be back tomorrow to check on him."

"Thanks, Doc," said Edwards.

"Anytime." The doctor pattered to the exit. Zestrum opened the door to let him leave.

"I'll see my client now," said Judd.

Edwards impatiently waved him into the interior. Judd sauntered down the aisle to the cell, out of sight.

Puzzle shook his head and muttered. "That brat's right. He'll be out by morning at the latest."

"Not this time," Edwards said with troubled confidence. "Everybody saw him draw on Louisiana and shoot Wilkinson."

"Manslaughter, not murder," Puzzle pointed out.

"Nevertheless, a conviction might discourage him."

"If we can hold him long enough for a trial."

Edwards's face crumpled in worry. "Yeah."

CHAPTER 10 – ANOTHER LONG EVENING

Zestrum lounged in the chair beside the door listening while Edwards explained what he'd witnessed to Sheriff Bodie. Puzzle leaned on his broom, grimacing and smiling at the twists and turns of the narrative.

Bodie summoned Louisiana into the office and had him relate his testament. The facts matched, with a grain of restrained rage.

Ephraim Judd emerged from the cells and addressed Bodie. "I'll see you tomorrow at the courthouse for arraignment." He departed.

Louisiana scowled at the attorney, then loomed over the desk.

"Thanks for your cooperation." Bodie didn't look up from writing on his notepad on the desk.

Louisiana watched him. "So am I free to go?"

"As soon as I finish this report." Bodie wrote some more while the red cyborg shifted weight from foot to foot, aggravated. The sheriff recognized broiling anger. "You got a place to stay, Louisiana?"

"I got a room at Colton House."

Bodie looked at Zestrum. "Ain't that where you're staying?" At Zestrum's nod, Bodie looked at Louisiana. "You two can go over there together. Make sure you get there safe. It's late and dark and late." His eyes narrowed to preclude argument from the newcomer.

Taking the cue, Zestrum stood.

"What about my gear?" Louisiana gestured at the weapons on the counter behind the desk.

"Tomorrow you come back, sign the report, and we'll return your gear." His gaze hardened to flint. "It's late."

"How will I defend myself if someone pays an unexpected call?"

"I'm sure a fit fellow such as yourself can take care of yourself if need be. You proved it tonight."

Louisiana glowered, but understood arguing wouldn't liberate his armaments. He headed for the door.

"Good night," Bodie said.

The red cyborg said nothing on his way out.

"Good night," Zestrum said to Bodie, and he followed Louisiana to Colton House through darkened streets. It was near midnight and most folks were in their homes.

They entered the foyer and walked to the stairs. Both men turned at footfalls behind them. Louisiana's hand leaped to an empty holster and he froze, realizing his disadvantage.

Jessica Colton stood in the hallway, holding a tray. "Gentlemen."

"Ms. Colton. Sorry to disturb you this late. Goodnight, ma'am." Louisiana tapped his hat brim and hustled up the staircase to his room on the second floor.

"Goodnight, sir." She watched him disappear into the darkness, then looked expectantly at Zestrum.

Zestrum felt no need to explain but waited for Jessica to precede him.

She remained at the foot of the stairs. "You're keeping late hours, Mr. Doniphon."

"Some trouble at the Majesty. I had to make a statement."

"I see."

He noted the tray with the hot water and tea. "You're up late, too, Ms. Colton. Is that to help you sleep?"

"Oh, this is for Mr. Bainbridge. Indigestion."

"You're on call 24 hours a day?"

"Well, I figure I can accommodate a guest if I'm already in the kitchen." She pulled a bottle of soda water from her pocket and smiled.

He smiled. "I see. Good night, Ms. Colton."

"Good night, Mr. Doniphon." She went up the stairs to deliver the curative.

Zestrum followed her, then entered his room, locked his door, pulled off his boots, and flopped onto the made bed, too tired to undress.

CHAPTER 11 – FAMILY TAKES CARE OF FAMILY

Claude Etcheverry was at the sheriff's office at 8 am when Bodie unlocked the doors. He had Doc Hartman with him. The medical man looked half asleep.

"I need to see my son," said Etcheverry.

Bodie allowed them into the cell and left the inner door open. He sat at the desk to complete the endless paperwork the job demanded, wondering why he bothered. No doubt Judge Roberts would dismiss the charges by the end of the day and exempt Chris from responsibility again.

It was a sad pattern of the local judiciary that Claude Etcheverry had veto power. Bodie feared the Widow Anderson would never receive satisfaction—and he'd bear the brunt of her wrath.

The hushed voices in the cell were indistinct. Puzzle leaned against the wall beside the door, scowling as he attempted to eavesdrop. He glanced at Bodie and shook his head: nothing.

Bodie glanced at Edwards, asleep on a bedroll on the floor behind the other desk. Edwards was a good man once, long ago. He'd shown a flash of that skill last night, apprehending the troublemakers. And Zestrum stepped up to help without a second thought.

Maybe Bodie should offer Zestrum the job again.

Louisiana arrived and filled the doorway, taking in the layout of the room before entering. He noted where each man was and that the inner door was open.

"Can I help ya?" Puzzle said.

"I came for my gear."

"Get his gear," Bodie said.

Puzzle went about the business of releasing weapons, presenting a form. Louisiana scrawled a signature and collected his guns and knives.

Puzzle openly admired the Rickenhower. "Nice piece. Don't see custom-made like that too often."

"No, you don't," Louisiana said. Evidently, he wasn't interested in sharing the story of how he acquired the weapon.

"You staying awhile or just passing through?"

Louisiana gave him a suspicious look. "I'm paying my way. I'm emancipated."

"Oh, sure, we all are. Just wondered if you're looking for work."

He holstered his pistol and sheathed the knives. "I'm looking for peace and quiet."

Bodie granted him a stern look. "Won't find that at the Dual Majesty."

Louisiana speared the sheriff with a hot glare. "A man's got a right to make a living. Gambling's legal. And I wasn't cheating."

"I believe you. Everybody knows Chris can't play poker worth a shit."

Puzzle chuckled and nodded. "Got that right."

"He's the one you should warn out of the saloon," Louisiana growled.

"If only I could," Bodie said grimly. Chris Etcheverry had been a sore source of trouble since the day he was born. Gabriel was a close second, and damn if Johnny wasn't coming up the same way.

Doc Hartman appeared at the inner door, clutching his medical bag. "The patient is recovering nicely."

"Is he up for a trip to the courthouse?" Bodie asked.

"As long as he's not on his feet too long."

Bodie nodded and the doctor departed.

Edwards yawned, sat up, and scoped out where he was. Bodie nodded to him, then turned toward the inner door as Claude Etcheverry strode into the office.

Claude's expression was forbidding. "What time's Judge Roberts opening court?"

"Eight-thirty," said Bodie.

Claude eyed Louisiana. "This the guy who shot him?"

"I am." Louisiana folded his arms across his chest defiantly.

Claude assessed him with disdain. "My boy says you pulled a weapon on him for no cause."

"Man called me a cheater. I can't abide a man calls me a cheater."

"You saying my boy's a liar?"

"That ain't the main dispute," Bodie said. "Chris shot Festus. Killed him."

Claude looked at the sheriff with cold calculation. "He says that was an accidental discharge of his weapon."

"That's what he says. We got statements. We'll let the judge sort it out."

Louisiana snorted derisively.

Claude regarded the red cyborg with contempt. "Looks like we're getting off on the wrong foot, then."

Louisiana gave him a wide-eyed challenging look. "Looks like."

The tense standoff was broken when Lawyer Judd strolled in, wearing his attorney best duds. "Good morning, gentlemen. We have a court date at eight-thirty."

"We do." Bodie motioned at Puzzle. "Prep the prisoners for transport to the courthouse."

Puzzle lifted handcuffs off a hook.

"Is that necessary, Sheriff?" said Claude, a chiding note in his tone.

"It's regulations," Bodie said sternly. "Wouldn't want to go against regulations."

Claude glowered. "Mind if I accompany my boys over?"

"Suit yourself." Bodie lifted another set of handcuffs from a hook and assisted Puzzle in cuffing the prisoners.

Edwards levered himself to his feet and stood watch, blinking as he came to full cognizance. "Etcheverry."

Claude scowled meaner. "Edwards."

Edwards looked at Louisiana. "You still here?"

"I've been out and back," Louisiana said. "Looks like you have, too."

Edwards lowered his head, inspecting his boots. "Some days it don't pay to go home."

* * *

Zestrum strolled down the street from Colton House and was surprised to see people clustered outside the courthouse on the corner. The arraignment had drawn a huge crowd. Everyone was waiting to hear the judge's mandate about a trial.

Zestrum entered the bank and found he was the only customer. Three employees stood at the door watching the crowd. One of them was Burt Davis.

Davis straightened his gray-and-black striped suit. "Mr. Doniphon. Can I help you?"

"Need to cash a check."

"Right this way." Davis craned his neck toward the courthouse, then scurried behind the cashier cage and locked the hatch. "Can I see your ID?" He smiled. "Merely a formality."

Zestrum pulled out his wallet to display his card. "Something going on at the courthouse?"

"Arraignment." Davis took the ID card and studied it with a quizzing glass. "Etcheverry's son Chris is charged with manslaughter. Waiting to hear if there'll be a trial."

"Is that up for debate?"

"Well, round here sometimes the judge just sentences a man if he pleas it out first thing. Tens or twenties?"

"Tens and fives."

He rapidly counted the cash. "Two hundred." He counted again on the counter on his side of the bars. He looked at the customer. "You want it in an envelope? Easier to carry, I say."

"Sure."

Davis tucked the bills into an envelope stamped with the bank logo. He slid the envelope across the counter underneath the bars. "There you go, Mr. Doniphon." He leaned forward and grinned.

"And may I say it's a pleasure to do business with you. Would you like to open an account?"

"That all depends on what happens in the next week." He tucked the envelope into an inside shirt pocket. "Thanks kindly."

"Thank *you*. Have a blessed day."

As Zestrum exited, Davis joined his co-workers at the door to keep watch on the justice building.

On the wooden sidewalk, Zestrum observed the crowd. He spotted people he'd seen at the saloon and the café. A spark of curiosity struck, then he decided he'd hear the outcome soon enough. He had better things to do.

At the stable on the opposite end of town the grooms were sweeping the dirt outside the barn, hampered from joining the throng by their chores. Zestrum signaled, and Charlie rushed into the barn to bring his horse. Minutes later Zestrum rode off toward the hills.

CHAPTER 12 – THE PRIZE

Zestrum reined in Shiloh on the mountainside under tall oak trees and checked the map. The coordinates indicated this was the border of Gerald Nowlin's property. He examined the map, then followed a game trail between trees and boulders to assess the terrain.

The Dicron Mountains presented much as the Striker Range had: an asymmetrical range with its crest and high peaks toward the east; granite and sedimentary rock; an upfaulted chunk of planetary crust that was rising a millimeter a year. The gentler western slope had streams and rivers emptying into the large Salinger River that Etcheverry had dammed.

When Etcheverry sold water to Copperbank, he demanded small fees and big favors from the Town Council, allowing enough through a private canal to support the city. He made a fortune selling meat and dairy in exclusive contracts with the retail markets and restaurants.

As Zestrum directed Shiloh along the faint path, he recognized the songs of the blackbird, torpe, and pheasant. Here and there he heard squirrels scurry in the branches above. His mind wandered to building track through the Strikers.

The precise design of trestles, bridges, and tunnels to conquer steep mountains was critical to opening up the interior of the continent. The downward thrust trusses used metal and wood, built in separate sections manufactured off-site and brought in by the locomotive behind them.

Zestrum had managed a construction crew working ahead of the track-layers. Workers chiseled roadbed from sheer cliff, hacking, drilling, and blasting while suspended by ropes.

Back-breaking labor through frozen winters and burning summers. Explosions, landslides, accidents, avalanches, and disease killed thousands. The vegetation was only ten years old and there was little shelter from the unchecked winds. Dust storms sandblasted painted metal to shiny steel. Snowstorms turned workers into shovelers to link camps and clear tunnels of ice and snow.

Owen never made it out of the snowslide that smothered Camp 8. Even after spring thaw they didn't find his body.

It took four years to build across the range through the only accessible pass. They laid track across the flat arid plains to the opposite coast at a much more rapid pace. Boomtowns sprang up along the route to supply alcohol, gambling, entertainment, and sex workers. As the railway moved on, the towns disappeared and reappeared in their wake.

He halted Shiloh and examined the map to clear his memory of the past. Designing and constructing an aqueduct would take years—unless Nowlin procured the best equipment. Something borgs rarely saw in the Strikers.

Training unskilled laborers would be time consuming, but the cyborgs he'd seen on Nowlin's ranch looked fit enough. The biggest obstacle was sabotage from Etcheverry once the rancher learned of the plan.

Zestrum didn't need that kind of aggravation.

While he formulated the design in his head from this brief survey, the prospect of devoting years to the project did not appeal to him, no matter how altruistic the motive or how high the pay.

Perhaps Nowlin would be satisfied with a detailed set of blueprints for a set fee. Zestrum preferred not to be tied to anything or anyone.

* * *

"You're certain I can't persuade you otherwise?" Nowlin offered a refill of his best brandy.

Zestrum let the man fill his glass and held it between his hands to warm. Refusing the employment was becoming tiresome. "I foresee at least thirteen months to trench the bed, lay the trestle, and construct the arches for an aqueduct."

"This is great country for an ambitious young man." Nowlin set the bottle among the others in his well-stocked bar. "The possibilities are endless. The potential wide open."

"The amenities are wonderful, Mr. Nowlin, I can't disagree."

"But you don't see yourself working for me?"

"I don't see myself working for anyone. I've done that, and I prefer to work for myself."

"There's a difference between working for the Consortium and working for a private company."

"May be, but it's still working for someone else."

Nowlin chewed his lower lip, trying to conjure more incentives. "But you think it can be built?"

"Anything can be built with the right crew and resources." He leaned his elbows on his knees. "I suggest a counteroffer."

"Tell me."

"I can draft a blueprint for the construction with detailed instructions. Your men follow the instructions and you get your aqueduct."

"For what compensation?"

"The land we spoke of."

He scoffed. "That was for a full employment through to a completed project."

"The blueprint would be a completed project. It's simply up to you to hire the men and the foremen."

"Hmm." He contemplated the ceiling, tapping a finger against his chin. "I'll have to think about that." He leveled a critical look at Zestrum. "I usually get what I want in the end."

"I have no doubt you'll get your aqueduct."

"Timeline on getting the blueprint done?"

"A week."

Nowlin swallowed down his drink and smiled. "Well. Let me show you the parcel of land that comes with my offer."

* * *

Gerald Nowlin and Zestrum rode across the range north of the main house toward the foothills. The meandering dirt road had several trails leading off into the distance, disappearing in trees and brush to nearby buildings. The road continued up into the hills and eventually into the mountain range through the canyon.

Nowlin turned right, down a narrow strip of rutted packed dirt carved through scrub brush and oak trees. Two miles in, he gestured at a weathered shack and a listing barn. "Ten square acres at the base of the hills."

Zestrum dismounted to walk the circuit around the structures. The barn needed a new loft and roof. There were stalls and rusty implements abandoned by the former inhabitants.

He stepped onto the creaking porch and walked through the residence. The house was small, three rooms meant as parlor, kitchen, and bedroom. An outhouse visible through the kitchen window, and a well.

He examined the well. He turned the handle to raise the bucket. Empty. He glanced into the distance and saw the dry riverbed that passed through the property.

The parcel of land was dependent on the water from the mountains.

Quite an incentive. The sooner the pipeline was laid, the sooner he'd have potable water to drink, to farm, and to raise livestock.

He scowled. Nowlin knew how to drive home his point about the urgency of the engineering project.

He walked around the back of the barn, scoping the landscape, noting the withering trees, the barren fields, and the possibilities. The arid plains had looked like this, dry as a bone, dusty, inhospitable. And yet there were now towns along the railway, thriving with the humans who wanted to live in open spaces.

He wanted his own open space.

Zestrum finished the inspection and rejoined Nowlin beside the horses. Nowlin was drinking from his canteen; he offered it as Zestrum approached. Zestrum took a swallow and returned the canteen.

Nowlin hooked the canteen to his saddle. "It was a beautiful place when Hollis lived here."

"What happened to Hollis?"

"He passed away last year. Most of my tenants moved to greener pastures. Losing those rents has affected my finances, Mr. Doniphon. I don't want to lose more."

"Understandable." He studied the horizon of purple mountains, the snowy peaks in the distance. "What would you think of expanding that aqueduct to the snowline?"

Nowlin frowned, blinked, and stared off the direction of Zestrum's gaze. "That's at least fifty miles."

"Fifty-two miles. But you'd have uninterrupted flow directly from the source."

"You mean—*around* the Salinger River?"

"Yes. Etcheverry wouldn't have any claim on it."

Nowlin slowly smiled. "I like that idea. Tell me your design."

"A gravity-powered system, open lined canal from the north end of the Salinger Hills across the Dundee Valley. A tunnel through the Fortram Hill, then down to this valley via an open canal."

"You make it sound simple."

"The design is simple. The execution is complex."

"But how do you get it through the Dundee Valley? The elevation drops a good thousand feet and goes back up on the other side."

"Steel pipe inside concrete frame. Water pressure builds in the downslope and forces the water through the upslope. Thirty tons of steel for pipes. Concrete masts to reinforce the stability of the sag pipes. A tunnel boring machine to cut through the Fortram Hill." He pointed toward the dry riverbed. "You've got the base for the canal right there."

Nowlin envisioned it in his head. "Mr. Doniphon, if you make it happen, this land is yours."

CHAPTER 13 – TOO MANY CHOICES

At the livery stable Zestrum slid the saddlebags off Shiloh and turned his horse over to Charlie with a coin tip for extra good care. On Main Street, he saw the Etcheverrys outside Barnes' General Store.

Gabriel was loading sacks of flour and rice into the family's buckboard. The grocer's boy was struggling to load heavy sacks into another rancher's wagon. Claude and Angie were speaking with two upstanding ladies in daytime finery on the sidewalk.

Zestrum spotted the weapon on Angie's belt. She had a carbon pistol, of course, but she also had a high voltage wand.

The wand was rare. One discharge disrupted cyborg components. Two could maim. Three could kill. The Consortium outlawed wands to protect their work force. But in the Badlands, wands were effective at repelling predators and herding cattle, particularly the fierce Blanken Ox.

Zestrum wondered if Angie carried the wand to tend livestock or punish errant ranch hands. She wasn't wearing it when they first met at the ranch.

Zestrum hadn't intended to stop but the sooner he spoke to the man, the sooner he would finish this business.

Gabriel saw him approach. "Pa."

Claude excused himself from the conversation. "Doniphon."

Zestrum touched the brim of his hat to the ladies, to the land baron. "Mr. Etcheverry."

Claude's eyes flicked to the saddlebags over his shoulder, then he got straight to business. "I hoped I'd see you today. You made your decision about that employment opportunity?"

"I have. I'm afraid I'm going to have to decline your generous offer."

The older man's eyes glinted with dissatisfaction. His son and daughter quieted, their eyes trained on their father.

Claude hooked his hands into his waistband near his guns. "You're going to pass up all that money?"

"I'm going to pass up all that money."

"Got a better offer somewhere else?"

"I did."

"Whatever it is, I'll double it."

Twice as much land? *Don't get carried away; you're not sure you can manage the acreage you've negotiated this far.* "It's not only the compensation, it's the nature of the work. Easier on the body." He smiled disarmingly.

"I see." Claude swept him with a dangerous look. "You're going to regret it."

"I live with many regrets, Mr. Etcheverry." He held the land baron's gaze without a quail, the way he'd learned to do on the crew. Never show weakness.

Claude drew a breath and exhaled it. "Well. I guess a man's gotta follow his instinct."

"Very much. I appreciate meeting your family and hope to cultivate your friendship in the coming days."

"Sounds like you plan to stay awhile."

"Awhile. We'll see how it goes." He touched the brim of his hat to the ladies, who were openly eavesdropping. "Ladies."

The upstanding ladies smiled. Angie's eyes contained a modicum of uncertainty as she nodded to him.

Zestrum entered the General Store and checked the shelves as he passed through to the rear wall where stationery supplies were. None of these were adequate for his needs.

He peeked through a wide arched doorway into a luncheonette with a black and white tiled floor, blue-upholstered swivel stools, and a brass foot rail along a 20-foot-long white marble bar. The soda fountain was bordered by intricate oak detailing.

The menu on the wall boasted egg creams, malts, banana splits, black and white sodas, milkshakes, and ice cream floats. Lemonade, orange juice, phosphates, and flavored colas.

Ralph Finkle was filling a glass from the fountain. "Morning."

"Morning," said Zestrum.

Four men seated on the stools turned in unison to look at him. Zestrum tipped his hat and the men acknowledged him with nods, then returned to their drinks. Apparently, this was a meeting place for the locals.

The display case contained a vast array of candy—mints, jelly bellies, candied fruit, hand-dipped chocolates, divinity, vanilla fudge, chocolate fudge, and caramel wafers. The space doubled as a pharmacy, with medicines, herbal remedies, and elixirs on shelves at the barback.

Zestrum wondered if Jessica Colton liked divinity.

Finkle walked through the General Store and set the glass of Coke on the front counter. Store owner Elijah Barnes thanked him and took a sip.

Zestrum approached the front counter. "Morning."

Barnes gave a courteous smile. "Morning. May I help you?"

"I need a piece of butcher paper." He used his hands to show the dimensions.

"Uh, a piece? Did you want to buy meat to go with it?"

"No. Just the paper." Zestrum reached for his wallet. He heard someone moving down the other side of the aisle and coming up beside him.

Chris Etcheverry plopped a can on the counter, making Barnes and Finkle flinch. Chris enjoyed the men's reactions. He gave Zestrum a sidelong look, unhappy he didn't elicit a similar reaction from the cyborg.

"Put this on my account." Chris produced a malevolent smile. The sling holding his arm didn't temper his attitude in the least. He picked up the can and sauntered outside.

Barnes breathed easier. "I'll get that paper for you."

Zestrum glanced out the window and watched as Chris and his kin had a quick confab beside their wagon. Angie shook her head in dismay. Chris glanced toward the store—where Zestrum was—and sneered. Obviously, Claude was informing him that Zestrum declined the job. Claude and Angie climbed into the wagon. Chris went to his horse at the post.

Gabriel secured a sheet of canvas over the bed of the wagon. Then he pulled out a knife and stabbed three of the sacks in the other rancher's wagon, making small holes that dribbled flour, sugar, and rice. He smiled and ambled to his horse.

Barnes saw the prank. He pressed his hands on the counter. "Shit. He did it again."

Finkle looked out the window at the leaking sacks. "Better tell Mr. Hoffstetter."

"Yeah." Barnes didn't move. "I'll wait till Gabe leaves."

"Yeah. Good idea."

And Zestrum knew at that moment he made the right decision.

* * *

At Colton House, Zestrum encountered Jessica in the front parlor. Again he was struck by the beauty of her eyes, her delicate eyebrows, her full lips. "Ms. Colton."

"Mr. Doniphon." She held a stack of folded sheets in her arms, noticing the saddlebags and roll of butcher paper. Her eyebrows lifted in speculation. "What do you plan to do with the paper?"

"Drawing, ma'am."

"Drawing of what?"

"I'll show you when it's done."

She slowly smiled at the proffered mystery. "Good enough."

He reached for the banister.

"I hope you don't mind, but I took the liberty of changing the sheets on your bed."

He glanced at her, surprised, then embarrassed because despite his cleanup he must have left dirt on her linens. "I'll try to do a better job cleaning up."

"Oh, it's not that. It's sheet-changing day." She hefted the sheets in her arms and those gray eyes twinkled with amusement.

He almost laughed. "Thank you, ma'am."

She continued to the door at the end of the hallway. He watched her disappear into the rear of the house and climbed up the stairs.

In his room, Zestrum hung the saddlebags over the back of a chair and withdrew his drafting tools from a leather pouch. He spread the tools onto the table by the window and unfolded his own map of the terrain—a detailed drawing with precise elevations.

A government map, which he technically shouldn't possess.

He laid a piece of butcher paper beside the map and outlined the imagined aqueduct from the mountain to the valley. By evening he had a rough sketch on paper and dozens of calculations in his moleskin sketchbook. He noted the time and went downstairs for dinner.

In the dining room, the other boarders were sitting at the table. He took the empty seat beside Louisiana and they exchanged a nod of greeting.

Jessica carried in a tureen of soup. She smiled when she saw Zestrum at her table. She served her boarders a pleasant meal, with special attention to him.

Louisiana flirted with Ms. Nolan, the schoolteacher. From the way the woman blushed, she hadn't garnered that much attention in a while. And, cleaned up, Louisiana presented a courtly picture. Zestrum wondered what his intentions were. He'd hate to see a friend of Jessica get hurt. Yet, Louisiana had taken a room here instead of the transient hotel. That hinted at a certain permanency.

After the meal, the lodgers left the dining room, tossing perfunctory compliments to the hostess. Jessica collected plates into a pile on the table.

Zestrum lingered behind for a private word. "That was a fine meal, Ms. Colton."

Her lovely eyes lifted to him and her lips curved into a smile. "Thank you, Mr. Doniphon."

"You set a good table."

"I strive to." She tilted her head. "Are you ready to show me what you have on the paper yet?"

"Not quite. I'll have something soon."

"I'll look forward to it."

"Can I help you here?" He gestured toward the table of leftovers and dirty plates.

"Absolutely not. You are my guest and shall be treated accordingly."

He cocked his head. "That is something I'm not used to hearing, ma'am."

"Well. I shall remind you at every opportunity." She lowered her chin, eyes locked on his. "If you'll let me."

"I will." He broke into a grin and picked up his hat. "Thanks again, ma'am."

She continued her work, smiling to herself.

The other boarders assembled in the parlor for an evening of reading, or cards, or some such domestic type activity. Zestrum stood in the hallway, debating his options. He would have preferred helping Jessica clean up the kitchen and getting to know her better, but—

Louisiana buttonholed him. "You plan to go to the Dual Majesty?"

"I haven't had the best luck over there," Zestrum said. "Somebody's always shooting somebody over something."

"Humans." He scoffed. "We shouldn't let them spoil our fun, though, should we?"

"Two hours waiting around for the investigation can sure put a crimp in it." He lowered his voice. "I saw Etcheverry the younger at the General Store."

Louisiana grimaced. "He made bail."

"That makes the town a little less safe, doesn't it?"

He puffed up. "Well, Sheriff Bodie had the foresight to hire on another deputy."

Zestrum's head slanted in speculation. "You?"

Louisiana moved his vest to show the badge cinched to his belt near the buckle. "I'm officially employed and no longer a vagrant."

"So this trip to the Majesty is a celebration of sorts?"

"Gotta get my kicks in before my midnight shift." He grinned. "Come on. I'll buy you a drink."

CHAPTER 14 – A WANTED MAN

The casino at the Dual Majesty was open for business. Revelers surrounded the gambling tables, shrieking wins and losses over the background music. The pianist was varying from jazz favorites to classical pieces with a honkytonk rhythm showing off her virtuosity if only to herself.

McConnell circulated among the game tables, pausing here and there to encourage customers to keep playing. He handed a blue chip to one of the losers at the blackjack table. The man pushed some green chips from his dwindling pile into the betting area. The dealer shuffled the deck to deal another hand, glancing at McConnell. McConnell smiled and ambled on.

Louisiana and Zestrum surveyed the room. When Louisiana spotted Chris at the blackjack table, he nudged Zestrum.

"Don't that beat all," Louisiana murmured.

"He looks happy to be out of jail."

Louisiana snorted, then gauged the poker tables before choosing his opponents for the evening. He gave Zestrum a wry look. "A man's gotta make a living."

Zestrum acknowledged that with a look and watched the red cyborg join a table. The three men eyed Louisiana as he sat down, aware of last night's deeds but agreeable to test their skills against a shrewd stranger.

At the bar, Zestrum ordered bourbon and observed the crowd. Many of the same men and women, but some newcomers. He was dismayed the showroom was dark beyond the open doorway.

"Buy a lady a drink?"

He turned to find Victoria Barkley at his side, wearing a jade green dress cut low across her bosom. She wore less makeup, looking softer than when he last saw her.

He signaled to the bartender, who poured her a drink. "Evening, ma'am."

She pouted. "Victoria, please. I'm not a ma'am." She lifted the glass. "Haven't seen you lately."

"Lots going on." He inclined his head toward the showroom. "Will you be singing tonight?"

"I will. Will you be listening?" She sipped her drink.

"I will. I enjoy a beautiful voice."

She leaned close, placing a delicate hand on his bicep. "You think I have a beautiful voice?"

"I do." He found it odd how desperate she sounded for appreciation and compliments. Surely she had dozens of admirers. Or perhaps their fawning no longer satisfied her.

She smiled and touched the rim of her glass to her lower lip. "How many more nights will I get to entertain you, Mr. Doniphon?"

"It depends on the next few days."

Her expression brightened. "You're contemplating a longer stay?"

"I am."

The fingers clasped around his arm. "I can't tell you how happy I am to hear that." She glanced over the crowd, a scowl marring her perfect features. "So many men think being strong is trying to prove it. A strong man doesn't need to. So few measure up." Her eyes returned to him and softened to admiration. "I can see a man such as yourself must have many options in life. I would surely like to discuss those options with you at some future point in time."

The blatant offer made his blood rush. Then his thoughts flickered to Jessica Colton, standing at the base of the staircase holding a stack of folded sheets. The fact that his landlord popped into his mind while he was speaking with a delectable songbird must mean something. "I look forward to that—when it happens."

She sidled closer, brushing her bosom against his arm. "Would you be—"

"Victoria."

She lost her smile and pulled away as McConnell approached from behind her. She painted the smile into place when she turned toward him. "Mr. McConnell."

"Show starts in five minutes." He gave a quick appraising look, assessing their conversation from their proximity and body language. "You should prepare."

"I'm prepared." She drained the glass and placed it on the bar with a clunk. She looked at Zestrum. "Front row's reserved for my friends. Take a seat center." She pressed a blue chip into his hand and strolled into the showroom.

McConnell noted everything. He leaned an elbow on the bar. "I hear you may be taking employment at the Etcheverry Ranch."

He'd turned down that job. McConnell's spies were lax. "I'm assessing options."

"If you want options, you could consider working for me."

"For you?"

"Yes. I've seen how you handle yourself. I can use a man with wit and muscle to help keep the place neat and clean." Here the man glanced at the patrons, noisily consuming beer and playing games of chance.

"As a bouncer?"

"You could work your way up." He nodded toward the bartender. "Geflos here started as a bouncer and he's making good wages as a bartender. Anselmo runs the roulette wheel. A man who can figure things might rise to an administrative position."

"I'll keep that in mind." At the start of music in the showroom, he set down his glass. "See you later, Mr. McConnell." He started toward the showroom.

Suddenly Johnny Etcheverry blocked him and moved in closer than Zestrum preferred. His eyes brimmed with challenge. "Is it true?"

Zestrum held his temper. "Probably." He moved to go around the boy.

Johnny stayed in his path. "Is it?"

"Depends on what 'it' is."

"That you turned down my Pa?"

"That 'it' would be true."

The youngest Etcheverry evaluated him a long moment, then strode away with enthusiasm equal to his arrival.

Zestrum ducked through the doorway to get that front-row center seat.

* * *

The same Moonshadow Clan cyborg guarded the red velvet rope separating the front row of tables. Zestrum showed his blue chip and the bouncer lifted the barrier to let him pass.

The two outer tables were full. At the center table sat Gabriel Etcheverry, feet propped on the lip of the stage. There were two empty mugs on the table while he worked on a third. He gave Zestrum a smile that reeked of venom.

Zestrum nodded to be polite and sat on the opposite side of the table.

Chris bulled through the crowd and dropped into the chair next to Gabriel. He hooked the arm of a passing waiter who juggled a tray crammed with drinks. Chris took a mug from the tray and released the waiter, who looked askance but skittered away as fast as possible.

Chris and Gabriel exchanged a smug look.

Zestrum wondered if Chris and Gabriel won—or stole—the blue chips from someone else. The songbird was classy enough not to give these privileged hooligans blue chips and McConnell looked smart enough to know the Etcheverry brothers at the front table could ruin the show.

Then the blackjack player showed the bouncer his blue chip and plopped down at the front row table to his right.

The lights lowered and the chatter ceased. The first song of the set was a bouncy tune with all the ladies dancing and singing. Victoria was conspicuously absent. At the end, there was applause—and calls for Victoria.

The dancers formed a V and struck poses. Victoria strutted out from the upstage curtain and the crowd went wild. One could hardly hear her song over the commotion.

At a particular juncture, the dancers came close to the edge of the stage. Gabriel grabbed at Victoria's shoe. She playfully kicked her foot loose and reversed out of his reach, never missing a beat.

Another lively song and then the ladies exited and a man came out to sing a rowdy drinking song. Chris and Gabriel interjected rude comments between lyrics which the singer acknowledged with a grin even when it threw off his rhythm.

That song ended, the ladies did another dance, and then another man appeared on stage in a puff of smoke.

The signboard on the edge of the stage bore the message "Imperio – Master of Aces!" with an illustration of the performer.

Imperio stood before a black velvet background dressed in immaculate suit and dress shoes. He produced a pack of cards and proceeded to shuffle and transfer and misdirect with impressive showmanship. Every trick earned applause and cat calls in equal number.

Zestrum marveled at the man's speed and command of the deck. His dexterity could have been the result of hours of practice or cybernetic enhancement, hard to tell.

"Get off the stage, Master of Asex!" shouted a cowborg from the back of the house, a deep voice that drew laughter from the crowd.

"Asex" was slang for someone that no one was attracted to.

Imperio peered into the darkened audience. "You, dear sir, are but a passenger in life's boat. I am a captain. And while you sit on your questionable assets, I spend my time with these beautiful ladies."

There came a dose of laughter.

"I guarantee all of you that your time spent with me will be well worth the while. For as we speak, the ladies are changing into something more revealing. Isn't that worth waiting for?"

Shouts and catcalls filled the air, answering *yes*.

Imperio completed his routine and took a bow as patrons applauded and stomped feet. The performer vanished into the wings as the stage blacked out. Lights came up on the ladies, music started, and dancing commenced.

For the finale, the songbird appeared alone in a baby spot. She wore a tight dress, more revealing than the last.

The room hushed to silence. The band struck a chord and Victoria sang a lovely ballad, wrenching the hearts out of every lonely soul in the room.

When you told me you were leavin',
you tried to seal it with a kiss
I told you you could keep it,
'cause it's not a thing I'd miss.

You've never been no damn good, and I told you so.
Take your second shirt, your cheatin' heart,
get on the road and go.

I miss your cheating heart
I miss your wandering ways
Since we've been apart
I've lived my longest days.

You're the only man I ever loved
Like I love you.

I miss the way you lied to me
when I asked you where you'd been.
I miss the way you cried to me when
I caught you in a sin.

I miss your cheating heart
I miss your wandering ways
Since we've been apart
I've lived my longest days.

*You're the only man I ever loved
Like I love you.*

*I can't live without you,
This much is true.
You're the only man I ever loved
Like I love you.*

Even Zestrum felt the tug of sentiment, and he'd had his heart crushed by the best. Thus, his policy of not getting involved.

By the time she finished, the men were sobbing in their beers and the women were misty eyed. But the audience leaped to their feet with applause as Victoria took her final bow.

Chris stood and started to climb up on stage. A flash of irritation crossed her face as Victoria planted her foot on his uninjured shoulder and pushed him back into his chair. The crowd roared. Chris looked a trifle angry—until she winked as if it were an impish gesture. Then he laughed.

Victoria backed upstage and the curtains closed. The musicians played while the lights brightened.

Chris and Gabriel hoisted out of their chairs and jostled out of the showroom, pushing aside anyone who got in their way.

Zestrum sat at the table until the room emptied, then took his leave.

* * *

At the end of the evening, Zestrum and Louisiana departed the saloon together. Louisiana regretted leaving the table—he was winning—but work called. He proceeded to the sheriff's office for his shift. Zestrum returned to the boarding house, enjoying the relative quiet of a Thursday night near eleven thirty.

He was halfway across the foyer when he heard a door open in the rear of the house. He slowed to identify the person in the dim lamplight.

Jessica Colton appeared, carrying a tray with a teapot and cup. She stopped short, startled, until she recognized him. "Mr. Doniphon." She came closer.

"Ms. Colton." He glanced at the tray. "Mr. Bainbridge's indigestion again?"

A crooked smile graced her face. "Afraid so. The chicken and dumplings didn't agree with his constitution."

"That is not possible, they were perfect. I suspect Mr. Bainbridge just wants the attention."

"I don't believe that."

"You don't give yourself enough credit."

They regarded each other for a moment until Zestrum felt awkward.

"You better not change those dumplings."

She chuckled, rattling the pot and cup. "I won't."

"I meant to tell you earlier. I'm headed out early tomorrow morning and I expect to be gone overnight. So you don't make more for meals than you need."

A troubled look dampened her cheerful expression. "You'll be gone overnight?"

"Yes. I should be back Saturday evening." Her distressed attitude pleased him. Was she going to miss him?

"What time do you plan to depart tomorrow?"

"Early." When she waited for an exact time, he added, "Five."

"I'll have something ready for you before you head out."

"That's awful early, ma'am. I can't rightly expect you to provide breakfast at that hour."

She shook her head decisively. "I can't possibly let you leave my house without a decent meal. That wouldn't be right." She lowered her chin, defiant eyes on him. "You paid for room and board, and that includes breakfast and dinner."

"And lunch on my own."

She held his gaze. "You take care of that and I take care of the rest."

He started to argue, then realized she was determined to feed him. He let it go with a smile. "I appreciate that, Ms. Colton. I was kind of lamenting not starting my day with your eggs and bacon."

"Eggs and bacon it is. And coffee. You'll need something to keep yourself warm." She put her foot on the bottom step. "Cream and sugar?"

"You know my weakness, ma'am."

She smiled, lifting her chin triumphantly, and proceeded up the stairs. He followed, watching the sway of her hips.

At his door he watched her stop outside Bainbridge's door. They traded a long look, then she knocked. When the door opened, she handed over the tray.

Zestrum entered his room and locked his door to keep himself in.

CHAPTER 15 – UNWANTED COMPANIONSHIP

When Zestrum came downstairs at five, he found a place setting with a cloth napkin, a coffee cup, and a thermos on the dining room table. He draped his saddlebags over a chair.

Jessica breezed in with the enamel coffee pot and filled the cup. "Good morning, Mr. Doniphon."

"Good morning, Ms. Colton."

"Sit down." She filled the thermos, then added cream and sugar. "I believe those are your proportions?"

He was impressed at her memory. "Yes, ma'am." He sat.

She went into the kitchen and reappeared with a plate of eggs and bacon which she set before him. "Don't eat too fast. No need to upset your stomach." She glanced at his abdomen, his chest, then at his eyes, her interest palpable.

If he wasn't leaving so early, he would pursue that interest. But he'd formulated his plan and the sooner he delivered on his commitment to Nowlin, the sooner he'd acquire his payment. Even a plot of dry dirt was solid land. A place to plant roots. Once they had water.

And something to offer a woman of substance.

She busied herself in and out of the kitchen and dining room, checking on his progress and setting places for the other boarders. As he finished his coffee, she set a leather satchel on the table near his hand. "I'm sure you're more than capable of rustling up your lunch, but I did promise you a dinner."

He stared at the bag, surprised she'd provided more victuals. "You didn't have to do that, ma'am."

"No, I didn't have to. I wanted to." She lifted her chin, gazing down at him. "And in case you don't find any game out there, there's extra for tomorrow."

Slowly he stood. Her eyes remained fastened on his as he rose, taller than her by half a foot so her head tilted back to hold his gaze. She wore the plainest of dresses, had no makeup or fancy coiffure, and she was the loveliest woman he'd ever seen.

He saw her chest rise and fall in an erratic pattern as if he'd stolen her breath. He was tempted to thank her physically. She appeared open to the possibility. But it would be the height of rudeness to kiss and run and leave them both in need.

Her lips parted and it seemed she was about to suggest something intimate. She altered her words. "You will be careful, won't you, Mr. Doniphon?"

"I will."

"I expect you here tomorrow night at the latest. Your plate will be on the table waiting."

"I appreciate that, Ms. Colton."

She placed a hand on the satchel. "Enjoy your voyage." Reluctantly she slipped her hand away from the bag.

He picked up the satchel and his saddlebags. "I will thank you properly when I return." He flashed a smile and she blushed and smiled.

"I will be waiting."

* * *

The half-asleep boy at the stable stumbled to fetch Shiloh. Zestrum bridled and saddled the loyal animal and then mounted up for the ride out into the foothills. He didn't notice a second pair of eyes watching him.

This early there was no traffic in town, only pigeons and stray dogs.

The road ascended into the mountains through pine trees and brush and detritus from flash floods and storms. Sunlight flickered through the canopy of branches. The crew who'd built the road had followed terrain alongside the river, and the pass narrowed at the higher elevations where eons of water and wind had eroded the granite walls.

The view was scenic. Spectacular. The thunder of churning rapids filled the air.

He halted Shiloh to take in the immense scope of nature. Movement far down the road behind caught his eye. Someone was following at a distance.

He continued up the trail.

On the west side of the pass was Righoletti Lake, the source of water for Etcheverry's property. From here the water ran down through the canyon in the river.

On the east side of the pass, higher in the mountains, was Sansano Lake, the source of water that could be tapped for Nowlin's aqueduct. The frozen snows higher up melted to fill the lake as a natural reservoir. As long as Nowlin didn't overtax the flow, the snowpack lake would remain a steady supply of water. Some humans got greedy and sucked lakes dry. Then everything died.

He let Shiloh graze while he sat along the bank of Sansano Lake and made sketches and calculations in his moleskin book. He noticed flickers of movement at the far left of the lake as his stalker attempted to spy on him and stay out of sight.

Not an experienced scout, for damn sure. More like some greenhorn idiot.

Johnny Etcheverry sprang to mind. The only reason the kid would follow was to bushwhack him and there was no way the little punk would pull that off.

Logistics played through his head and he recorded his design in the book. One tunnel through the mountain would suffice for the canal, emerging in the pass south of the main canyon, connecting with the existing riverbed in the valley. Siphons and weirs would direct the path of the water, bypassing Etcheverry's property entirely.

He rode around the lake to inspect where the water cascaded down from higher elevations and trickled over granite rock in glittering sheets of liquid life. The power of water, so easily underestimated.

When the temporary dam broke apart on the Sullivan Ridge, the valley below flooded within minutes, tearing up trees and brush and leaving a scar on the side of the mountain. Sixteen cyborgs died in that catastrophe. The Consortium assigned blame to the engineer, who was one of the casualties. Easier to blame the dead, close the investigation, and continue the work.

Zestrum knew the true cause was shoddy materials and unreasonable deadlines.

At noon he took a rest under a willow tree on the shore of Sansano Lake and opened the satchel Jessica provided. A chicken sandwich and shortbread cookies. He finished the coffee and washed out the thermos, filled it with fresh water, and tucked it into his pack.

On the breeze he heard the singing of a gentle call. Not an animal, but a howler tree. Its gentle melody would likely turn into a ghostly symphony when the wind picked up.

Howler trees were among the few bits of flora reintroduced after the planetary cleansing. One of the biologists choosing the right mix of vegetation must have liked them; most folks thought they were creepy.

Zestrum leaned back against the trunk of the tree and tilted his hat to deflect the fierce sunlight.

Blanken 9 reminded him of Earth in many ways—the beaches, deserts, valleys, mountains. His childhood home had been in a green valley where he learned farming and raised animals before being consigned to the Consortium. His education changed abruptly after that, and his days filled with tedium and hard labor.

And then came the grueling surgeries.

He missed the long lazy afternoons of his pre-teen years, where he lay under a tree and dreamed of the future he would never have.

He breathed deep the fragrances of grass and lake around him. Could he have that future now?

His sixth sense activated, pulling him to the moment. The elusive intruder had pursued him up the slope to this side of the lake. Kid was going to have a long ride back tonight.

An hour or so later Zestrum rode slowly along an ancient trail winding up the side of the mountain, tracking his position and distance from the lake. The higher the elevation, the more native plants and trees appeared. Some species survived the sterilization program to spite the Consortium, and no amount of weeding exterminated them. Above 10,000 feet, the cleansing process was ineffective.

Seeding valleys and highlands with Earth plants was successful most of the time. Scientists repopulated the planet with Earth animals, including predators. Biologists roamed the Continent to measure and maintain the balance of nature.

The Blanken bees proved to be critical to crops. They made good honey, superior to Earth varieties.

The Consortium fabricated base camps to establish places for cyborgs to live. They tailored coastal cities to resemble Earth to attract humans. By the time the second wave of cyborg laborers arrived, the edges of the continent were strikingly similar to Earth shores.

When Zestrum, Virgil, and Owen arrived on Blanken 9 for their contracted work detail, coastal cities were established on the west and east sides of the continent. The next phase was building the railroad over extreme mountain ranges.

That was where Zestrum first encountered the Malivino Trees.

The tree had a nice canopy so a person might sit underneath it to rest in the shade. The tree's fragrance compelled one to sit because you became dizzy. If you knew the plant, you realized you'd been poisoned. If you retreated quickly, you might survive. But if you became confused and sat down, chances were you'd be toxified by the aroma. In the next hours the roots crept up out of the ground and wrapped around you. That meant death.

Zestrum could smell the tree from a distance.

The scent came to him now as he rounded the bends of the twisting road. He spotted the tree, a towering 40-foot survivor of the cleansing, in full bloom of spreading branches and brilliant orange leaves rustling in the heat.

Underneath the tree, ten feet from the thick trunk, roots wrapped around the bone and steel skeleton of a cyborg. The roots had long since done their work and dried to desiccated stalks. The perfume in the air warned that the tree was eager for its next victim.

The unfortunate cyborg probably had ID—someone somewhere might want to know he'd met his end—but attempting to retrieve that ID would invite the tree to emit fresh roots. Someone wearing hazmat gear or wielding a grappling hook would have to accomplish the identification.

Zestrum gave the tree a wide berth and hurried Shiloh past the grisly sight.

He ended up on a narrow plateau overlooking the canyon and river flowing down into the valley. This was the crevice where the pipeline would best serve the needs of his plans if the water source could be channeled here.

He pulled out binoculars to examine the hillside and damned if the trail he was on didn't lead to where he needed to go. He scouted for another route.

He had a good view of the mountainside and the landscape below—and, hell, that little bugger was making his way up the primitive trail after him.

He scowled and focused his binoculars on the figure. It was the Etcheverry brat, urging his horse up the grade. Did his pa send him on an errand to shadow him? To see what he was doing up in the mountains around the river?

More likely Johnny just wanted to kill him.

On the other hand, if the kid went missing, they'd never find him.

Dusk was coming on. In two hours the sun would set and cold would set in. While Zestrum had a thermal blanket and supplies for overnight, he doubted the kid had any expectation he'd be spending the night.

Zestrum also possessed the advantage of augments which regulated his body temperature in extreme cold and heat. That gadget had saved his skin several times in the past.

He walked Shiloh down the trail, backtracking. He knew the moment the kid spotted his reverse; the kid stopped in the middle of a switchback, then turned his horse to start down in a hurry. Zestrum could have made things worse by maintaining his usual speed, but he preferred to give the kid time to get the hell out of his way and rush home.

By the time he reached Sansano Lake, the kid was hustling for cover in a grove of cottonwoods. His mount's hoof prints were all over the place, as if the kid was unable to figure out where to hide.

Zestrum chose a comfortable spot by the lake among four trees, ample cover from wind and easy access to water. He removed the tack from Shiloh and dropped forage onto the ground for his dinner. He assembled a ring of stones and collected tinder, kindling, and firewood.

The space between here and the road was visible; the kid would have to show himself to reach the road. After another hour he hadn't abandoned cover to depart. Maybe he'd wait for nightfall. He probably didn't know modified cyborg eyesight functioned equally well at night.

The temperature dropped. Zestrum slung a warming blanket over Shiloh, then positioned his bedroll on a bed of grass. The breeze picked up and the howler trees began their ghostly nighttime serenade.

He set his saddlebags and packs on the ground beside a flat boulder, his seat for the evening. In a half hour the sun would sink below the horizon and. . .

. . . dammit, that kid was going to freeze to death in the brush.

"You might as well come out," he called across the empty expanse between here and there. "I know you're there."

There was a long silence. And then the kid emerged from the brush. It took him five minutes to cross to Zestrum's camp. He stopped under a tree and glared. "What are you doing out here, borg?"

So it was going to be like that.

Zestrum sat regarding him a moment before speaking. "What are *you* doing out here, boy?"

"I ain't no boy."

"Following me?"

"I ain't following you."

"Then why are you skulking around in the bushes?"

"I ain't skulking."

"I saw you trailing me up the path."

"It's a free country. I can go where I want."

"Who do you think paid for that free country you're enjoying?"

"My Pa staked his claim and paid his taxes."

"Cyborgs paid for that free country. With their blood."

"My Pa paid for his land. Etcheverrys pay their debts."

"He's been paying your way your whole life."

"I pay for myself."

"By stealing from other folks."

"I don't steal."

"Like that couple on the highway."

"I wasn't stealing!"

"You sure as hell were. You were just about to put your hand on a woman and if you'd done that, I'd have had to kill you. You should thank me for stopping you."

"I didn't mean nothing by it."

"And your pa buys your way out of trouble."

"He does not!"

"You ain't even worth arguing with."

"I'm better than you are!"

Zestrum lost patience. "You're a little tyrant, aren't you? Selfish brat. You got everything you need and everything you want and it doesn't make you happy. You're not happy unless you bully somebody. No wonder your pa don't pay you any attention. You don't deserve his attention."

"My pa pays plenty of attention to me!"

"Then what are you doing out on the road stealing things don't belong to you? What are you doing stalking me in the middle of nowhere?"

"I want to be like you."

Even the crickets went quiet.

Zestrum stopped. He hadn't expected that. Johnny's expression indicated he hadn't either.

The kid hunched his shoulders and dropped his chin, avoiding the cyborg's eyes. "Nobody messes with you. You're the first man that ever said no to my Pa without a beating, and he's not even planning one. You do what you want and nobody tells you different. I want to be like that."

"You want to be like me," Zestrum growled, angry.

Desperate eyes lifted to meet his. "Teach me how you do what you do. Show me what you do to get folks' respect. How do you do it?" That last sentence squeaked like a frantic plea.

"First thing you do is treat others with respect. The respect you want from them. You learn manners and use them. You finish school and listen to your elders. Then you might be ready to be like me."

"School's useless. Ms. Nolan only teaches simple stuff. Not the stuff I need."

"You got to have a foundation, boy. Otherwise the rest collapses. Education is the basis for the rest. And Ms. Nolan seems pretty damn smart to me. You wanna learn anything you gotta admit who's smarter than you and listen to 'em."

He sneered—then concealed the disdain. "I listen all the time. Folks always telling me what to do."

"You ever wonder if that means you're doing stuff wrong?" Arguing was useless at the moment. At the moment it was growing dark and within a half hour the sky would be pitch black and they were out in the middle of nowhere. "I can't send you to town this time of day. There are creatures in the mountains that'll eat you alive. So I guess we'd better make camp and have some chow, then bed down for the night."

Johnny's eyes widened at the mention of being eaten, then brightened at the mention of food. "I brought my bedroll." He pointed toward wherever he'd tied his horse among the trees.

"You bring food?"

He puffed in indignation. "Sure I did. I've camped out before. When I saw your saddlebags loaded down, I gave Charlie cash for travel goods."

"Go get 'em."

He hurried across the empty space into the brush. Ten minutes later he returned with his horse. He tied the critter next to Shiloh and pulled a canvas sack from a saddlebag.

Zestrum arranged kindling within the ring of stones. He struck the flint and started the fire, feeding small sticks until they blazed. Then he retrieved the satchel Jessica had given him this morning. The thought of her made his blood heat and he started to drift into imagination—then recalled there was a brat sitting three yards away.

He hardened his expression and sat on the flat rock to check the contents of the bag. Bread, cheese, smoked meat, and four small cartons of almond milk. There was also some kind of dessert wrapped in wax paper tucked at the side. Thoughtful woman.

He looked at Johnny. "What have you got?"

Johnny pulled things out of the canvas bag. "Ham. Beans. Corn." Three cans, which he set on the flat rock beside him. He gave Zestrum a look of self-sufficient triumph.

"You bring a can opener?"

The triumph faded and alarm flickered in his eyes. He ransacked the bag and came up with more cans—but no opener.

Zestrum almost said it—*what an idiot*—then decided not to. No doubt Claude Etcheverry said it regularly. Instead, he pulled out his army knife and pried out the can opener attachment. He set it on the rock between them.

Johnny laboriously hacked open his beans. The army knife wasn't a quick clean cut like a conventional can opener. It was for men on the move who traveled light. A real can opener was a luxury on the rail crew.

Zestrum pulled the six-inch skillet from his pack and proceeded to heat the meat. He saw Johnny looking mournfully at his cans, the lids three-fourths cut and jacked open. "Why don't we share."

Johnny eagerly agreed and handed over the cans. Zestrum warmed the beans and corn alongside the smoked meat and shared his dinner, but not the dessert. That was his.

Over dinner, he watched his uninvited companion. The kid ate like a starving urchin.

The conundrum was explaining his presence in the mountains overnight. This wasn't a pleasure trip; it was business. But that business involved matters pertaining to Nowlin, an enemy of Johnny's father. Best to keep the boy quiet about this.

"It's interesting you came along today," Zestrum said, breaking the silence. The boy's wary eyes shot over to him. "In Vaclya, where I come from, it's a tradition that men prove their intelligence and bravery in a hunt on a summer solstice."

He saw he'd snagged the boy's curiosity.

"It's a symbol of decisiveness and maturity, to show that a boy has become a man. Part of a week-long celebration."

"How do they prove they're a man?"

Zestrum prolonged the suspense by peering out into the darkness beyond the campfire. "Well. One tradition dictates that a man camp for a night at the graves of his ancestors to pay homage. To show loyalty and grace. On that night the women sing ancestral songs until dusk, then meet together in the public hall and tell tales of their departed loved ones."

"That must make for a long meeting."

"There are new stories every year. New graves every year." He looked at Johnny. "Kind of like the cemetery in Copperbank. There are new graves there this week."

Johnny averted his gaze, aware of the cause of that. "People die all the time."

"That they do. That's why the meeting gets longer every year." He let a pause build in the cold night air. "There's another tradition in that celebration. When a boy turns fourteen, his father takes him along to hunt together, to show him the ropes, teach him how to survive on his own. Then, when the boy turns fifteen, he goes alone to prove he's learned from his father."

"What kinds of things?"

"How to find water. How to trap game. How to dress and cook the meat. How to navigate by the stars. How to stay warm through the night. How to get back home alive."

"My pa taught me how to hunt." He slapped a hand on the knife at his side.

Zestrum glanced at the cans on the flat rock.

Johnny saw the direction of his gaze and straightened his spine. "He's taught me lots of things."

"That's good."

"He showed me how to wrangle cattle and take care of a horse." He trailed off into silence. Then the dam burst. "He ain't taken me out on the trail. He says I'm too young. He ain't taught me those things you learned."

Zestrum didn't mention that his father taught him those skills to fetch a higher price when he sold him to the Consortium. All of his brothers learned things at their father's hand to bring a better price. He tucked away that rancid memory.

"He might teach you if you acquire a better attitude." He caught the angry glare from the kid. "You become a helper round your pa's ranch, he'll respect you and share more."

He snorted. "You don't know my pa."

"Then you need to listen and learn by what he ain't doing."

"That makes no damn sense."

"You've lived with your pa your whole life. You know what he values. Is it the same as what you value? If you want to be a man, take a man's responsibilities, a man's pride."

He fiddled with a stick, drawing patterns in the dirt at his feet. "Will you teach me them things?"

Zestrum sighed at the thought of acquiring an unwanted apprentice. He'd tutored plenty of green kids during his tenure on the crew, but he no longer wanted to be a role model to anyone. Still, this was his opportunity to ensure silence about his travels. "I can only do that if you agree not to divulge where you learned it."

The kid regarded him with a puzzled expression. "Why not?"

"How would it look, a stranger teaching you things outside your family?" He pressed the point. "How would your pa feel? The only way we can do this is if we keep it strictly between us. You wouldn't be able to tell anybody else."

"I wouldn't tell." He sat taller on the rock. "I won't tell. I swear."

"You do and we're done." Zestrum pointed a finger at him. "Just don't point a gun at me again."

"I wasn't going to shoot you."

"You don't draw unless you intend to shoot. Someday you might draw on somebody who ain't as tolerant as me. Hell, I'm a tolerant man and I've nearly shot you twice in a week."

"I said I was sorry about that."

He cocked his head. "When did you say that?"

He mumbled, then spoke louder. "I'm sorry about that."

"Well." He left the matter dangling. "I'll think it over and let you know tomorrow."

"Tomorrow?" The disappointment was sharp.

"It's late. Best way is to start fresh in the morning. You can watch what I do and start your lessons."

Johnny's attitude improved considerable. "Okay. Anything you say, Mr. Doniphon."

The sudden courtesy was impressive. Zestrum kept his voice serene. "Lay out your roll and get to sleep. I'm rising at the crack of dawn and you'll need your rest if you're going to keep up."

Johnny unrolled his sleeping bag and tucked himself inside. Within minutes he was asleep.

Then Zestrum pulled the lovely apple tart out of the waxed paper and enjoyed dessert in the tranquil moonlight and the glow of his campfire. The cry of the howler trees filled the air with a mournful song.

CHAPTER 16 – NOT THE JOB HE WANTED

Zestrum woke at five and took in the surroundings. Nothing dangerous; nothing had attempted to approach his camp. Shiloh was a good guard, always alert, and he was giving Zestrum the eye, wanting breakfast.

At the birth of dawn, the sky gave a spectacular display of aurora borealis with waves of green and yellow. While his logical mind knew this was a result of gases and other particles interacting with oxygen and nitrogen in the atmosphere, his primitive mind propelled him back to scary stories around campfires in the fall when they slept under the stars during the roundup.

Zestrum was normally silent as he performed his morning routine, but this morning he was supposed to teach the kid how to survive in the wild, so he made noise to rouse him.

Johnny sat up abruptly inside his sleeping bag, disoriented and frightened until he recalled where he was.

"Time to get up." Zestrum rolled up his bedroll.

"It's still dark," Johnny complained.

"It's a long day ahead." He lowered his voice. "You wanted to learn what to do."

The reminder spurred him to action. "Yeah. I do." He wriggled out of his bag and started folding it.

"Roll it up from the bottom."

Johnny glared—then remembered their deal. He smoothed out the bag and rolled it into a neat bundle.

Zestrum tied his roll securely with the leather strap. "Takes less room in the pack." He set that aside. "Time to eat. Fetch some kindling and we'll re-stoke this fire."

Again there was a hesitation as the kid started to object to being ordered about, then he reached for a dry branch on a nearby tree.

"Downed wood," Zestrum said. "Don't take branches from standing trees."

"It's dead."

"Critters and birds use the dead trees. Downed wood."

The kid scowled, then stalked off to forage for fallen sticks.

Zestrum grinned. Turned out it was kind of fun having someone do basic scutwork for him.

When the boy returned with the wood, Zestrum inspected the stack. "Not this one. Not that one. And I don't even know what that is." He threw the pieces aside.

"Why ain't they good?"

"They're native wood that survived the sterilization. The first two have toxic smoke and I don't recognize the third."

He had the kid place wood on the fire, then cook the breakfast, ham and biscuits. The kid only had a canteen of water, so Zestrum shared some of the almond milk. Just to be sociable.

"Now we put out the fire." Zestrum filled empty cans with water.

"Can't we just dump dirt on it?" Johnny said.

"Dirt covers hot embers. If something disturbs the dirt, the coals are exposed. That could cause a fire. Believe me, you don't want to be here if there's a fire."

At Zestrum's direction, Johnny sprinkled the fire with water, stirred ashes, and applied more water to extinguish every hot spot. He scooped up the ashes and spread them around the campsite and refilled the hole with dirt.

Zestrum handed the kid a sack to collect their garbage to pack out.

"Why can't we leave it?" Johnny said.

"Cause we ain't barbarians."

They fed the horses and packed their gear. They saddled and bridled the horses, filled canteens, and did their intimate business behind bushes. By the time the chores were done, the sun was up, heating the air.

"Where we going today?" Johnny asked.

"Up there." Zestrum pointed toward the side of the mountain he hadn't explored yet.

The kid scowled. "What for?"

"The view." He mounted Shiloh and set off.

Johnny scrambled up onto 5card and galloped to catch up.

Along the way, Zestrum pointed out the formations in the hillsides. The range stretched more than 240 miles north to south, and varied from 20 to 40 miles wide. The highest peak was 13,000 feet above sea level, with lower summits of 5,000 to 6,000 feet. There were bands of metamorphosed sedimentary rock. Ancient glaciers had created beautiful cirques, moraines, and lakes.

It was no surprise the kid had never heard of tectonic plates or glacial climates, but he seemed ignorant of the local wildlife. Zestrum quickly ascertained Johnny had not ventured out of the valley beyond the canyon and the lake where they'd camped. Was that from Claude Etcheverry keeping a tight rein on his kid or was Johnny a disinterested delinquent?

They stopped for a rest on the plateau. While Johnny gawked at the vista, Zestrum made sketches and calculations in his book. Here and there he collected rock samples. The mountains were home to chickadees, owls, goshawks, badgers, Ferrobian cats, beavers, and treehoppers. One could hear the woodpeckers tapping against the tall trees.

Zestrum pointed out the sheep perched on the ledges of a steep hillside, demonstrating their incredible balance. He identified the tracks of wolves and bears. He explained the purpose of balancing nature.

Without the predators, the prey animals would overpopulate and die a slow death of starvation. Without the prey animals, the soil would lack the nutrients of their fertilizer and decay of their bodies. The plants would die out as their seeds would not be spread by the animals. Without the animals that ate them, the insects would proliferate unchecked. Every living thing was a link in the chain.

Except mosquitos. The Consortium went to great pains to work around introducing them.

Zestrum photographed the area, including Johnny in several of the photos for scale.

"Mr. Doniphon, will you teach me to defend myself?"

"You don't think that Ginwalt is gonna do it for you?"

He grimaced. "I can't use that on. . . some folks." He hunched his shoulders. "I want to learn boxing or wrestling. Something I can use on anybody."

Zestrum recalled seeing Claude Etcheverry slap Johnny in front of the General Store. "Anybody in particular or just general like?"

"Just general like." He stuffed his hands in his pockets. "Sometimes Gabe gets mad at me."

"I see."

"If you could just. . ." He shrugged again like a helpless fish.

"Let's move over to that grassy spot."

Johnny followed Zestrum to a patch of grass among a copse of oak trees.

Zestrum had long ago discovered his training in multiple forms of combat gave him options in any situation. "The first rule in learning to fight is learning to fall."

Johnny looked astonished. "Fall?"

"Otherwise you're gonna injure yourself if you take a bad fall."

"The ob-*jec*-tive is to throw the *other* guy."

"The ob-*jec*-tive is to keep yourself in one piece to accomplish that. You can't do anything if you get injured at the start."

Johnny stared at him for a long moment before acknowledging the logic of that.

"You need to learn how to take a fall and overcome the fear of getting thrown. When you eliminate the fear, you can take the initiative. First, you gotta relax. Feel the ground. Breathe. Here's how we start. You're gonna sit and fall back and strike down at the ground with open palms."

Zestrum demonstrated the breakfall on the grass.

Johnny cocked his head. "Well, that looks easy."

"Then you oughta be able to do it."

He did the fall.

"All right. Now, you practice that every day for ten minutes for the next week and we'll move on."

"*Week?* You mean—that's it?"

"That's it for falling from sitting. After you get proficient, I'll teach you how to fall from squatting and standing. After that, you gotta learn how to take a punch."

"*What?*"

"You want to minimize your opponent's blow. Relax. Watch the man's eyes to see where he's going to strike. When you see his aim, tighten your core muscles and absorb the impact."

"But I don't wanna get hit!"

"You're gonna get hit. Accept that and we'll move on."

Another fuming moment of opposition and then Johnny nodded.

"For right now, I'll show you a few ways to deflect a blow. Hands up, chin down, you parry. When the man throws a punch, you strike his hand to misdirect. We'll do it slow motion so you get the idea."

Zestrum demonstrated the defensive position—chin down; hands up, left under the cheek and right under the chin; feet shoulder-width apart, weight evenly balanced on both feet; upper body relaxed; spine straight.

Johnny mimicked his stance. Zestrum slowly extended his right hand. Johnny did a clumsy parry.

"So I just block punches?"

"You'll tire out doing that. You can slip aside like this." Zestrum demonstrated the slip, rotating hips and shoulders to cause the opponent to miss. "You can roll your body to deflect hits." He pressed his fists at his forehead, tucked his elbows to his body, and rolled his hips and torso to the side.

Johnny mimicked the movements.

"You need to do exercises to develop endurance. Train with weights. Do core exercises to build strength."

He sneered. "All that?"

Zestrum gave him an unadorned glare. "All that."

Again the kid took his time accepting the regimen. "Okay."

"Last, let me show you how to make a fist."

"I know how to do that." Johnny stuck out his hand, thumb inside his fingers.

Zestrum held out his hand straight and extended his four fingers, then pressed them together into a solid mass, bent them into his palm and curled the fingertips to touch their bases. He curled his bent fingers inward so the joints were tucked in. He folded his thumb across the top halves of the index and middle fingers.

Johnny bent, curled, and folded his fingers into the same shape.

"Not too bad." Zestrum shook out his hand. "Next time we'll do some shadow boxing to practice stance and footwork."

"What if somebody comes at me before then?"

"That's why you practice falling. Let's get lunch."

They had a cold lunch on the plateau. To Zestrum's relief, Johnny did not interrogate him about what he was doing up here in the mountains. The kid must have figured Zestrum was sightseeing. More sketches, more photos, and then it was time to head to town.

Zestrum looked at the kid. "What have you learned today?"

Johnny tried to conjure the right answer. "About rocks and plants and animals. Camp food and fires. And how to fall."

"It's a start. Your town have a library?"

"Yeah."

"Take advantage of it." He walked over to Shiloh. "Let's go."

Johnny pouted. "Do we have to go just yet?"

"If we want to be in Copperbank before nightfall, we do."

"What if we spend another night out here? I got the time."

Zestrum mounted up. "I have an appointment tonight. You can't respect a man who doesn't keep his word."

Zestrum expected an argument, but Johnny just cocked his head a little, then silently moved to his horse.

* * *

They encountered no one else on the route through the canyon to the valley floor. Five miles from town, Zestrum reined to a stop for a final chat with his apprentice.

"Remember our deal."

"I remember," the kid said.

"Go on home and rest up. You need to be fresh for school tomorrow."

"Tomorrow's Sunday."

"Then do your homework. Then your exercises."

Another long sigh of disinterest. "You don't have to sit in that schoolhouse all day listening to the teacher drone on and on."

"No. I have to work all day to earn money. Be grateful your pa lets you attend school and doesn't send you off to work someplace. Some kids don't get to go to school and they end up ignorant and poor. Don't waste what you've been gifted, boy."

Johnny looked away, then glanced back. "When we gonna talk again?"

"I don't know. I'll be around. Better get on your way. The sun's going down." Zestrum prodded Shiloh to a trot and headed toward town.

Johnny called to him. "Zestrum?"

Zestrum quarter-turned Shiloh and glanced back. "Yeah?"

"Thanks for stopping me."

CHAPTER 17 – A GOOD NIGHT

The clouds in the sky glowed red and orange as Zestrum directed Shiloh to the livery and dismounted. Charlie hurried over to take his horse. Zestrum slid off the pack and saddlebags, then headed down Main Street toward Colton House.

The Dual Majesty was open for business, lights on, music playing, luring customers through the doors. He heard the clamor of raucous cowborgs as he passed by. He was far too tired to enjoy the entertainment tonight.

He saw Louisiana strutting along toward the entrance, dressed in his red leather vest and matching boots. Almost like a uniform. They exchanged a nod. Louisiana was working the tables for extra income.

Down the block and across the street, Zestrum saw Bodie in his rocking chair on the porch in front of the jailhouse. They waved to each other. Zestrum wondered about Chris Etcheverry's bail. Having that man loose must have rankled the sheriff.

At Colton House, Zestrum stepped into the foyer and heard folks chatting in the parlor. He was late for dinner.

He trudged up the stairs, unlocked his door, and washed his hands at the basin. He soaked the washcloth, washing his forehead, cheeks, and the back of his neck, the cool water soothing sore muscles.

He stowed his goods and checked to ensure his moleskin book was safe in his pocket. Then he went downstairs to the dining room. There were only a few leftovers on the platters.

Jessica entered from the kitchen in the process of clearing the table. She stopped short at the sight of him. "Mr. Doniphon. You're back."

"A little too late, I reckon." He surveyed the remnants.

She pointed at a chair. "You sit down right there." She disappeared into the kitchen.

He sat in the nearest chair.

Two minutes later she returned and set a plate of food in front of him. "You eat every bite of that. I'll get your coffee." She was out the door before he could respond.

He smiled, picked up a fork, and took a bite of beef pot pie. Delicious, as he expected.

Did she make the pot pie because she thought I might be late and the pie wouldn't dry out as quickly?

He decided he'd let himself believe that.

She breezed in and set a slice of apple pie next to his cup. She poured coffee for him, set the blue enamel pot on a trivet, and sat opposite him.

He paused digging into the plate. "What about you, ma'am?"

"I've eaten. I eat before I serve the folks or else I can't get through the dinner."

"Oh." He continued eating.

"Was your trip successful?"

He thought about the sketches, the beauty of the landscape, and the brat that pestered him. "It was largely successful."

"And the roll of paper? Did it meet your needs as well?"

"That'll be tested tonight."

She studied him, deep in thought. "You need rest more than anything else after a journey like that." She assessed his clothes and determined the level of dirt on him. "I take it you had no opportunity to bathe while you were away."

He laughed and then gave her an apologetic look. "I failed to take into account the amount of filth I am tracking into your house."

She waved a dismissive hand, then her eyes wandered over him again. "You finish that meal, fetch some clean clothes, and then come downstairs for a real bath."

"A real bath?"

"There's a tub in the bathroom up there, but my tub is bigger and closer to the hot water." She pointed at him. "Take your time 'cause it'll take about 20 minutes to fill the tub."

"Please, Ms. Colton, don't go to any trouble."

"Come down when you're done. Bring fresh clothes so I can launder these. Leave the dishes here." She strode out of the dining room into the rear of the house without waiting for agreement.

He chuckled at her businesslike attitude. She was a fiery one, assertive and so attractive.

Eating a full dinner at a dining table was a pleasure after the past few days of plain meals under the stars. Open skies provided wonderful panoramas, but the cozy dining room reminded him of better times and places with friends.

He was beginning to consider Jessica Colton a friend.

He finished the slab of apple pie and leaned back in the chair, enjoying the sugar rush and the solitude. While he heard the chatter in the front parlor, the voices were far enough away to ignore.

He followed orders—he left the dishes on the table and went to his room to get his spare clothes, then came downstairs to the foyer. He heard movement from the back of the house but waited at the staircase until Jessica appeared through the door at the end of the hallway.

She wiped her hands on her apron. "How was your meal?"

"Excellent."

"Good. This way." She turned smartly and marched through the doorway to the rear of the house.

He hadn't been in the back rooms before, only in the front parlors and dining room. Through the door at the end of the hall was a second parlor, furnished with personal items, done in pastel blue with rich oak furniture, a leather couch and matching chair, sheer curtains at the windows, and heavy drapes drawn for the night. One small lamp glowed on the table.

She crossed left to another doorway that led to a bedroom—her bedroom, he realized as he entered the space. He was surprised that made him a little nervous. A mahogany dresser, matching four-poster bed and nightstands, two small lamps, and a rug on the polished hardwood floor.

She stopped at the door on the other side of the room. "Through here, Mr. Doniphon."

He lowered his head, embarrassed to be tramping through her bedroom in his filthy clothes and boots.

The bathroom was large, almost as big as the bedroom, with a door that led directly outside, two frosted windows, and an enormous claw-foot porcelain bathtub. A large square mirror hung over the basin, magnifying the room's illusion of size.

"I hope it's not too hot." She leaned to run a hand through the water in the tub, then straightened. "Leave your dirty clothes outside the door and I'll wash them."

"That's not necessary, Ms. Colton."

"I insist. You brought your fresh apparel?"

He lifted his hand in which he held the clean jeans, shirt, and underwear tucked inside.

"Soap here. Towels. Washcloth. Rinse water. Please take your time. I'll check in on you in a half hour." She strode out and shut the door.

He glanced around the pristine room, so tidy and organized, clean, feminine. He hadn't been in a woman's boudoir in ages. Plenty of rooms, but none that told the story of the woman that held them.

Slowly he removed his garments, bundled them, and pushed them out into the bedroom, then shut the door. Standing naked in the bathroom, he caught sight of himself in the mirror and noticed the dirt that had penetrated through his clothing. He also had three days of beard he hadn't bothered to shave.

He'd do that later. In his own room.

He eased into the tub. Hot water, but not too hot, comfortable, soothing. He settled in, watching the water level rise to within two inches of the rim. Had she judged his size when she filled the tub? Possibly. She looked like she could calculate a man's volume on sight.

He gripped the rim with both hands to steady himself.

Soaking in warm water was a luxury in the Badlands. Water was scarce, baths usually reserved for the rich. This house appeared to be one of the first constructed in Copperbank, in a cluster of similar fine residences on large lots. Possibly the city fathers made the initial properties plush with conveniences to attract settlers.

Or maybe Ms. Colton's late husband was an engineer. He'd never considered that. But it explained her boldness in interacting with cyborgs. Most humans had that nervous tic of apprehension when speaking with cyborgs. Jessica seemed comfortable with all strata of society.

Or perhaps she was a Free Thinker, who believed humans and cyborgs were equal. Fearless. Independent. He liked that.

He'd completed the plans for the aqueduct during the wee hours of last evening, before turning in for sleep. Now all that remained was transferring the details to a sheet of paper and delivering that to Nowlin.

A piece of land. . .

That was all he needed, a little piece of land of his own. He'd tap into the aqueduct running past the boundary and get his own hot water to fill his bathtub.

A soft rap on the door startled him. Was he falling asleep?

"Yes?" he called.

Her voice came through the door. "I was just checking on you, Mr. Doniphon. To see if you need anything?"

He was surprised where his mind went on that—*You, Jessica Colton, I need you.* He shook off the drowsiness so he could answer without sounding coarse. "I'm fine, Ms. Colton."

"Do you need more hot water?"

He hadn't noticed the water had cooled. He could ask for more. . . but that would be gratuitous. He'd already put her out way too much. "No, ma'am, I'm fine."

"All right. I'll leave you be."

He focused his augmented hearing on her footsteps padding away across the hardwood floor, over the rug, and out of the bedroom. Then he noticed his manhood had swelled at the sound of her voice.

"Never lose control. Lose control and you lose everything." The memory echoed unbidden.

He picked up the bar and soaped himself, washing off the grime, and pulled the plug to drain the tub. He rinsed with the kettle of clean water and stood to wipe off with the washcloth. The swelling persisted, interfering with his concentration.

He reached for a towel and dried himself, then stepped out of the tub onto the soft rug. Again he caught himself in the mirror and saw the glint of lust in his eyes, in his body. He set down the towel and reached for his clothes to dress.

He needed to get out of this woman's boudoir before he made a fool of himself.

* * *

He opened the door and stopped on the threshold. She was in the bedroom, folding laundry on the bed, a full basket on the floor at her feet.

She looked up at him. "I hope you enjoyed the bath, Mr. Doniphon."

"Very much, ma'am. Thank you."

"Your clothes are presently in the laundry." Her gaze swept over him in keen appraisal. "I found this in your vest pocket. I imagined you didn't want it washed." She picked up the moleskin notebook from the dresser.

"No, ma'am. I didn't."

He felt his cheeks flush. There were more than aqueduct plans on those pages. He quickly took the book from her, noting the strap was secured over the unbound side. Had she looked inside? Surely a woman of her integrity wouldn't invade his privacy?

She placed a hand on her hip, regarding him closely. "Did you finish your drawing? The one you started before last evening's adventures?"

"Preliminary work is done. I need to finalize it."

"Oh. I see."

"Perhaps tomorrow I could show you. If you're still interested."

Her lovely dark eyebrows rose in amusement. "I am still interested, Mr. Doniphon."

She was within reach. He could have pulled her close and expressed his feelings, but. . .

He lowered his chin. "It's been a long time since I've had such pleasant hospitality, Ms. Colton."

"It's been a long time since I've had such a pleasant tenant, Mr. Doniphon." She raised her hand to brush her hair back. "I enjoy having you in my residence."

Her hands had touched the notebook he held. "You have a fine house, ma'am."

"I've done my best to maintain it. My father built the original structure. We added these rooms to the back, to make it larger." She smiled. "I wanted a big bathroom, not one of those little washrooms most houses have."

"Your bathroom is just the right size."

"Some might say it's a little large for one person."

"One who shares her house with so many deserves any sanctuary she can get."

"I agree."

They stood gazing at each other for a long leisurely moment in perfect silence.

"I suppose I should finish this." She gestured vaguely at the laundry basket.

"Can I give you a hand?"

"You need to finish that drawing."

"I do indeed." He nodded to her, having a hard time breaking their communion. She hadn't moved but somehow it seemed she was closer to him. He made his exit through the parlor to the front of the house and hustled up the staircase to his room.

* * *

The draught came through his hand quickly and efficiently, the way it did back in the railway days. He'd always had a keen talent for maneuvering through obstacles and difficult terrain. The canal would span a scant fifty miles and provide sufficient water for the

Easterbrook Ranch and that plot of land Nowlin pledged to Zestrum.

He'd detailed the specs at each juncture and compiled a list of materials for each phase of the build in his moleskin book. The moleskin was a gift from an admirer back in those days. Elaina had been a denizen of the mobile boom town that followed the crew across the plains. She'd been blonde and willowy and generous. Many nights he thought about her.

He completed the diagram on the sheet of butcher paper. In the old days, he used vellum, but that wasn't available at the General Store. The largest paper in stock was the butcher paper. He transferred the relevant notes and calculations to the key along the right side, then signed his name at the bottom claiming ownership of the design.

Tomorrow was soon enough to deliver this to Nowlin and collect his payment.

He turned to the pages in the back of the moleskin, to the sketches of Jessica Colton in various attitudes—pensive, cheerful, soulful, longing, the way he'd imagined her looking at him.

A glance at the clock showed eleven o'clock. She'd be busy preparing for sleep right now. He wouldn't risk bothering her until he knew she had time, though a hotelier was always busy. Witness her late-night deliveries to Mr. Bainbridge.

Best to stay out of her way. And he could use a rest.

He pulled off his boots, turned off the lamp, lowered the window shade, and stretched out on the bed. He hadn't realized how much tension had coiled in his body. He recalled feeling fatigue like this during the work on the railway. Endless hours of hard labor in twelve-hour shifts. Never enough time to recover between those shifts. Constant exhaustion.

He stared at the ceiling, recalling his conversations with Jessica today. Recalling the curve of her smile, the curve of her hips, the soft footfalls, the delicate fingers she ran through his bath water. He imagined those fingers touching him in the most delicious fashion.

* * *

A soft knock on the door woke him from enjoyable dreams. The clock showed 8:45. He'd overslept and missed breakfast, dammit.

He opened the door and found Jessica holding a tray with silver covers and a small coffee pot.

"Mr. Doniphon."

"Ms. Colton."

"May I come in?"

He backed up and she carried the tray to the table by the window. She proceeded to pour coffee and settle the napkin and silverware for him.

"You shouldn't have gone to this much trouble," he said, embarrassed at causing her extra work.

"You are entitled to your breakfast, Mr. Doniphon."

"I figured I'd grab something at the Opal."

"You figured wrong." She pointed at the chair, an order to sit, and continued laying out his meal.

He sat on the hard-backed chair. "I can do that."

She ignored him and lifted the covers, revealing fried eggs, sausage, and biscuits with gravy on the side. His protests declined amidst the intoxicating aromas of culinary perfection.

"You deserve a bit of quiet time." She piled the covers together on the end of the table. "Did you complete that project you were working on?"

"Last night."

She interpreted that to mean he was up late finishing the task. "Did you get enough sleep last night?"

"Almost enough."

"I'm afraid your clothes aren't dry yet."

"I have extra." He indicated the duds he was wearing.

"Do you need anything else?" She gestured at the tray.

"This is excellent, Ms. Colton."

She nodded and went to the door.

He speared a sausage. "If you're upstairs in about 20 minutes, I could show you that drawing I promised."

She paused, giving him a long look. "I will definitely be upstairs in about 20 minutes." She closed the door on her way out.

CHAPTER 18 – A VERY GOOD NIGHT

After the meal, he cleared the table and wiped down the surface to save her the trouble. He hated being a burden to her—being late for meals, invading her personal space for a luxurious bath—but in another way, he liked having her tend to him. He doubted she'd draw a bath for Mr. Davis or Mr. Bainbridge.

At the soft knock, he opened the door.

Jessica stepped in. He debated leaving the door open for propriety, then decided the tenants were gone for the day. He shut the door but did not turn the lock.

He gestured at the table and she sat. He pulled out the roll of butcher paper and spread the blueprint across the table, weighting it with his pocketknife and his box of writing tools.

"This is the project I've been commissioned to do." He pointed out the details on the blueprint. "The Dicron Mountain Range. The Salinger River. And this is the proposal." He ran his fingertip along the drawing of the aqueduct.

She followed his finger with her eyes. "You propose to build a canal?"

"An aqueduct. From the Sansano Lake to the Easterbrook Ranch."

She breathed deeply at the massive scope of the project. "That is. . . a formidable construction."

"It is." He pointed out the specs in the key. "The materials. The estimated timeline."

"Almost two years."

"If conditions are favorable. Winter weather could impact progress."

She laid a hand on the edge of the table, wary of soiling the paper. "Do you plan to oversee the project as well?"

"I haven't committed to that. Mr. Nowlin has agreed to grant me a piece of land as payment for the design. I plan to settle there. The aqueduct would provide water for that land."

"I see." She was silently ticking off the same things he had—the land was incentive to have him work on the construction. "That is hard labor."

"Yes. And I've done my share on the railway. I'd prefer to sit in the shade, but the sooner the aqueduct is built, the sooner I can work the land."

"You plan to farm your acreage?"

He scrunched his nose in skepticism. "I'm not really a farmer. But every homestead needs a garden, chickens, sheep, other animals. They need water."

"Where is this parcel?"

He touched the map to indicate the location.

She took another deep breath, her mind ticking on that. "That's not too far from town, Mr. Doniphon."

"Not very far at all."

Now she looked at him and in the orange morning light her face glowed. "Perhaps you might need to come to town from time to time. For supplies and such. Until you're self-sufficient."

"Probably after that, too."

Her gaze returned to the blueprint. "This could irrigate the valley. Transform the landscape. Make this property valuable."

"And break the Etcheverrys' stranglehold on water."

"When will you deliver your plans to Mr. Nowlin?"

"This afternoon." He rolled up the butcher paper and tucked that inside a cylindrical case.

Her gaze fell upon the moleskin on the edge of the table. "Is this what you've been collecting in your book?"

He paused, then secured the blueprint case and set it aside. "Among other things." He pulled the other chair beside hers, sat, and opened the book to display the sketches he'd made of the terrain during his trip in the mountains.

She studied each image as he slowly turned pages. "Is that Johnny Etcheverry?"

"It is."

She frowned. "Did he accompany you on your trip?"

"He was an uninvited guest."

She nodded acknowledgment. "He invites himself most of the time." She watched as he turned the page, displaying a scene of Johnny sitting under a tree. "He sat long enough to pose for you?"

"He fell asleep."

She smiled and watched his hand turn to a two-page drawing of the view from the plateau. "You have a good eye for detail, Mr. Doniphon."

"I studied the arts in my spare time on the work crew."

"When you worked on the railway?"

"Yes, ma'am. From west coast to the east coast."

"That was an arduous construction. I understand many men died."

"Many men died." He turned the page and displayed a view of the lake.

"I've never been up the canyon," she said. "Is the water cold?"

"Very cold. But crystal clear to the bottom."

"I'm not much of a traveler. I've never been much further than the edge of Copperbank."

"You were born here?"

"No, but my parents shipped over when I was three. My father built the hotel to accommodate the miners and traders. He saw great opportunity here, but riches seemed to bypass him for the most part. He did hold onto the house, though, so I have that."

"And what did your husband do?"

"He was a teacher. He came here for his health—the dry air. But it turned out he had kidney disease, so the clean air didn't help."

"I'm sorry to hear that, ma'am."

She shrugged as if the loss had lightened over time. "I miss him from time to time. It wasn't really a love match. We were among the few single people living here of a certain age." She studied the drawing. "How about you, Mr. Doniphon? Were you born on Blanken 9?"

"I was born on Earth, in the Continental US. My father commissioned me and three of my siblings to the Consortium when we were small. We each came over when we turned 16."

"I've. . . heard of people doing that to their children."

"We funded my youngest brother's university education. He's a scholar. A gentleman."

"That's barbaric. Trading in people should be abolished."

"More folks would have to believe we were people for that." He liked that she thought so.

"I don't believe people realize the sacrifices cyborgs made to make this planet livable for all of us. And then they're denied land and votes and civil rights. Treated like they're not even human." She licked her lips, cast her eyes down, then met his gaze. "I don't mean to rant."

"It's nothing I haven't ranted about myself. It's nice to be appreciated." He turned the page—and there was a sketch of Jessica Colton standing under an apple tree.

She inhaled sharply. "Mr. Doniphon. . . is that me?"

"Yes, ma'am." He left his hand on the edge of the page, anxious for her honest response.

"I know I never posed for such a picture."

"I drew from memory."

"You have a keen memory as well as a keen eye." She appeared mesmerized by the image. "Is this the only one?"

He turned the page to another sketch of her, a portrait with incredible detail.

Another sharp inhale, then she slowly released the breath. "You must have met many beautiful women in your travels."

"I have." He turned the page, an illustration of her standing beside the lake. "But I only draw the exceptional ones."

A smile tugged at her lips and she steadfastly avoided his eyes. "I think you've enhanced my appearance beyond the reality."

"Not in the least." He traced the outline of her shoulder and hip on the paper. "I've detailed your silhouette exactly. I've captured your beauty as it exists."

Slowly she raised her gaze to his. "I'm very plain in real life."

He shook his head once to contradict that, then kissed her. She closed her eyes, allowing the invasion with a lush sigh. Following instinct, he settled his mouth more firmly upon hers and she shifted her body for a better fit. For the longest time they connected fully with this simple touch.

Then he withdrew to gauge her true reaction. After a moment her eyes fluttered open and the strongest desire swirled within the gray irises.

"Mr. Doniphon, I believe you have captured more than my image."

"I have carried you in my mind since we met. I've thought of you. . . many times."

"And where have those thoughts led?"

He glanced toward the bed, then looked at her.

"You do realize that's a single bed."

He chuckled. "Well, it's plenty wide for me."

"Perhaps you would find the bed downstairs more. . . accommodating."

He leaned close and she took initiative and kissed him, daring him to deepen the kiss with flicks of her tongue. The connection grew stronger and he wasn't certain he could wait the time to go downstairs. But this was not a woman he wanted to rush, and it was imperative she understood what this romance entailed.

He drew back. "Before we take this further, I should tell you about my implants."

Her eyebrows shot up in interest. "Your. . . implants. You mean. . . ?"

"The cybernetic components. You understand how they work?"

Her head tilted. "Not entirely." She smiled nervously, embarrassed.

"Sixty percent is organic. Same as you. Forty percent is enhanced with cybernetic mods. Modifications. Everything you see or touch is just like any other man." Here he smiled wryly. "Maybe not most men."

She laughed and relaxed a little. "Oh. Yes. Of course."

"The mods are chiefly in my arms and legs. To be stronger. To have increased stamina."

"Stamina. Does that mean you can. . . ?" Her gaze flicked toward his crotch, then to his eyes.

"I don't get tired. But most women are satisfied with two or three hours."

"Two or three. . ." She trailed off, staring at some faraway place in her mind. She drew in a long breath. "I'll be honest with you, Mr. Doniphon. My husband never lasted more than twenty minutes. Anything past that would be new territory for me."

He acknowledged that with a nod. "You set the pace. You set the limits. If I do something you don't like, if you tell me to stop, I will."

"What if I do something you don't like?"

He smiled. "Well, that would be new territory for me."

"Anything else I should know?"

"I'd never let anything happen to you that you didn't want." He pulled a set of packets from his pocket to prove he had condoms at hand.

"Armed and ready," she whispered.

"Pardon?"

"You're prepared for, um, this. Today."

"I am. The question is, are you?"

Her lips parted and her eyes darkened. "Mr. Doniphon." She smiled. "I am prepared."

He smiled. "Zestrum."

"Zestrum." She leaned eagerly into him and angled herself for a deeper kiss. Gradually she broke the kiss. "Please come downstairs with me right now."

CHAPTER 19 – ROOTS

Late morning Zestrum veered off the road at the stone markers denoting the path to Gerald Nowlin's homestead. The scrubland was even more parched than before if that was possible. He crested the hill and crossed the bridge over the dry creek bed.

Ranch hands noted his arrival with suspicious looks. No, he wasn't here to displace anybody. In fact, if Nowlin liked the blueprints, they would have more work than they knew what to do with.

He dismounted outside the front door.

A boy hustled over. "Water your horse, Mr. Doniphon?"

"Thanks."

The kid led Shiloh toward a trough near the barn. As Zestrum put his foot on the first step up to the front porch, the door opened.

Rachel Nowlin smiled. "Good morning, Mr. Doniphon."

"Morning, Ms. Nowlin." He touched the brim of his hat, waiting with one foot on the step. "Is your father in?"

She gestured toward the left. "Wallace is going out to let him know you're here. Won't you come in?" She cleared the doorway and ushered him into the parlor. "A drink?"

"Water would be welcome."

"Please sit down." She poured from a clear carafe as he sat on the sofa. She handed him the glass. "Perhaps you'd like something to eat?"

"Water's fine, ma'am."

"It's a long dry ride from town. I find it unbearable in the high summer."

"There's a hot heat in the valley in the summer," he agreed.

"How are you liking Copperbank, Mr. Doniphon?"

He sensed an underlying question about his future plans. "It's like most towns, ma'am. Good people and bad people. Assets and incommodities."

"Which assets are the most advantageous?"

"The possibilities of irrigation."

Her smile broadened. "I'm glad to hear that's a distinct possibility." Her watch beeped. "Oh, excuse me a moment?"

He nodded and she left. He inventoried the room, noting the family photos on the wall, old photos of the Nowlin ranch in its infancy with a sod house and skeleton of a barn.

Rachel set a plate of shortbread cookies on the end table beside the sofa. "In case you might like to try my cooking." She smiled and sat in the rocker.

He sampled a cookie. "Very good, ma'am."

"My specialty is shortbread. I make a mean chocolate chip cookie and pretty fine pecan pie. Not to mention macaroni and cheese and meatloaf, which I did just mention."

He smiled and hefted the cookie. "I believe you."

"Cooking is the fun part. But I've got company, so I have an excuse to avoid the cleanup." Her gaze darted round the room. "I apologize for the condition of the house. The dust. Wednesday is the day we deep clean. There's so much dust out here, it coats the room before you finish wiping down the furniture."

"I didn't notice dust, ma'am."

Another smile crossed her face. "You're so kind."

The front door opened and boots thunked through the entry to the parlor. Gerald Nowlin tossed his hat on the hook beside the door. Zestrum rose to shake hands with him.

"Mr. Doniphon."

"Mr. Nowlin."

Rachel popped up to let her father take the rocker. Zestrum sat on the couch. Rachel sat on the adjacent sofa.

"I apologize for not making a proper appointment," said Zestrum.

Nowlin settled in his rocker. "We're informal around here."

Zestrum pulled the roll of paper from the case and unfurled the blueprint on the coffee table, weighting the two ends with his pencil box and the case. "The plans we spoke of."

"That was quick." Nowlin leaned forward, eager to see the details.

Rachel scooted to the edge of the sofa to study the paper.

Nowlin scrutinized the drawing. "This looks efficient."

Zestrum explained the general plan—the siphon at the lake, the concrete canals and steel pipes, the use of gravity and water forces. He estimated the amounts of materials and manpower required.

The rancher shook his head in wonder. "This is exactly what I was looking for. Mr. Doniphon, you have fulfilled your part of the contract." He looked at him. "I can sign over the grant deed to you this afternoon."

"That would be amenable."

"We can go to the Land Office together and sign papers."

Rachel pointed at the valley between mountains. "Are you proposing to cement the riverbed?"

"No," said Zestrum. "We need to restore that water back to the aquifer and attract the critters that used to live there. If you let the trees along the shore die, the animals don't come back and the wind blows harder."

"That would be something to see. All that water pouring down the mountain into our riverbed."

"That will be a welcome sight." Nowlin looked at Zestrum. "Now the challenge is persuading Mr. Doniphon to oversee the project." He grinned.

Zestrum smiled and cast his eyes upon the blueprint. "Well, sir, that remains to be seen."

"Ah, that's better than the flat refusal you gave me last time. We'll have to work on convincing him, Rachel."

"We will." She picked up the plate and held it within his reach. "Have another cookie, Mr. Doniphon?"

***

Zestrum rode Shiloh alongside Gerald and Rachel Nowlin in their buckboard to the Land Office on Main Street. Over the course of luncheon and chocolate cake, Zestrum had agreed to supervise construction of the aqueduct. Nowlin and his daughter were a formidable team.

Plus, the enterprise was too challenging to pass up. For the first time, it would be his project from survey to construction to implementation. And he would benefit from the fruit of his labor.

First order of business was acquiring the last of the land through the mountains to the lake. Then staking the route. Purchase of materials. Transport of those materials. Employing competent workers who would follow orders.

Zestrum agreed to assist in every phase for set prices along the way. This gave him steady employment for the next two years and a useful mission to occupy him. With the income, he could improve his new homestead.

At least as far as no water allowed.

Nowlin stopped the buckboard at the curb and disembarked. Rachel drove the wagon to the General Store further on.

When Gerald looked toward the right, Zestrum followed his gaze to see a horse approaching at a steady trot. The woman in the saddle rode easy. She didn't scan the street; she knew exactly where she was going.

Her sun-worn canvas vest, cotton shirt, and thick denim boot-cut jeans bore years of outdoor work. A bandana hung loose at her neck, patterned in deep red. She stopped at the Land Office and dismounted in one fluid motion, low heeled boots hitting the packed earth like punctuation.

No wasted movement.

Gerald stepped forward and they greeted each other with a smile and a kiss that spoke of deep affection.

"Calves are tagged and moved to the north pasture. That sorrel steer finally took to the mineral lick—might've been the molasses." She handed him a folded note from her vest pocket. "I ran into the Murdoch boy. He's got pinkeye in two heifers and asked if we'd loan him the salve. Told him to stop by later."

Gerald tucked the note into his shirt pocket and turned to Zestrum. "Zestrum, this is my wife, Aaliyah."

Aaliyah extended a hand to Zestrum. Her eyes met his with a steady, intelligent gaze that indicated she'd seen enough to know what mattered. "Good to meet you."

"It's a pleasure to meet you, ma'am." Zestrum shook her hand, noting the calluses, the strength in her grip. He recognized that she wasn't just a part of the Nowlin enterprise. She was the backbone.

She smiled and gave him a once-over, taking in everything as if reading a ledger in his very posture. "I hear you're a man with a plan. I'd certainly like to hear the details."

"Tomorrow, babe," Gerald said. "Today we're taking care of step one." He gestured toward the door and they entered the Land Office.

At the front counter, Zestrum and the Nowlins transacted the change of title over the next hour. Darrin Banachek, the clerk, seemed especially interested in this transfer of ownership. He laid out at least a dozen forms for them to complete.

Gerald signed. Aaliyah signed. Zestrum added his signature.

Banachek lifted each paper to study the names. Zestrum half expected him to pull out a quizzing glass for closer inspection.

The clerk examined their ID cards, though he knew who the Nowlins were. He took the forms to another desk to notarize and stamp with the county seal. He recorded the change in the official county register. He printed a new deed on an ancient photocopy machine that must've come over on the first Consortium supply ship.

At last he placed the authenticated certificate with Zestrum Doniphon's name as owner of the tract on the front counter.

Gerald plucked up the brand-new deed and presented it to Zestrum. "Congratulations, Doniphon. You are now a landowner."

Zestrum held the precious parchment in his hands, admiring the fancy script that proved the land was his.

Gerald shook his hand, grinning. "And now that we're neighbors, I hope to be seeing more of you. To discuss the weather, the crops, and other important matters."

"That would be most agreeable." Zestrum tucked the parchment into his moleskin book.

The three walked out together onto the wooden sidewalk.

"Meet us tomorrow morning to get started?" Gerald said.

"I will stop by."

"We'll have a celebratory lunch," said Aaliyah.

"And the good wine," Gerald added. "G'day."

"Good day."

Looking powerfully pleased, Gerald and Aaliyah headed off in the direction of the General Store.

Zestrum gazed up and down the street. Copperbank looked different with a piece of real estate in his custody. More like a home than a stopover.

Now he might court a woman of substance.

* * *

Walking from the livery to Colton House, Zestrum passed the Dual Majesty and heard quick light footsteps on the wooden sidewalk ahead. Victoria Barkley rounded the corner and intercepted him. In a ruffled day dress and a hat with fringe on the crown, she looked the picture of demure respectability. Only the carthy glint in her eyes hinted at her true nature.

He stopped to be sociable. "Ms. Barkley."

"Mr. Doniphon." She moved closer than appropriate and grasped his forearm, a light possessive maneuver. "I was hoping I'd see you today. I didn't see you last evening." Her voice had a disappointed edge on the last words.

"I was otherwise occupied."

"Will you be our guest tonight or tomorrow? I'll be singing some new tunes. I'd love to have your opinion of my music."

Her intense desire for his involvement swept over him. Flattering, but futile. A week ago he would have been completely in her thrall, responding to her cues all the way into her bed.

Today he had other objectives in his life. However, there was no need to be harsh.

"I'll have to drop in soon to hear you sing, Ms. Barkley."

His refusal to commit to a date disheartened her. Her fingers tightened on his arm and she blinked rapidly as she absorbed the blow. They were in public; making a scene would attract attention.

Slowly she adjusted to the new parameters of their relationship. "I will certainly miss you, Mr. Doniphon."

"I will miss you, Ms. Barkley."

Recovering her poise, she tossed her head and presented a winning smile. "Perhaps we'll meet again in the street from time to time."

"That would be a pleasant meeting, ma'am."

"Very pleasant." She released his arm and offered her hand for a formal handshake. "So nice to see you this afternoon, Mr. Doniphon."

"Until we meet again." He clasped her hand and her hand slipped away gradually.

Her smile saddened, then she attuned her expression to mask the disappointment and strolled on down the sidewalk.

* * *

After the series of errands, Zestrum did not reach Colton House until Jessica was preparing dinner for the tenants. He didn't want to interfere with her routine. In his room, he tucked the deed among his valuable papers in the portfolio hidden within his saddlebag. Besides his birth certificate and his emancipation credential, the land deed was the most valuable document he possessed.

He smiled. He would surprise Jessica tonight, after dinner, with his acquisition.

He spent a long time washing up in the upstairs bathroom to make himself presentable to decent company. The land deed represented freedom—his own parcel—and encumbrance—he had to be responsible, respectable, and upstanding.

He hadn't always been.

At six he came downstairs to the dining room. Dinner was an exceptional main dish of macaroni and cheese—four kinds of cheese—a sumptuous hot meal. The tenants chattered about the day's events—mostly mundane activities that happened in every town this size. With no new murders or assaults, the conversation centered on social gossip.

Zestrum noticed Louisiana stealing glances at Irina Nolan across the table. During the chatter, the red borg was unusually soft-spoken, not at all the brash gambling man who shot Chris Etcheverry. He looked downright. . . domesticated.

Jessica avoided voicing opinions as she served the meal and cleaned afterward. Bainbridge and Cole wandered into the parlor to continue discussing the upcoming election in November. Louisiana nursed his coffee a few minutes more before exiting the room. Davis remained planted at the table with his cup of coffee.

Irina chatted with Jessica about clothing she'd seen in the latest Sears Catalogue. When the Consortium took the contract to terraform the planet, an entrepreneur seized the opportunity to revive the popular concept of catalogue sales. Zestrum had seen the catalogue frequently on the Coast.

However, fashion in the Badlands lagged about a year behind couture on the Coast. Zestrum chose not to mention ladies had moved on to other styles and colors this season. He'd have to explain how he knew, and that could be embarrassing.

He caught Jessica's eye several times during dinner, letting her know he was anxious to speak to her in private once they had an opening. He even carried a few platters into the kitchen for her, waiting for that opportunity.

At length, the fashion talk drove Davis out of the room. Zestrum stacked coffee cups onto a tray.

Irina picked up the hefty catalogue and headed toward the door. She looked back at him as if she wanted to ask a question but then thought better of it. "Good night, Mr. Doniphon."

"Good night, Ms. Nolan."

She went up the stairs.

The kitchen door opened and Jessica peered at him. "I think you wanted to speak to me?"

He gave her a significant look, lifted the tray of cups, and followed her into the kitchen. The door swung shut. He set aside the tray and bundled her in his arms.

She squealed a small playful objection. "I'm all wet from dishes! I'll soak through your nice shirt."

He kissed her, pressing her closer to him. Her arms snaked around to embrace him. After a long indulgent kiss, he drew back.

"You are kissing a genuine, certified landowner."

Her mouth opened into a wide smile. "You secured your stake?"

"This afternoon."

"Congratulations."

"I hoped you might help me celebrate."

Her eyes darted toward the door behind them, indicating the tenants beyond that door. "I have evening chores to tend to first. If you're willing to wait?"

"I would wait for you however long it took." He raised his eyebrows and lowered his voice to a suggestive tone. "And I will help you."

She smiled, her fingers entangled around the nape of his neck. "Will you show me the deed to the land?"

"I'll show you whatever you want to see."

She licked her lips and tilted her head. "We should get started on those chores right away, then."

"We should." He crushed his lips against hers.

CHAPTER 20 – FRIENDS AND ENEMIES

He woke shortly after 5 am, his arm curled around her in the queen-sized bed. The sense of peace and completion astonished him. He'd found something unexpected in this town, something he'd resigned himself to living without.

She'd astonished him last night, too, adventurous and exciting, leading him into a devotion he'd long avoided.

He wanted to stay in bed with her all day but. . . he had obligations. She had obligations, too, and he didn't want to embarrass her by leaving her suite in front of the other boarders this bright morning.

As if she'd heard the thought, she clamped a hand around his forearm to hold him fast. She sighed and wriggled tighter against him. "Mr. Doniphon."

"Zestrum."

"Zestrum. I hope you slept well."

"Better than I deserve, ma'am."

"Jessica."

"Jessica."

"I had a question for you last night but we got. . . distracted. I meant to ask you. . ." She slid her hand up to his bicep and traced a finger over his intricate tattoo. "This tree with the river running by. It's a landscaper emblem, isn't it?"

He was surprised she knew the symbol signified rank. Most humans considered the markings graffiti or "cattle brands." "It is."

"Tell me about these pictographs."

He pointed at the tree in the center of the circle. "This is the foundation of a Landscaper. I was good at mathematics and science, so I was recruited straight up as an engineer." He indicated the river. "This starts out as two lines, empty inside, a path showing you've learned design and analysis." He pointed out the cryptic symbols among the leaves on the tree branches. "Mechanics. Thermodynamics. Fluid mechanics. Control systems. Project management." He indicated the various plants along the river. "I pursued architecture—technology, sustainability, urban design, and technical drawing. When I earned my license, the path became a river."

She traced along the ripples in the stream. "I recognized the compass and the drafting tools, but not all these others."

"These represent the engineering skills I have at hand."

"Is there one for drawing sketches of beautiful landscapes?"

He smiled. "Several of these have double meanings. The tree signifies growth and life. The eye is perception and inner vision. The circle shows completeness."

"And the butterfly?" Her finger touched the butterfly among the leaves.

"Metamorphosis."

"What metamorphosis have you undergone? Besides from engineer to architect."

"I went from a greenhorn kid to an emancipated man in the time it takes most folks to master one profession."

"I would suggest you have embraced authenticity."

He pulled her closer. "I hope so."

"You know the right thing to say." She took a deep breath and stretched, her body pressing into his so he hardened everywhere in response. "I'm afraid it's time for me to get up."

"I should leave before your lodgers get up."

"Perhaps you merely came downstairs early. To help set the table."

He smiled. "I think I would be inclined to do that."

She turned in his arms and touched her nose to his. "I'm certain you have tasks to perform today."

"Later today."

In the next breath they were kissing, warming each other, inciting, then joining together in passion. When he next noticed the clock, the hands pointed at 6:20.

"I've made you late," he murmured.

"You'd better get busy setting that table." She untangled from him and slipped out of bed, displaying her nude form in the glorious dawn sunlight. She picked up her undergarments and rushed to dress—then saw him watching and slowed, letting him watch.

When she pulled on her dress, he rose from the bed and gave her an unobstructed view of his body. She froze mid-buttoning to admire that view. He pulled on his briefs and jeans and slid on the cotton shirt, breaking her trance.

"What would you like for breakfast, Zestrum?"

"Anything you care to make, Jessica."

She smiled. "We should get cooking."

In the kitchen, they playfully bumped into each other getting out plates, silverware, and cookware. While he set the dining room table, she mixed cathead biscuit dough and dropped handfuls onto a baking sheet. Then eggs into the skillet for scrambled eggs and bacon slices onto the griddle, weighted with an iron press. Back in the kitchen, he helped.

Around 7 they heard footsteps in the dining room, chairs scraping, voices. Jessica handed him the plate of thick fluffy biscuits, giving him a lusty look as encouragement. He entered the dining room and set the plate on the table.

Louisiana, Davis, and Bainbridge glanced up in surprise at seeing him serve the breakfast.

"Good morning, Mr. Doniphon," said Bainbridge.

"Morning, Mr. Bainbridge. Mr. Davis. Louisiana." Zestrum took a seat at the table and poured coffee into his cup.

Bainbridge and Davis traded curious looks. Louisiana smirked. The four men stood as Ms. Nolan entered and exchanged greetings. They sat at the table. Cole arrived and took seat next to Ms. Nolan, grinning widely at her. She bestowed a polite smile and ignored him.

Louisiana's expression was priceless jealousy.

Jessica delivered platters of bacon and scrambled eggs. "Good morning." Her businesslike manner discouraged questions about Zestrum's assistance serving breakfast.

Instead, they discussed the weather, the arrival of the mail coach this afternoon, and other ordinary topics. As they finished the meal, they left the dining room.

Louisiana's eyes followed Irina as she walked out the door. The red borg looked petulant as he finished his coffee and then went back upstairs. Since he gambled in the evenings and worked the graveyard shift for the sheriff, he came in for breakfast and then went to bed to sleep till late afternoon.

Zestrum remained at the table, watching Jessica clear the dishes. He carried platters into the kitchen and caught her around the waist, halting her in the midst of chores.

"I have to go out," he murmured at her ear.

"I figured."

"I'll be back this evening and we can. . . continue?"

"I will be here," she said softly. "Thinking about you."

One last luxuriant kiss and he forced himself to go out the door to officially begin his job for Nowlin.

* * *

Using a giant Blanken 9 Continental Map spread over his billiard table, Gerald Nowlin outlined where he had purchased land between the boundary of his ranch straight across to the Sansano Lake in the Dicron Mountains. Considered useless parcels, the State sold the tracts without question to acquire property taxes.

Thus, an entire five-mile-wide stretch between the lake and his ranch belonged to the Nowlins.

Aaliyah studied the map, noting developed areas between the ranch and the mountains. No doubt the Blanken Ox grazed on those hillsides, so she probably knew the terrain better than anyone.

The initial task involved blasting a 12-by-12 hole through solid granite to form the tunnel through Fortram Hill in the foothills. Then they needed to construct a cement mill nearby and mine for limestone, clay, and tufa to produce cement. One crew would dig the canal and another crew would pour concrete in sections. Other crews would construct steel siphon pipes and concrete masts for the above-ground conduit through the valley.

Zestrum devised a carefully worded Help Wanted advertisement to attract emancipated cyborgs from the West Coast and the East Seaboard. They would build a base camp in the mountains to house everyone for the duration. And there would be contracts for each worker along with a lengthy vetting process.

"We should wire this to the Coast papers now to recruit," Zestrum said.

"We'll do that today," Gerald said. "I'd also like to connect telegraph between the ranch and the camp."

"That would ease communication considerable. Radios are fine on the job site, but Vikite makes long-range radio near impossible." That was a problem Zestrum had struggled with during his career as a landscaper.

"We'll have to factor in staking poles and stringing wire."

"And find some good electricians. Going through mountains ain't the same as going over the valley."

"Let's talk to Hugh Pennyworth. He's the local expert." Gerald looked at Zestrum. "I'll leave the hiring to your discretion."

Rachel rubbed her hands together, smiling at the map. "I can't wait to get started."

Gerald glanced at Rachel, amused at her enthusiasm. "I can't either, honey."

"We can revive our garden and grow fresh vegetables again." Aaliyah checked her watch. "Speaking of which. It's time for lunch." She and Rachel strode out of the game room.

"Join us, Mr. Doniphon."

"I can't impose on you for another meal," said Zestrum.

"Bullshit. You're family." He planted an easy hand on Zestrum's shoulder and directed him into the dining room where plates were laid out for four. "Sherry? Or something stronger?"

"Sherry. I've got to keep a clear head to manage all this."

Gerald poured drinks for four. "I can't tell you how much I will enjoy having control over how much water I use for my land."

Zestrum smiled. "I think I might kinda like that myself."

"This is going to transform the valley, mark my words. People have been under that man's boot too long." He held up a conciliatory hand. "Not that I haven't done questionable things. I think everybody does, once in a while. It's the steady underlying mendacity and degradation of basic human decency that galls me. And he's getting away with it again."

"Something new happen?"

He lowered his voice. "There was trouble last night at the Majesty. Nobody got killed, but some boys got beat up pretty bad. And Gabe and Chris walked out of there with bruised knuckles."

"They like to squabble."

He scoffed. "They like to *kill*. They *settle* for squabbling." He cut short the diatribe as the ladies entered the room.

Aaliyah set a platter of biscuits on the table. "Have a seat, Mr. Doniphon."

"Zestrum," he said as he sat at the table.

"And you can call me Ali." She surveyed the table one last time, then smiled at Gerald as he held the chair for her.

Rachel set a platter on the table and sat opposite Zestrum. "More of that good beef you were praising the other day. Nowlin Blanken Ox." She pointed at the small steaks, lighter in color to the beef.

Aaliyah proceeded to put one on each plate.

The meat of the Ox was such a delicacy that prices had soared to over one hundred dollars a pound. Zestrum felt a little guilty about the expense, but appreciated the gesture.

The flavor was good—nearly sensuous—but for 100 bucks he'd keep his money.

Breaking bread with the Nowlins was extraordinarily pleasant. They treated Zestrum with respect and accepted him as an equal. There was no condescension or sharp remarks about the limitations of cyborgs.

For the second time in a long while Zestrum felt at home. The first time was with Jessica earlier today. And that was truly a marvelous feeling.

* * *

Zestrum left Shiloh at the stable and went to the post office to check for mail. There was nothing with his name on it. Virgil must have been incommunicado, otherwise he would have written to let his brother know he was well.

He emerged from the building and adjusted his hat. Commotion down the road caught his attention.

Two men burst through the doors of the Dual Majesty in a fit of fists and heels. One man shoved the other into the middle of the street. The second man fell. While he was righting himself, the first man pounced and assaulted him with both fists. Both boots.

Onlookers watched, horrified, but didn't dare intervene.

Even from a block and a half away, Zestrum recognized Gabe Etcheverry's build and kinesics. He headed toward the brawl.

Gabe was intent on his objective and did not let up until his victim stopped moving. Then he straightened, loomed over the man to ensure he was good and beat, and strode into the Majesty with an inebriated lurch.

Zestrum reached the fallen man and knelt to check on him.

From south on Sixth Street Doc Hartman scuttled over to the man. A few citizens crept in for a closer look.

Doc Hartman grimaced and shook his head. He beckoned to Zestrum. "Help me get him to the clinic."

Zestrum and Doc Hartman half-carried the victim the two blocks to the medical clinic on Sixth. A shingle above the door with a giant skull surrounded by the words "Physician and Surgeon" designated this as offices of "Tim Hartman, Doctor of Medicine."

Inside the converted residence, they crossed through the lobby into a big exam room and laid out the patient on a padded exam table. Zestrum noted the modern sophisticated medical tools on the counter. Doc Hartman might be a country doctor, but he had big city supplies.

"Just hold still, Allan." Doc Hartman examined the man's bloody face.

"I think he broke my nose."

"That he did." Doc Hartman placed his hands on either side of the nose and aligned the busted cartilage with a nauseating *crack*.

The man moaned in pain.

Doc Hartman went to work cleaning up the blood and disinfecting the wounds. "What're you doing in the Majesty so early in the day?"

"I just stopped in for a beer." He winced and flinched under the ministrations.

"Uh huh." Doc Hartman finished preliminary cleanup and gestured at Zestrum. "Help me get his clothes off."

"My clothes?"

"Gotta check you for injuries."

With Zestrum's assistance, Doc Hartman removed Allan's vest, shirt, and jeans. Bruises mottled his torso, arms, and legs.

Doc Hartman glanced at Zestrum. "You see what happened?"

"I saw the fight in the street." Zestrum had no doubt Gabe provoked the quarrel. It was a gut feeling.

"Hmph." Doc Hartman cleaned Allan with alcohol wipes. "What happened, Allan?"

"I dunno. I was having a drink. I guess I. . . got in his way or something."

"Well. Gabe doesn't need much reason. He spends more time at the Majesty than on the ranch." He continued the physical exam. "You got two busted ribs, boy. I need to wrap you up."

"I gotta work, Doc."

"Can't work with two busted ribs." He wrapped a beige bandage around the patient.

"I got no insurance."

"You go swear out a complaint with the sheriff. Sue Etcheverry for damages and mental anguish."

Allan winced. "Ain't gonna do no good."

"Yeah, but it's the thought that counts. Someday the weight of all those charges is gonna collapse on him."

Allan almost laughed and then grimaced in pain. "That'll be the day."

Doc Hartman sighed. "Can't come soon enough for me."

CHAPTER 21 – PRELUDE TO WAR

Zestrum backtracked to Main Street. At the corner, he heard loud voices from the Dual Majesty—Bodie, Edwards, Gabe, and Chris Etcheverry. There were others, too, arguing and posturing. He crossed the street and peered through the plate glass window into the bar.

Bodie and Edwards flanked Chris, hands ready at their weapons. Chris was sitting at a poker table with buddies. Gabe stood nearby.

"You ain't taking me anywhere," Chris was saying in belligerent tones.

"Got no choice," said Bodie. "Got a warrant."

"For what?"

"For the killing of Festus Wilkinson."

Zestrum eased through the double doors into the saloon for a clearer view of the impasse.

Chris snorted with derision. "That old drunk?"

"He's not an old drunk," said Bodie. "He's a person whose life you took."

"He was a *bum*."

"He was Senator Hiram Wilkinson's son. The Senator has sworn out a warrant for your arrest and trial."

Chris sat taller in his chair, pulling an accusing tone. "I didn't know he was a Senator's kid. Nobody knew he was a Senator's kid. How was I supposed to know that?"

"Even if he wasn't a senator's son, you'd be on trial for manslaughter. Let's go."

Gabe bulled into Edwards' space, making the deputy take an involuntary step back. "I don't think you can execute that warrant, Sheriff. Not with all our friends here." He glanced around at the other customers, many of them Etcheverry employees. The mutter of the mob filled the air.

Bodie sighed. "Don't make it harder than it is."

Chris was instantly savage. "I'll make it as hard as I like." He reached for his sidearm.

The click of a pistol being cocked made him freeze.

"Don't." Zestrum aimed his pistol at Chris.

Chris faltered, hand on the butt of his gun, surprised at the intrusion.

"Really. Don't." Louisiana stood at the bar behind Gabe, his elbow resting on the bar, his Rickenhower aimed at Gabe.

Bodie noted his allies. Caught in a possible crossfire, Chris and Gabe did not draw their weapons.

Gabe glared at Louisiana. "Stay out of this, borg."

Zestrum looked to Bodie for instruction, letting the sheriff know it was his show.

Bodie acknowledged the assist with an imperceptible nod and drew his pistol with his right hand while removing Chris's sidearm with his left. "Let's go, Chris."

Edwards drew his gun. "Step aside there, Gabe, or you might get hurt."

Gabe fumed and moved away from the deputy.

Chris slowly got up and headed for the door. Zestrum backed out onto the sidewalk as Bodie followed Chris while Edwards took post at the door to hold off the mob. Louisiana sidled in beside Edwards, one eye on Chris, one eye on Gabe.

Bodie and Zestrum escorted Chris to the sheriff's office where Puzzle waited on the porch with a rifle in his hands.

Puzzle brightened when he saw Zestrum. "Doniphon."

"Puzzle." Zestrum followed Bodie into the office and noted the open boxes of ammunition on the counter behind the desk. The Sheriff had been preparing for this arrest.

"This is an unlawful detention," said Chris.

"Show him the warrant, Puzzle," said Bodie.

Puzzle held up the arrest warrant so Chris could see his name inscribed on the document. He set the paper on the desk and readied his rifle. "Gonna frame that one."

Zestrum looked at the old deputy. "You gonna put it over your chair?"

"No, over the window so I can see it without twistin' my neck around."

"That looks forged," said Chris.

"Came over the wire today," said Bodie.

"You're all gonna face charges of false arrest. This is an *unlawful arrest*."

Bodie gave him a baleful look. "Empty your pockets."

Puzzle and Zestrum provided backup as Chris removed his remaining weapons and set them on the desk.

"I want my lawyer."

"I'm sure he's on his way by now." Bodie patted down Chris and located another knife. He gave Chris a warning look.

"I forgot about that one."

"Uh huh." Bodie set the knife on the desk.

"I got rights."

"So did Festus."

"Pa ain't gonna like this."

"I don't imagine he will."

Bodie directed Chris through the inner door into a cell and locked the door.

"You're gonna be real sorry you done this," Chris promised.

"I'm real sorry now. The variety of your conversation appears to be extremely limited." Bodie walked into the front office and closed the inner door.

Puzzle locked the door and grinned. "That's a sight I like to see."

"Don't be too happy. Now we gotta hold him till the marshal gets here."

Zestrum holstered his gun. "When'll that be?"

"Tomorrow at one."

"That's a long 24 hours."

"Yeah. And with a whole lot of his friends outside chomping at the bit to liberate him." Bodie took a rifle from the rack to prep it. "Things've gone downhill since we last spoke."

"I heard there was an altercation last evening."

"Chris and Gabe celebrated their liberty by bashing some heads. Kramer ended up at the Doc's clinic with a concussion."

"Tore up the Majesty pretty good, too," Puzzle said.

"Today I saw him assault someone named Allan," Zestrum said.

Bodie shook his head. "Another victim. Another complaint."

"I got a whole drawer full of 'em," Puzzle said. "Gonna make a collage."

The front door opened. Puzzle and Bodie both swung their rifles in that direction. Edwards held up his hands, waiting till they recognized him and lowered their weapons.

"Is the prisoner secured?" Edwards said.

Bodie nodded. Edwards entered the office, closing the door. The door stalled and swung inward. Edwards drew his pistol. He, Puzzle, and Bodie aimed their weapons in that direction.

Louisiana held up empty hands. "Just me, Sheriff."

They lowered weapons and breathed easier. Louisiana shut the door. Then there was a loud knock on the door and everyone aimed their weapons at the exit.

Puzzle opened the peephole hatch.

"Ephraim Judd, Esquire, here to see my client."

Puzzle scowled as he snapped shut the hatch and opened the door to allow the attorney to enter. The lawmen lowered their weapons.

Judd presented as he had before, with infinite clarity and condescension. He walked to the inner door and waited as Edwards pulled the locks and swung the door open.

"I'll require privacy, Deputy."

Edwards gave a curt nod. Judd sauntered into the interior room and Edwards shut the door—and locked it. "There's your privacy, pettifogger."

Puzzle cackled.

"He's not getting out again, is he?" said Louisiana.

"Not on a federal warrant," said Bodie. "Judge Roberts got no jurisdiction."

Louisiana nodded. Edwards checked his rifle.

Bodie looked at Zestrum. "I thank you for your assistance."

"Think nothing of it," Zestrum said.

Louisiana perched on the other desk. "I gotta tell ya, the folks at the Majesty are pretty riled."

"I expect they'll stay that way indefinitely," Bodie said.

"Will it end once this one's on his way to Steelreach?" Zestrum indicated Chris with a tilt of his head.

"I ain't convinced Claude Etcheverry won't ambush the marshal on his way out of town to rescue his boy. The marshal's office assured me they could handle transport." Bodie shook his head, heavy with doubt. "Won't be an easy task, but I'll be glad to hand this over to the Feds."

"It's a piece of cake," said Louisiana.

Zestrum sensed the red borg had no idea how hot things would get holding a prisoner for 24 hours among hostiles.

Bodie had the same thought. "It's gonna get dirty."

"I've been dirty before," Louisiana said.

"It'll be a help to have a fourth hand till the marshal gets here."

"How about a fifth hand?" Zestrum said.

Bodie's eyes narrowed. "You offering your services?"

"Sure."

Bodie considered that. "Guess I should deputize you, to make it official."

Bodie raised his right hand. Zestrum did the same.

"As Sheriff of Copperbank, I hereby authorize you to serve as my deputy, to discharge the duties of said office with fairness, integrity, diligence and impartiality, and to uphold fundamental human rights to all people, according to law." He lowered his hand. "You're deputized."

"Don't feel no different," Zestrum said.

Bodie gave him a look. "It feels a little heavier when you walk down the street."

Puzzle rooted around in a drawer and found a badge. "Here's the weight."

Zestrum studied the badge before pinning it to his vest. "I ain't been a member of law enforcement before. What's the pay?"

Bodie laughed.

Puzzle cackled. "You get a decent burial if they kill you."

Bodie gave a wry smile. "Now you got incentive to face death. I'm acquainted with your specialties, Zestrum, but not yours." He looked at Louisiana.

Louisiana blinked in confusion. "My what?"

"Your gadgets," Edwards prompted.

Louisiana frowned. "That's kinda personal, sheriff."

"Consider it part of the arsenal." Bodie waited for disclosure.

The red borg shifted on his feet, uncomfortable. "I got eyes, ears, aim, and muscle."

"Good enough. We got a foundation, gentlemen."

Louisiana jutted his chin in challenge. "What's Puzzle bring to the table?"

"Experience. Why don't you two go get your dinner and come back after. I suspect Judd will be in there the next two hours getting Chris's story straight."

* * *

Zestrum and Louisiana strolled to Colton House together.

Louisiana gave him a sidelong look. "You ain't been a deputy before?"

"No," said Zestrum. "Though at times I was enforcer for the Consortium."

He grimaced. "The Consortium. I hated those fuckers."

"I hated myself. Were you in landscaping?"

"I was security for Ralph Jordan's bordello on the East Seaboard. He was mean as a snake. Used to beat the women and men if they didn't bring in their quota for the night. But he was untouchable. Consortium said so."

"We had those, too. Human supervisors got special privileges."

"I hated those fuckers."

"Seems to me you hated a lot of fuckers."

"Well, there's a lot of 'em to hate."

They reached Colton House and entered the foyer. Voices from the dining room indicated dinner was beginning. They paused in the doorway to scope out the layout. Zestrum saw Louisiana glower when he spotted Cole sitting next to Irina Nolan.

Irina did not look comfortable with her table companion. When she noticed Louisiana, her expression brightened.

Zestrum and Louisiana sat at the table opposite her.

"Did you hear what happened at the Majesty?" said Bainbridge.

"What?" said Davis.

"Sheriff arrested Chris Etcheverry and took him into custody."

Zestrum saw Jessica at the kitchen door, coffee pot in hand, hearing this news. Her eyes came to his eyes and then landed on the badge on his vest. Her forehead furrowed.

"That's gonna provoke Claude for sure," said Cole.

"That's gonna provoke a *war*," said Bainbridge.

Irina gasped.

Bainbridge turned a silky smile on her. "No need for us to worry, Ms. Nolan. All that'll happen down on Main Street and we're well clear of that."

Irina frowned. "I'm more concerned about who might get killed in the melee, Mr. Bainbridge."

He looked surprised and chastised.

Jessica braced herself and poured coffee for the lodgers. "I'm certain whatever happens, Sheriff Bodie will handle it."

"He'll have plenty of help," Louisiana said.

Everyone looked at him.

Louisiana spooned sugar into his coffee and noted their interest. "He'll have additional deputies."

Davis noticed the badge on Zestrum. "You, Mr. Doniphon?"

"And me." Louisiana sipped the coffee.

"You boys know what you're getting into?" Davis said.

"Probably not," Zestrum said.

Louisiana laughed, nearly spilling his drink.

"I don't think that's funny," said Cole. "Law enforcement is dangerous work. It's. . . Around here, it sure is."

Louisiana sobered and met his gaze with a firm eye. "I worked security on the East Seaboard. This is cake."

"This is the Badlands," Irina said softly. When Louisiana looked at her, she added, "I hope you will adjust your expectations accordingly."

"I will do that, ma'am." He held her eyes, giving Cole fits at the interest he showed in Irina.

Zestrum felt Jessica's gaze on him and knew she had a million questions for him. He'd wait till after the meal to speak to her in private.

Conversation remained irritatingly focused on the Etcheverrys' criminal behavior and antics over the decades.

They didn't play well with others.

Several people had died at their hands, and a few disappeared without a trace out in the Badlands.

After dinner, the lodgers migrated into the parlor.

Louisiana glanced at Zestrum. "See you over there." And he strode out the front door.

Zestrum was left alone with Jessica in the dining room. She gave him a quizzical look.

"I've got a shift tonight," he explained. "I've been deputized."

Her mouth opened and her jaw worked silently for a moment as she digested the information. Worry clouded her dark gray eyes. "I see."

"It'll all be over by noon tomorrow."

"One way or another," she murmured. Her worry escalated. "You don't. . . *need* the work?"

"I'm helping out a friend."

"I see. You won't. . . take any unnecessary risks, will you?"

"I never do."

"I wouldn't want to see you. . . miss your dinner tomorrow night."

"That's about as strong a motivator to avoid a stray bullet as I can think of." He gave her a smile, waiting while she processed his intentions.

"Well. The least I can do is provide some solid food for you and the boys at the sheriff's office." She darted into the kitchen and he could swear those shining eyes were filmed with tears.

CHAPTER 22 – BEHIND LOCKED DOORS

On his way to Main Street, Zestrum slowed as he heard someone approaching from the alley. Johnny wheeled into his path like a wild hog under hot pursuit.

"Mr. Doniphon—" His eyes zeroed in on the badge on his vest and his attitude hardened. "You're not gonna join the sheriff, are you?"

"I'm helping out an old friend."

He appeared offended and a trifle injured. "What about our agreement?"

"Our agreement stands unless you want to terminate it."

His features twitched as he wrestled with a new dilemma. "But. . . I thought you were gonna help *me*."

"You been practicing your falls?"

Diverted by the question, he gave a quick nod, then returned to the dilemma. He lowered his voice. "You can't go up against Pa. He'll kill you."

"He may try."

"You ain't seen him at his worst."

"He ain't seen me at my best."

Johnny stared at him, at a loss for arguments in the face of Zestrum's resolve. "Why you wanna go do that? It ain't your problem."

"Like I said. I'm helping out a friend. Same way I'm helping out you."

"But he's my *brother*."

"If the jury acquits him, he'll be a free man."

"What if they don't? Those folks in Steelreach don't know us like these folks here."

"So he oughta get a fair trial."

Johnny didn't like the implications of that slice of truth. "Pa ain't gonna let the marshal take him." He averted his gaze. "Just saying."

"I expect it'll be a rough night. You need to stay out of this." When the kid opened his mouth to protest, Zestrum interrupted. "This is my advice. You asked for advice, on how to be responsible and mature. How to earn respect and be a man. There are times it's damn hard. This is one of those times."

Another truth he didn't like facing. He stuffed both hands in his pockets and hunched his shoulders. "I gotta stand by Pa and Gabe."

"Then that's your decision. I respect your choice. Respect mine."

Johnny scowled, then nodded, spun around, and hustled into the alley.

As Zestrum approached the corner, he picked up the sound of angry voices—lots of them. Below that was the murmur of calmer voices, gawkers probably. His hand went toward his gun as he leaned forward to get a look at the jailhouse.

A restive mob of men and women, human and cyborg, undulated in the street outside the sheriff's office. Claude Etcheverry, Gabriel, and Angie stood at the forefront. Johnny observed from the sidewalk in front of the Land Office.

Zestrum noted Claude's exact position to target. He wished he'd have brought his rifle.

On the wooden porch, Bodie and Louisiana held rifles at the ready. And down the road a piece, Harris Black scribbled words on a little notepad as if his life depended on it.

"You men and women disperse or I'll start arresting folks," said Bodie.

The multitude grumbled and retreated like an ebbing wave but did not disband.

Claude didn't budge from the center of the street. "I suggest—strongly—that you release my son."

"I got a federal warrant," said Bodie. "Your lawyer explained that to you."

"You got no cause to hold him."

"He's going to trial for the death of Festus Wilkinson. Your lawyer explained that to you."

"It was an accident, pure and simple."

"It was manslaughter, and it ain't the first time. The judge in Steelreach will provide an impartial judgment."

"I'm not letting that corrupt judge try my son." He dipped his head like a bull. "You don't want trouble, do you?"

The sound of a gun cocking made Claude and his companions look up. Edwards was perched on the jailhouse roof, his rifle trained on Claude.

Claude glowered. "I won't forget this, Bodie."

"I don't imagine you will. But if there's any gunplay, you'll be the first one shot." Bodie leveled his rifle at the man.

Claude spent a long moment contemplating his situation. Then he turned toward his crew. "Disperse, folks. Let's have a drink."

The majority of the mob wandered into the Majesty. Some lingered on the sidewalk in front of the saloon. Claude stood on the sidewalk across the street, opposite the jail, talking with Gabriel and Judd. Reporter Black snapped pictures with his camera, then hustled over to speak to them. Johnny stood behind his father.

Zestrum chose to stay where he was as he was interested in Claude's conversation. It was mostly Judd ticking off unlikely legal tactics to skirt justice.

Angie stood outside the jailhouse porch, regarding the sheriff with pleading eyes and a soft voice. "Be reasonable, Sheriff Bodie. The death was an accident. The jury will see that. Why waste taxpayers' time and money on a trial that ends with acquittal?"

While she kept her voice quiet and calm, Zestrum heard her words. Enhanced auditory modifications came in handy at odd times.

Bodie kept his tone calm and quiet to match hers. "Ms. Etcheverry, I appreciate your sentiment, and you're probably right about that acquittal. But there's been entirely too much violence round here, and your brother is usually at the center of it. There's a limit to tolerance, and I've reached it."

She gestured toward her family and the people milling across the street. "Won't this situation merely engender more violence? You'll be the cause of that, Sheriff. And for what outcome? More deaths?"

"I'm upholding the law, ma'am, like I'm sworn to do by the Blanken 9 Constitution and the Treaties Natural. If I don't arrest a man for a crime, there's no need for a sheriff. You don't want to live in a territory with no law enforcement." He lowered his voice to cold steel. "You don't want that, Ms. Etcheverry. You really don't."

She studied the old cyborg, her mouth forming a stern line, her brows furrowed. Zestrum read her thoughts from that expression—she rated Bodie an obstacle and a fool. She turned on her heel and joined her father and brothers outside the Dual Majesty's entrance.

McConnell appeared sympathetic to their plight. From what Zestrum had heard around the dinner table, Claude always paid for his boys' damages, plus a little extra.

Zestrum approached the jail. Bodie's gaze darted round at the folks on the street. He gestured, and he and Zestrum entered the office. Louisiana remained on the porch, cradling his weapon.

In the office, Puzzle stood sentry at the closed inner door, a rifle in his hands. He lowered the weapon and smiled. "This is real law enforcing, ain't it, Mitch?"

Bodie shook his head in disgust and set his rifle on his desk within reach. "Claude'll be back soon and next time he won't back down."

"They have to get through the walls first." Puzzle sounded confident the reinforced structure would withstand the attack.

Bodie looked at Zestrum. "Had your dinner?"

"I did." Zestrum took in the lay of the office. The inner door was shut and barred. The ammunition was at hand.

Bodie sat at his desk and started processing paperwork.

Puzzle secured the outer door and picked up his broom. "What'd she have tonight?"

"Lasagna." Zestrum set his leather satchel and the basket of vittles on the desk across the room from the sheriff.

"I could use some of that myself." Puzzle flicked the bristles of the broom around the edges of the room. "What's in the basket?"

Zestrum checked the flooring. "Our midnight snack, courtesy of Ms. Colton."

Puzzle headed over to take a look-see.

Bodie smiled. "She is a generous woman."

Zestrum selected a rifle from the rack and loaded ammunition. "Who's the guy with the notepad?"

Bodie scowled. "Harris Black of *The Copperbank Sentinel.* Bought and paid for."

"Etcheverry's man?"

"Have you seen a copy of *The Copperbank Sentinel?*"

"Around the parlor."

"You may have noticed the rather large advertisements for Etcheverry Dairy and Beef. 'When you think dairy, think Etcheverry.'"

"Catchy."

"Etcheverry is the *Sentinel's* biggest advertiser."

"I see."

"I tend to ignore Black and let the mayor do the talking."

"Who's the mayor?"

"Frederic du Beauchez."

"Don't think we've met. Where is he as the pie hits the fan?"

"Been on an extended fishing trip since the warrant came in. I suspect he don't want to talk to Black either. Or deal with this." Bodie indicated the current situation with a gesture toward the cells on the other side of the wall.

Zestrum stepped outside to inspect the front of the jailhouse. This time he took a rifle.

Sturdy wooden planks, reinforced posts, and only one door. Thugs would have a hard time getting inside with only one entrance—but that left the men inside with only one exit.

No snipers yet.

Then Zestrum saw an unexpected sight—Claude Etcheverry consulting with a priest outside the General Store. The priest—unmistakable in a black cassock—held a canvas bag as if accosted in the midst of shopping.

Claude spoke with persuasive gestures, no doubt asking for intercession.

Zestrum wondered how often Claude attended church. He himself was not a religious man, and he suspected the elder Etcheverry was even further removed from the pulpit.

"Look at that," Louisiana said. "Satan's gone to church."

Puzzle appeared behind him, shutting the door. "Seeing the priest? Claude's getting desperate."

Puzzle, Zestrum, and Louisiana watched the interaction in front of the store.

After ten minutes or so, Claude accompanied the priest to the jailhouse.

Puzzle opened the door and spoke to Bodie. "Claude couldn't convince you to release Chris, so it looks like he convinced the pastor to convince you to release 'im." Puzzle renewed the grip on his rifle. "Coming this way, Mitch."

Zestrum hefted the rifle in his arms, holding it ready but not threateningly. It wouldn't be right to aim at a man of the cloth no matter his intentions—but Claude was a different book.

Louisiana held his weapon under his arm, finger on the trigger, moving to the other side of the door.

"Good afternoon, Puzzle," said the priest. "Deputies."

"Father Monaldi," said Puzzle, flashing a quick smile at him, a scowl at Claude.

"Afternoon," said Louisiana.

Zestrum tipped his hat.

Father Monaldi addressed the deputies pleasantly enough. "I don't believe we've met. I'm Father Bonaventure Monaldi."

"Father Monaldi wants to speak with Chris," Claude said, interrupting the introductions to press his business.

Louisiana gauged whether the priest was coerced. "That true, Father?"

"I'm frequently summoned to aid the infirm and the destitute in their bleakest hours."

Zestrum knew Chris was neither of those. He glanced at Bodie for instructions.

"Good afternoon, Sheriff. May I come in for a moment?" Monaldi waited for permission.

"Come on in," said Bodie.

Puzzle scowled again at Claude, then cleared the doorway. Monaldi entered the sheriff's office.

Stepping into the street, Claude preened and strutted diagonally across to the Dual Majesty with the confident stride of a malefactor who expected to get his way.

Zestrum couldn't resist. He stepped inside to eavesdrop. Louisiana listened from the porch. Puzzle observed as Bodie greeted Monaldi with a handshake.

"Father."

"Sheriff. How are you this fine day?"

Bodie almost laughed at the absurdity of the question. "I'm doing well. How about yourself?"

"I've been quite busy." He set his canvas bag on the floor by the desk. "I'm here to speak with Chris. Is he available?"

Bodie scoffed. "He's available. I'm afraid you'll have to visit through the bars."

"Naturally."

At Bodie's signal, Puzzle unlocked the inner door and allowed the priest into the rear room. He brought the door halfway shut, open wide enough for cyborgs with enhanced auditory mods to overhear. This wasn't privileged conversation as no one requested the sanctity of confession.

"In case he calls for help," Puzzle whispered to Bodie and Zestrum.

"Father Monaldi, am I glad to see you," said Chris.

"Chris. I encountered your father at the General Store. He told me of your plight."

"I've been railroaded, Father. The charges are bogus. I mean, the gun fired, but it was totally an accidental discharge of my weapon." He gave an extraordinary fabrication of his innocence.

"Have you prayed about this?"

"Every night, Father. I asked Jesus for forgiveness and He give it to me. I felt it in my heart."

"Well, I'm glad to hear you've prayed to God. Would you like to make your confession? We could do that right here, even with the bars between us."

"You think that would help?"

"I think it would help immensely." And Monaldi shut the inner door for privacy.

Puzzle pouted. "Damn! Just when I was fixin' to hear the championship mendacity of all time."

"Chris confessing?" Bodie shook his head.

A while later Monaldi emerged from the back room. Puzzle secured the door and waited eagerly for some remark. Bodie waited, too.

Monaldi folded his hands together. "Sheriff, I have spoken to Chris regarding his unfortunate circumstances. I believe he is genuinely sorry for his crime. I believe he will long regret that crime." He lowered his voice. "And I believe you are doing the right thing." He glanced at Puzzle, Louisiana, and Zestrum. "Good day, gentlemen."

The priest picked up his canvas bag and glided out of the jailhouse.

Puzzle stared after him. "Chris must be climbing the walls by now."

"Father Monaldi is a wise man," Bodie said.

There came the sound of boots on a wooden ladder and Edwards appeared at the closet door. "Nothing stirring yet, but plenty in the pot." He hobbled to the desk and set down the rifle, stretched his spine.

Zestrum noted the man's hands were shaking, a sign of Vestal tremens.

Then they heard banging on the other side of the inner wall.

"Better check the prisoner, Puzzle," said Bodie. "See how far he is up the wall."

Puzzle opened the inner door and found an agitated prisoner pacing his cell.

"Where's my dinner?"

Puzzle scowled. "Ain't time yet."

Chris shouted. *"It's past dinner time.* I'm a *human.* You gotta *feed* me. It's in the Constitution."

"Hold your horses!" Puzzle slammed the inner door. "Human. Huh!"

Zestrum gave a sarcastic look. "That true? We gotta feed him?"

"'Fraid so," said Bodie.

"I'll go fetch a meal from Pete's," said Edwards. "I need the exercise." He grasped his rifle and shuffled out.

"I'll spot ya." Puzzle picked up a rifle and stepped outside.

"I'll spot *you.*" Louisiana checked his rifle and walked onto the porch with Puzzle.

"I don't need no uppity youngster—"

"Wind down, Old Timer."

"Who you calling Old Timer?"

"You, Old Timer."

"Why you cotton headed, low life, turd bloss—"

The outer door slammed shut.

Bodie leaned back in his chair, glancing to verify the inner door was firmly closed before speaking. "I ain't gonna lie to you, Zestrum. We may not live past tonight."

"We'll give 'em a hell of a fight, though."

He smiled wanly. "I wish I had your energy. Or Louisiana's."

Zestrum tilted his head in the direction Edwards had gone. "He's going to get a hit."

"I know. It'll fortify him. He gets the shakes if he goes too long." He studied him. "I noticed your absence the past two days."

Zestrum looked at the sheriff. Could he trust the man? They *were* old friends. . . "I was surveying for a project."

"For Etcheverry?"

"For Nowlin."

His eyebrows lifted in wonder. "Shifted sides?"

"I never took a side. I'm making an income."

"You took a side if you took his money. Etcheverry will make you pay for it."

"Worse than he's gonna do if I survive till morning?"

Bodie regarded him a moment, then chuckled. "Guess there is one advantage to getting killed tonight."

"How long since *you* took a respite, Mitch?"

"Can't afford to sleep till tomorrow afternoon round one o'clock."

"In the meantime. You got something you need me to do besides keep watch here?"

"Not right now. I'm just sorting the papers." He lowered his chin and gave a weighty look. "Can you keep yourself occupied without a broom?"

"I can." Zestrum sat at the desk and opened his sketchbook, took out his pencil. "Let me know if the noise bothers you." He wriggled the pencil in his hand.

Bodie laughed and resumed sorting through the forms.

* * *

Edwards returned a half hour later with a covered platter of something. His hands were no longer shaking and he seemed hyper alert.

Puzzle secured the outer door, then scurried to open the inner door.

Edwards delivered the food through an opening in the bars wide enough to accommodate a plate and cup. "Dinner is served."

Chris glared at the meal. "You call that dinner?"

"Unless you'd rather have nothing."

"This ain't good enough to feed a borg."

Edwards bristled. "This food meets the nutritional requirements of the Blanken 9 government for one meal. If you don't like it, you can vote for a change of prison menus the next election. Oops, I forgot–you'll still be incarcerated then."

Chris glowered and maneuvered the items through the bars. "I'm having a word with Pete after this."

"You do that." Edwards sauntered into the office and shut the inner door to forestall further complaints.

Puzzle picked up his broom and skimmed the edge along the baseboards by the door.

Bodie watched with irritation. "Go get your dinner, Puzzle."

Puzzle frowned in dismay. "I was gonna have Pete deliver something here."

Edwards smirked. "You don't want that."

"You need a break," said Bodie. "Go on. And don't come back for at least two hours."

"Two hours?" Puzzle paused in hanging the broom on a hook beside the tiny closet. "That's long enough for six meals." He looked crestfallen.

"Take a nap. I need you sharp for midnight shift."

"Oh." He brightened at that suggestion. "Then I'll be back here at nine. Sure thing." He grabbed his hat and lumbered out of the office, favoring his injured leg.

Zestrum secured the door and tossed the sheriff a skeptical look.

"He's a good man when the chips are down," said Bodie, "but he sweeps the floor till I can't stand the sight of the broom."

Edwards flopped onto the bedroll behind the vacant desk and glanced at Zestrum. "You wanna take a turn on the roof?"

"Sure." Zestrum picked up his rifle.

"Access through there." Bodie pointed at the closet.

Zestrum climbed up the ladder inside the closet onto the roof of the jailhouse, a flat surface with brickwork wall at the edges for cover.

From this vantage point, he had a view down Main Street in both directions and the buildings on all sides. Neighboring buildings were a good 15 feet away, plenty of alley between for a wagon to pass. The lot behind the jail sloped down to several small houses that faced Baker Street.

He saw Louisiana strolling down the sidewalk on a leisurely patrol of Main Street. Zestrum sat cross-legged with the rifle across his knees and scanned the terrain.

Being above street level provided a new perspective. He was even height with the second story of the Land Office and Assay Office across the street. He saw the rooftops of one-story warehouses and residences in the surrounding blocks. He had a glimpse of the courthouse in the Civic Square. The clock in the tower chimed eight and the sun began sinking in the distance.

Without a doubt the private militia would strike after dark. The question was—how long after?

* * *

At dusk, the streetlamps glowed pale orange light at the corners of each block. Not the bright white lights used in the big Coast cities that enjoyed priority for meager supply shipments, but small gas bulbs scavenged from places converting to liquid bulbs. The Badlands seemed to be the place of remnants, whether it be lightbulbs or lawmen.

Zestrum felt the deficiency tonight, sitting on the roof risking his life to help out a buddy from the way back. This would be a most ridiculous end to him, dying the same day he acquired his very own real estate.

He should write out a quick will, deeding the property to Jessica Colton "in case of." Someone should benefit from his labors if he lost the battle.

His dark adaptation vision adjusted so he detected Etcheverry's hired guns shifting in the shadows of alleys and crevices, a change of guard to keep the observers fresh. Some of those cyborgs probably had the same night vision mods.

The Consortium only provided components necessary per the job.

The misery of surgical modification had been equated with the process of dental implants—loss of tissue, severe pain, installation of titanium, and then fitting the module. The discomfort faded with time until the augmentation became natural. Though he'd heard some older cyborgs complain about the torment returning in old age.

He wondered if that was what happened to Puzzle.

In the early days of implants, surgeons used a raw unfiltered form of Bellingerine that caused severe adverse reactions in many patients. It took a decade for specialists in immunology, biomedical engineering, and prosthetics technology to identify the cause and formulate the cure. Some cyborgs recovered. For others, it was too late—the damage was irreversible.

Zestrum was glad he received his fifth generation mods after the solution was set in medical stone.

Below, the front door opened. Bodie stepped onto the porch to assess the surroundings, with Edwards at his side, holding rifles bold and visible to the public. Louisiana came down the sidewalk from the east, rifle at ready. Civilians paused in their evening walks, then hurried off the street at the show of force.

Bodie, Louisiana, and Edwards withdrew inside the office.

"Come on down," called Bodie.

A last glance around, then Zestrum climbed down the ladder to the inner office.

Bodie secured the exit with the deadbolt and bar. "Get your rounds done?"

"Yeah." Edwards set his rifle near the chair. "Etcheverry is at the Majesty with Gabe and Angie."

"For the time being." Bodie laid out a map on his desk.

Louisiana gazed at the map. "What's this?"

"This here's a diagram of the town," Edwards said. "Mitch is laying out some plans. Care to hear them?"

"Sure thing, but make it simple because I'm just a country cyborg, not your fancy landscaper model."

Edwards gave him a long icy sidelong look.

Bodie outlined where he expected the attack to originate and whip toward the jail. They discussed strategy and signals.

There came a knock on the door. The three deputies provided backup as Bodie opened the peephole cover and then admitted Puzzle, locking the door after he entered.

Puzzle looked brightly at his boss. "Anything happen yet?"

Bodie shook his head at the chirpy question. "Not yet. They're waiting for you, Puzzle."

Puzzle's chest puffed smugly. "We'll hold 'em off, Mitch. We got the best borgs in the business."

Bodie exchanged looks with the others. Zestrum knew the sheriff was calculating the odds of five law enforcement officers against a horde of hoodlums.

Bodie indicated the map. "Let's go over the plan again now Puzzle's here." At the desk, he detailed what they'd discussed so far.

Puzzle added some insights of his own—and he verified the location of Claude and Gabriel Etcheverry at the Dual Majesty. "I seen them in there playing a hand."

"I'd say the attack is coming within the hour," said Louisiana.

"It ain't coming within the hour," Edwards said flatly.

Louisiana looked insulted. "You contradicting me?"

"He'll wait three or four hours so we tire and let down our guard."

"It's dark enough now to assault on two or three sides to get in and out fast."

"The crowd ain't left the Majesty yet and it don't close till one. He don't want witnesses to a jailbreak."

Louisiana guffawed. "He don't seem all that worried about witnesses from what I've observed of him and his kin."

"Nevertheless." Edwards held himself together with a deep breath. "He'll wait till after one in the morning. When the rest of the town's asleep and we're fatigued from a long spell of waiting."

"I agree," said Bodie. "We'll need to take shifts resting up to get through the night."

"Well *I'm* fresh as a dappled daisy," said Louisiana. "What do you want me to do?"

"Take a shift on the roof."

"Sure thing, boss." With that, Louisiana scrambled up to the roof with the agility of a gymnast.

CHAPTER 23 – THE EDGE OF BATTLE

The night wore on toward midnight. Bodie recorded information in his log, then sorted paperwork. Most of it was trifling forms, but it was part of sheriff duties. Endless reports to prove to some spineless bureaucrat they were risking their lives every day.

Puzzle peeked out the peephole, then closed the cover. "Don't see nobody in the street. They must be hidden good."

Louisiana lounged in the chair beside the front door, flipping cards into his hat on the floor. Puzzle swept the room around the furniture. Edwards took watch on the roof.

Zestrum sat at the other desk and wrote out a brief last will and testament in his Moleskin. He left everything to Jessica except his horse and his weapons, which he left to Virgil—if he ever showed up. Zestrum wanted Jessica to have the land and this book.

"Ya writing a chronicle of our adventures?" Puzzle asked.

"No. A will."

Puzzle's face twitched.

"Want to be my witness?"

"Sure." Puzzle took the pen and signed his name under Zestrum's signature. Then he froze. "You own land?"

"Gerald Nowlin granted me a parcel near the foothills."

Bodie, Louisiana, and Puzzle looked amazed.

"Then you have become a bona fide resident of Copperbank County," said Bodie.

"You done that?" Puzzle shook his head in amazement. "I ain't ever heard of any cyborg owning land before."

"It may not even be entirely legal," Zestrum said.

"Law is fluid out here," Bodie said. "And possession is nine-tenths of that law."

Zestrum presented the book to Bodie. "Probably need a second witness to make it legitimate."

Bodie eyed him, then scribbled his name. "Bad luck drawing up a will like that."

"I'm counting on it preventing my early demise." Zestrum tucked his book inside the satchel. "The more prepared I am, the less likely I'll need it."

"Good strategy," Puzzle said. "Murphy's Law."

Bodie snorted. "I'd make a will if I had anything to leave to anybody."

"You're leaving a *legacy*," said Louisiana.

Bodie scoffed. "I got a change of clothes and a gun."

"And a hat," said Puzzle.

"And a hat." Bodie contemplated the paperwork on his desk. "You got a will, Puzzle?"

"My wife took everything in the divorce."

Louisiana squinted at him. "You had a wife?"

"Course. Everybody picks up a wife eventually."

The declaration astonished Louisiana.

Bodie cocked his head and smiled. "You never mentioned her before."

"Ain't worth mentioning. We parted on less than amicable terms." Puzzle paused in sweeping. "Not exactly a good match from the get-go. Don't remember the wedding. I do remember I'd just won a big hand at cards that night. Guess we celebrated my good luck."

Louisiana chuckled. "*She* celebrated your good luck."

"We both had a good time." Puzzle gazed heavenward. "She was a pretty thing. Sometimes I wonder what happened to her." He shrugged and resumed sweeping.

"How 'bout you?" Zestrum speared Louisiana with a keen look. "You ever been married?"

"Not even a little." Louisiana tossed a card.

Bodie looked at Zestrum. "You?"

Zestrum shook his head no.

Louisiana glanced mischievously at Zestrum. "Considering it in the near future?"

The question bothered Zestrum more than he cared to admit. Marriage? To a human? What would people say? "Ask me again in the morning."

Louisiana smirked.

"And I could ask you the same question."

Louisiana stiffened and lost his smartass expression.

Puzzle brightened at the man's reaction. "Something we oughta know?"

Louisiana scowled. "No." He bent to scoop up his cards and shuffled them expertly between his hands.

"Marriage is not to be entered into lightly," said Bodie.

"I wish I'd known that before I did it." Puzzle swept his way to Louisiana and gave him a stern look until Louisiana lifted his feet so he could sweep under the chair.

"Don't you have something more productive to do?" Louisiana said.

"Nothing more productive than housekeeping."

He chuckled, dismayed. "About a *thousand* things more productive than housekeeping."

"Not that you can do while keeping vigil." Puzzle completed the sweep around the chair and moved along the baseboards toward the second desk.

"It keeps us awake," Bodie said. "Unlike paperwork." He stacked forms and shoved them into a drawer.

"Maybe we need a snack," Louisiana said, his eyes going to the basket.

Zestrum gave him a sardonic look, then checked Jessica's basket. There was a thermos of oatmeal, a dozen muffins wrapped in waxed paper, and a carton of almond milk. Plenty for a midnight snack and breakfast as well. He set five muffins on the desk.

"We can pass the time telling stories," Puzzle said. "I heard you spent a couple days in the mountains."

Zestrum was surprised he'd heard that. "From who?"

"I got ears, boy. I hear things."

"I camped overnight by the lake."

"Pretty country up there." Puzzle swept along the wall behind Zestrum, making the man move his chair to accommodate him.

"What did you do up there?" Louisiana said, intent on switching attention from himself.

"I took a swim."

"Water's pretty cold," Puzzle said.

"I found that out."

"How's the road up there?" Louisiana asked.

"Needs work," Zestrum said.

"A town the size of Copperbank can't maintain a road 50 miles out in the wilderness," Bodie said. "It'd be a county responsibility. If we had a county."

"Nobody's doing anything out there except Etcheverry," Puzzle said. "He thinks owning the water means he owns Copperbank."

"Water baron," Louisiana muttered, his expression intense.

"Which is why he's so upset his son's going to federal court," said Bodie. "He ain't got as much influence over Judge Apatow as Judge Roberts."

"Judge Apatow is a hanging judge," Puzzle said cheerfully.

"He won't hang a human," Louisiana said.

"There's always a first time," Bodie said.

"It'd make our job easier," Louisiana said.

Puzzle scowled. "Claude Etcheverry could-a made this a nice place to live if he'd-a wanted to."

Zestrum scoffed. "Humans." Then he thought of Jessica Colton. *She's an exception to the rule.*

"Humans." Puzzle sneered. "They send us out here to colonize, creating a perfect balance of nature, and then show up and undo everything."

Bodie nodded. "Yep."

"Humans ain't all bad," Louisiana said. The others peered at him. "I mean, some of them are okay. Some of them are downright nice."

"Which ones?" Puzzle challenged.

"Well. . . Irina Nolan, the schoolmarm. She's right nice."

"What's she teachin' you?"

His eyes shifted. "Stuff."

"Yeah," Zestrum said. "I saw you making time with her at the boarding house."

"We're just amicable," Louisiana insisted, his eyes saying otherwise.

Zestrum and Puzzle gave him a skeptical look, then traded a look with each other and chuckled.

"We discuss the big questions," Louisiana said.

Puzzle cocked his head. "The big questions? Like what?"

"You know. Life and stuff. Sometimes I wonder about things."

"Only sometimes?"

He glared. "Things, yeah. I don't suppose an old timer like you wonders about things."

"Boy, you think I ain't got no sense of wonder? I wonder things all day long. I wonder what I'm having for breakfast. I wonder what I'm gonna do when I get home."

"I mean Big Things. Things like. . . where did we come from? What are we here for? You know?"

"We came from our mothers. We're here doing our job. What else do you need to know?"

Zestrum snickered. Bodie laughed.

Louisiana bristled with insult. "Not that stuff, you old geezer. There's Things bigger than us. Spiritual things. Life things. Don't you wonder about a purpose in life? There's gotta be more than money and fighting."

"And cards?" Zestrum ventured.

Louisiana hesitated. "Cards is easy. But what else is there for us?"

"Well, there's these here muffins." Puzzle snatched up a muffin.

Louisiana shook his head. "You're worthless, old borg."

"Well, you ain't got nothing but spite."

"And a hat," said Zestrum.

"And a hat." Puzzle cackled and tossed a muffin to Bodie, who caught it and inhaled the aroma. Puzzle took a bite and smiled. "Right good."

Louisiana grabbed a muffin and a rifle. "I'm going up." He crossed to the ladder and scrambled to the roof.

Edwards slid down the ladder and stepped into the office.

Puzzle shook his head. "These young borgs. 'Where did I come from? What am I here for?' You're here to do your job, man, do your job."

"I guess they want more," said Edwards.

"Sooner they realize they ain't getting more, better off they'll be. It's like this muffin wantin' to be president. He can want all he wants, but all he's gonna be is lunch." Puzzle peered at Zestrum. "You want more, Doniphon?"

"I used to," Zestrum said. "I couldn't figure out how to get it, though. I guess I stopped looking."

Bodie gave him a wry look. "Seems like you're looking pretty hard at something."

Zestrum crossed to the front door and seized a rifle. "Gonna take a look out front."

On the porch, his vision instantly adjusted to the darkness. The lamps glowed fainter but the lights at the Dual Majesty remained bright. Music drifted from the establishment.

He walked to the end of the block, aware of the shadowy figures watching him. His auditory mods allowed him to pinpoint each one so he would hear if they moved toward him. Apparently, they were waiting for a designated time or signal. No one accosted him.

He returned to the jailhouse.

Bodie stepped onto the porch to assess the surroundings with his expert eye. Suddenly his old friend looked weary and defeated. He shook his head. "Can't tell you how tired this makes me."

"I'll bet."

"Waiting makes me extra tired." He took a breath and scanned the road. "Gonna do one more round."

"You want me to come along?"

He gave Zestrum an amused look. "Think I can't take care of myself?"

"No."

"I'll be back before the Majesty closes."

"All right." Zestrum watched the sheriff amble down the sidewalk through shadows and pockets of light. He had a suspicion the man was inviting trouble—attempting to trip the switch to get the assault started and finished. Waiting for the ambush was arduous.

He took post at the front of the sheriff's office and kept watch on the street and sidewalks.

Noise from the next block attracted his attention as the Dual Majesty expelled its patrons. The customers scattered in different directions. The front door closed, the wooden shutters locked, and the ground floor lights doused.

The street appeared vacant. The quiet was eerie and ominous.

The peephole cover in the door opened and Puzzle peeked out. "See anything?"

"Plenty." Zestrum lifted a hand to indicate nothing was happening yet.

"So I got time for another muffin." He closed the cover.

Zestrum entered the office. "Bodie ain't back yet." He crossed to the ladder.

Up on the roof, he saw Louisiana poised behind the "Sheriff's Office" sign. They exchanged a nod and Zestrum knelt to scan the terrain behind the jail.

"Any sign of Bodie?" Zestrum said.

"No. You want me to go look for him?"

"We can't afford to be one more man down before the shooting starts."

Zestrum watched the oval moon rise and the stars creep across the night sky. He identified the constellations, skewed from this perspective from the classic configurations visible from Earth. Everything on Blanken 9 was skewed.

The streetlamps slowly dimmed and extinguished, confident that everyone was inside for the night. The streets were deserted—except for the hired guns staked out at uneven intervals. In the midnight murky air, everything was gray and obscure.

Then shots exploded in blasts of gunpowder.

CHAPTER 24 – SIX TO ONE

The lead came from all directions—targeting the front of the jailhouse, the roof, walls, the back of the building. Bullets ripped through the top layers of wood, splintering and embedding but not penetrating the steel-reinforced walls. Chris Etcheverry was behind a second layer of walls and doors in the cell but the noise would be nerve-jarring.

The flashes of gunpowder revealed the shooters' locations. Taking precise aim, Zestrum and Louisiana cut down four assassins in quick succession.

Under cover of gunfire, four thugs dashed to the jailhouse. Two were shot down. The other two attached a charge to the door and ducked into the alley beside the building. The small defined explosion blew a hole in the front door wide enough to disable the lock.

A rifle muzzle appeared at the peephole and blasted the two men who rushed the door.

Zestrum guessed Etcheverry promised these borgs a fortune for them to throw themselves into the path so recklessly. Or he chose the young stupid ones for the initial assault, saving the seasoned ones for the second wave. Or he liquored them up so they believed themselves invincible.

The fire concentrated on Zestrum and Louisiana and they took cover, and that allowed the next two thugs to yank open the front door despite another blast from the rifle.

The scuffle at the porch became frenzied, with gunfire and shouts and then an explosion at the rear of the building.

Zestrum scuttled across the roof and poised his rifle at two cyborgs who were prying off splintered boards to get inside. With that steel-reinforced wall, they wouldn't get far without a blowtorch.

Zestrum picked them off with deadly accuracy, then crept to the front of the building for a view of the street.

There was a momentary pause in gunfire and Zestrum's senses blared warning as his auditory mods picked up the sound of boots behind him. He pivoted, dropping onto his left knee in the spin, and fired at three oncoming thugs. While the bullet ripped through one, the other two reached him and knocked the weapon out of his hands, kicking it across the roof.

Both pummeled him with iron fists. His augmented defenses activated, deflecting the pain. His mods could delay pain receptors, but later he'd feel every bruise.

Louisiana was focused on firing at the men rushing at the front of the jailhouse.

Zestrum scuffled with the bushwhackers, cyborgs who worked as a team to subdue him.

He covered his head and used his left leg and elbow to protect his stomach. Zestrum slumped deeper into his crouch.

When one cyborg took a step toward Louisiana, Zestrum levered up on his left leg, sweeping his right heel into the other one's ankle, throwing her to the rooftop.

The first thug turned back toward Zestrum to continue the assault. Zestrum used the thug's momentum against him, seizing his arm and sidestepping to fling him forward off the roof to the street below.

The remaining thug scrambled to her feet and assumed a Jiu-Jitsu stance. Zestrum stepped into a Muay Thai stance. The Consortium trained its employees in all forms of combat and his body remembered the moves before his mind did.

The actual battle was over within seconds.

The thug rushed in quickly for a throw, expecting Zestrum to strike. At the last second, Zestrum shifted to a judo stance and threw her hard onto the rooftop, dropping an elbow into her torso.

The thug sprawled on the ground with three broken bones.

Zestrum's elbow felt like it impacted something—probably ribs. He dragged the thug to the edge and dumped her off the building, then retrieved his weapon and resumed his post at the sign.

Louisiana reloaded. "Where ya been?"

"I needed to stretch my legs."

Gunfire escalated around the jail as two dozen thugs converged in overwhelming force. Zestrum and Louisiana picked off as many as their ammo allowed. The attack slowed and stopped, with the attackers positioned behind barrels, posts, and wagons at strategic points. Those more experienced warriors.

In the sudden quiet, Claude Etcheverry's voice rang out from across the street.

"Deputy Edwards! Shall we continue the battle or have a parlay?"

A pause before Edwards responded. "We can hold out quite a while, Mr. Etcheverry. What do you want to talk about?"

"A truce. To discuss your surrender of my son."

"Well, I'm afraid that's not on the table."

"We don't want to have to burn down the jail, Deputy."

A longer pause. Burning the jail would incinerate the entire block. Possibly the adjacent blocks. The roads weren't that wide a gust of wind wouldn't blow the flames into the other buildings. The entire town could burn—all the way to Colton House.

"I don't think that will get your son back, Mr. Etcheverry."

"At least not in the condition he's in." Puzzle cackled.

Zestrum counted the attackers around them. At least twenty, plus their boss, and the prisoner inside would lend a hand once he had a weapon.

"I can't rightly negotiate with you, Mr. Etcheverry," Edwards said. "I ain't got the authority. You need to talk to Sheriff Bodie."

"Sheriff Bodie is indisposed, Deputy. Therefore, you are authorized by right of succession to negotiate."

Edwards allowed a long pause before speaking. "In that case, I guess we oughta talk about how I'm gonna have to arrest you for assault on a peace officer."

Etcheverry chuckled. "You come right on out and do that, Deputy. I'm here. I'll wait."

There was a round of laughter from his hirelings, giving away their positions. Zestrum wondered how many he could take out before the others concentrated their firepower on him. He glanced to Louisiana, who caught his eye and shook his head: *Too many.*

Edwards' voice called out. "You have the right to remain silent—"

Boisterous laughter from Etcheverry and his army, drowning out the recitation of custodial rights. Edwards continued to the end, though, then tossed handcuffs out into the street.

"Please comply with my orders and place these handcuffs on your wrists."

Etcheverry's shadow moved under the awning of the assessor's office across the street. "I'm afraid I don't recognize that order, Deputy. If you want to arrest me, come out and do it like a man. If you're actually a man."

More laughter—from the hired cyborg soldiers. Zestrum shook his head in dismay at the abuse cyborgs tolerated from their human bosses.

"Please comply with my orders," Edwards said. There was no pleading, only demand in his tone.

Etcheverry chuckled, then signaled. Down the road, a cyborg struck a match and flung a projectile into the center of the street in front of the jail. The chemical cocktail splattered on the dirt and burned in a ring of red, yellow, and white haloes.

"Next one goes on the porch," Etcheverry warned.

"I'll have to add arson and threats on a duly appointed law enforcement officer to the charges," Edwards replied.

Zestrum glimpsed movement where the incendiary device had originated as the cyborg prepared a second cocktail. Then he discerned another borg wearing a fireproof kit. So they would set fire and have the suited cyborg rescue the prisoner from the inferno.

"I don't want to have to burn down the place," Etcheverry said. "But I will."

"That's terrorism, Mr. Etcheverry," said Edwards.

Etcheverry signaled and his henchman wound up for the throw—and then staggered sideways at the single shot from Louisiana's rifle. As he dropped to the ground, the henchman attempted to complete the throw. The fiery device splattered onto a wagon parked in front of the barber's shop. Two cyborgs hiding behind the wagon rushed for new cover behind barrels further down the sidewalk.

Zestrum fired and winged one. The man lost his gun and scuttled into the alley out of range to tend his wounds.

Angry, Etcheverry thrust another signal. The man in the fireproof suit plucked the burning can from the bed of the wagon and threw it onto the wooden sidewalk in front of the jail. The flaming cocktail spread over the porch and whooshed up the posts onto the awning.

Zestrum flinched at the impact and sudden heat, instinctively dipping his head to let his hat shield his face. When the Stetson smoldered, burning his scalp, he knocked the hat off his head and renewed his aim at the shadows behind the barrels.

Etcheverry pointed both hands toward the jail and his henchmen abandoned cover to storm the office. Each one held a shield to deflect bullets. They advanced quickly to overwhelm and breach defenses. The man in the fireproof suit followed close behind.

Inside the office, Edwards activated the fire suppression system. Water burst from pipes underneath the awning, extinguishing the fire in a blast that rolled out into the street. Steam rose from the combination of cold water on hot medium over wood and dirt.

Caught by surprise, the henchmen stopped in their tracks.

"Keep going!" Etcheverry yelled—and then he froze as Bodie pressed the muzzle of his .38 against the side of his head.

"Belay that order," said the sheriff.

"Stop!" Etcheverry croaked loud enough to be heard.

"Now tell them to drop their weapons or your brains are going to be all over the street."

"Drop your weapons," he called obediently.

Confused, the hired thugs dropped their weapons.

"Tell them to lie down face first and lock hands behind their backs."

Grimacing with frustration, Etcheverry repeated the order. The gunmen complied. As they surrendered, Edwards and Puzzle emerged with handcuffs and manacled their wrists, one by one, until they were all trussed. Zestrum and Louisiana held their rifles at high ready while Bodie held Etcheverry at gunpoint.

Edwards approached the person in the fireproof suit. "Take off that gear."

The person lifted off the helmet, revealing Matt Dillon. He slid off the suit and got down onto the ground. Edwards enjoyed cuffing him.

Then Bodie stiffened as a gun cocked behind him.

"Drop your weapon, Sheriff," said Gabriel Etcheverry, standing at arm's length behind Bodie to prevent the lawman from reaching him.

Bodie lowered his hand and let the piece fall to the wooden sidewalk. Edwards and Puzzle paused in their work. Louisiana and Zestrum tried to zero in on Gabriel.

Claude smirked in triumph. "Good work, son."

"Step into the street and order your deputies to stand down," Gabriel directed.

Bodie stepped toward the street as if to comply–then shouted. "Ethan! Kill these sons of bitches!"

He sidestepped toward Claude, exposing Gabriel. A bullet fired from the jailhouse roof lodged in Gabriel's shoulder, lifting his feet off the ground. Claude spun round in time to see Bodie's fist smash into his face. Gabriel sprawled on the ground.

Bodie snatched up his piece and aimed at Etcheverry senior. "I think we were interrupted."

On the roof, Zestrum looked over at Louisiana and saw him holding his Rickenhower in his hand. "Impact round?"

"Plumb ran out of everything else." Louisiana kept his pistol aimed at the hoodlums below.

An impact round from a pistol from this distance? He definitely had Deadeye.

"My boy needs a doctor!" Claude shouted.

"We'll summon him in due time," Bodie said.

Puzzle approached with a pair of handcuffs. "Mr. Etcheverry." He gestured at the man's back.

Broiling mad, Claude placed his hands at his backside and Puzzle applied the cuffs. "Why ain't you dead?" Claude grumbled at the sheriff.

Bodie glared. "It ain't from your lack of trying." He lowered the .38. "That's murder for hire, Mr. Etcheverry."

"I didn't hire anybody."

"The dead man in my room with your red coin in his pocket is a pretty fair indication you did."

"Obviously a rogue or some disgruntled civilian."

"We'll let the evidence speak to the judge. Murdering a lawman is a federal case."

"But you're not dead."

"Don't worry. We'll sort out my state of health before the marshal gets here. We got time." He nodded to Puzzle.

Puzzle prodded the man across the street. "Cell's gonna be a little crowded, Mr. Etcheverry. But since they're friends of your'n, it's okay." He smiled amiably and directed the rancher toward the jail.

On the roof, Zestrum noticed his Stetson was still smoldering. Louisiana stomped it out, then looked at him. Zestrum looked at him, then the hat, then at Louisiana, and then he snatched up the squashed hat.

CHAPTER 25 – FULL HOUSE

Doc Hartman tended Gabriel on the bed in the doctor's exam room, extracting the bullet and patching the hole with 19 sutures and a thick layer of bandages. The doctor's assistant Roy kept averting his attention from the sedated patient to the unsympathetic deputy, uneasy in the presence of both.

Zestrum observed the surgery.

Doc Hartman finished the bandaging and checked the patient's vitals. "He'll be out awhile, deputy."

"Thanks, Doc. Let me know when he wakes up." Zestrum cuffed Gabriel to the bedpost and exited the room.

The outer reception room was a triage of moaning battered men and women holding gauze and fabrics to their wounds. A few had bandages to staunch the flow of blood. Most had to wait until the boss's son was patched up. A chain wrapped around chairs linked them all with handcuffs or manacles to whatever limb was uninjured. They gave Zestrum the stink eye as he strode past them to the outer door.

Roy hurried after him, catching him at the doorway. "Deputy, you can't leave them here. We're not equipped to hold. . . prisoners." He glanced at the captives locked to the chain.

Zestrum paused at the door. "When you can move them, we'll take them."

"What about. . . ?" Roy glanced toward the exam room containing Gabriel.

"When Doc says he can be moved."

"Where will you be?"

"Sheriff's office." Zestrum opened the front door.

The spindly man caught the edge of the door. "What if they—get loose?"

"You have soporifics?"

He nodded.

"Use them if you need to." Zestrum exited the medical office and started to put on his hat—then scowled at the damage on the hat. He defiantly settled the hat on his head and proceeded down the block toward Main Street. As he approached the corner, movement at his left caught his eye. He slowed. Someone lurked behind one of the barrels. A stray gunman or an overcurious spectator?

He crossed the road and came upon a boy crouched behind the barrel. "Johnny?"

The kid flinched and flopped onto his ass on the sidewalk, eyes wide.

Zestrum noted the Ginwalt was in the boy's holster, but the strap was tied down. "What are you doing out here?"

Johnny spent a moment getting to his feet and dusting off his jeans. "I saw it. I saw it all."

"Then you know what happened."

Johnny braced. "I know."

Zestrum lowered his voice. "You ought to get home and take care of your household."

"Did you have to arrest them?"

"It's only by luck they ain't dead."

He shook his head in confusion. "All that stuff you said before."

"It's valid."

He studied the cyborg. "Did Pa really send someone to kill Sheriff Bodie?"

"Yes, he did."

He stared at the deputy for a long while. "Is he going to hang?"

"That's up to the judge in Steelreach."

"Why can't the trial be here? It'd be quicker."

"Federal court is in Steelreach."

Every answer made the kid more miserable. "What do I do now?"

"Take care of your house. This is the time when you show what you're made of."

Johnny stood frozen for a long moment. "I'll show everybody." He sprinted away toward the next block where his horse was tied.

* * *

Processing the 18 surviving prisoners that could be moved occupied the next few hours. Zestrum stood watch at the front door while Edwards and Louisiana frisked each one, took their ID card, then guided them to a cell. They housed Claude and Chris Etcheverry in separate cells.

The injured prisoners who could walk were escorted at gunpoint from Doc Hartman's reception room to the jailhouse and contained in a cell where they could commiserate their suffering. Four could not be moved and would have to be transported later.

Gabriel remained unconscious in the medic's exam room. Doc's assistant Roy may have let his fear of Gabriel affect the dosage of his anesthetic.

His long recovery was a bonus for the lawmen.

When the deputies finished the task, the four cells were at capacity. Puzzle closed the inner door.

In that time, Mercado the local carpenter installed a new door with new locks on the sheriff's office. City garbage men swept up debris from the battle, clearing the street. Onlookers gawked and gossiped from a safe distance. Harris Black, clad in a cheap black and white business suit with wide lapels, snapped pictures with an upscale camera.

Zestrum spotted the doctor's assistant Roy scuttling down the sidewalk as if his pants were full. He stepped out to meet him.

Roy tangled his hands together. "He's awake. And he's mad. When are you coming to get him?"

"Before noon."

Roy didn't like the answer. "Do I send the bill to the City Council or the marshal's office?"

"Send it to the Etcheverrys."

Another answer he didn't like. His face screwed up in distaste. "Very well."

"Thanks for the update, Roy."

Roy scurried away. Zestrum entered the sheriff's office.

"How's the patient?" Bodie asked.

"Awake and angry." Zestrum secured the new front door.

"Figures." Bodie regarded the tall stack of papers on the desk. He looked at his deputies, sitting around the office. "Long night, boys."

They nodded.

"Full of adventure," Louisiana chimed.

"This'll take a lot of riffraff off the street," Puzzle said cheerfully. "I think McConnell is gonna miss the business, though."

"Angie Etcheverry will have to hire new hands to manage the place," Bodie said.

"Johnny's gonna need to grow up fast," Zestrum said.

"That punk?" Puzzle shook his head, scoffing. "He'll be avoiding chores and leaving it to his sister."

"Not if he wants to earn that respect he keeps demanding," Zestrum said.

"Can't worry about the kid," Bodie said grimly. "And we ain't done yet, boys. The marshal ain't due till noon. We gotta keep this lot under lock and key three more hours."

"Is the marshal van big enough to accommodate this many?" Zestrum asked.

"Don't know what vehicle they're sending," Bodie said. "I guess I should've requested the extra-large wagon."

They chuckled with black humor.

Bodie flipped a page onto the stack. "I asked Tandy to rig up something just in case."

Puzzle looked up from his broom. "What happened to ya, Mitch?"

"It's a long story," said Bodie. "When I finished my rounds, I stopped by home to feed my dog. He wasn't interested in eating but kept trying to go upstairs. I took care of things quiet."

"Can I go take a picture for my wall?"

"I need you here, Puzzle. Do that later."

A bang on the door triggered them to full alert. Louisiana, Edwards, and Zestrum reached for their weapons. Bodie drew his .38 to the ready. Rifle in hand, Puzzle waited for a nod from the sheriff, then opened the peephole cover.

"Let me in, Sheriff, I need to see my Pa."

Puzzle glanced at Bodie. "Angie."

Bodie holstered his weapon. "Let her in."

The others held weapons ready while Puzzle admitted the woman.

Angie looked like she'd rode in fast and hard from her ranch, her windblown hair and rumpled buckskin vest and skort coated in dust. She confronted the sheriff over his desk. "Why are my father and brother in jail?"

"Your father and brother and their hired reprobates tried to burn down the jail this morning," Bodie said.

She glanced toward the porch as if recalling the blackened sidewalk and posts she'd walked past, then glared at him. "I demand you release them so they may consult with our attorney."

"Mr. Judd will have to come here, ma'am. And he'll have to get here before the marshal. They're going to be arraigned before the federal judge, in federal court."

"Judge Roberts can handle arraignment and set bail."

"There's no bail, ma'am. Your father hired a man to murder me in my house. He paid and directed men and women to attack this law office. Folks died. He's facing charges for that in Steelreach."

Her delicate features screwed up in defiance. "The Consortium will hear about this."

"I expect they will. Feel free to lodge complaints, Ms. Etcheverry. In the meantime, you might want to see about hiring some new ranch hands to tend your spread."

Her eyes flashed red hot venom. She launched out through the front door that Puzzle opened in the nick of time.

Puzzle shut the door and looked at Bodie. "Think she's mad, Sheriff?"

Bodie gave a mirthless laugh.

Louisiana glared toward the inner door. "Do we have to feed these guys, too?"

"It's past 9," Bodie said sternly. "Their next meal's coming at 11."

"From Pete?" Edwards asked.

"Slade's. We'll send over an order." Bodie scribbled a note and handed it to Louisiana. "Deliver this and do a perimeter check."

Louisiana raised his eyebrows. "Should I send the coroner over to your place?"

"Yeah. And tell Adams at the mercantile that I need a new mattress."

Louisiana snorted and departed with his errands.

CHAPTER 26 – AND NOW THE SPIN

Zestrum sat guard at the inner door leading to the cells, rifle within quick reach. Bodie filled out paperwork at his desk while Edwards stood watch on the roof. Louisiana returned and posted himself on the porch. Puzzle swept the floor relentlessly.

While the majority of the troublemakers—and the leaders—were in custody, they had no idea how many of those cowborgs hiding in the shadows had slipped away back to the ranch.

Around 10 Angie Etcheverry returned with Ephraim Judd, Esquire to confer with Claude.

"I need to consult with my client in private," Judd said, glancing toward the door leading to the crowded cells.

"You'll have to consult in the cell," Bodie said.

"That's not proper procedure, Sheriff." Judd handed over legal papers. "Here's my request to speak to my client in a clean private space to discuss his situation."

Bodie glared at the papers. "These are extraordinary circumstances, Mr. Judd. I'm exercising the Manfred Law to supersede procedure. You'll have plenty of time to confer with your client after he's in Steelreach."

"I must object, Sheriff Bodie." He handed over another writ. "In anticipation of your refusal, I filed these papers with the court to demand you comply with my request." He folded his hands together over the handle of his briefcase. "Judge Roberts has made a room available at the courthouse."

"You want me to form an escort to take him one block over for a private word?"

"I so request, Sheriff."

"I'll have to cuff and shackle him. You want to parade him down the street like that in front of the whole town?"

Judd raised his chin. "If you desire to make a spectacle of an upstanding citizen of the community, that's your choice. I'm certain the voters of Copperbank will remember your actions on this day."

"I'm sure they will." Bodie glared, contemplated, and decided. "Well. Zestrum, Louisiana, you feel like taking a walk down to the courthouse?"

Louisiana rose from the chair on the porch. "I can always use a stroll."

"Then you will prepare my client for his interview at the courthouse. I shall wait." Judd stepped aside and assumed a statue pose.

Angie radiated triumph in forcing the sheriff to buckle to her demands.

Puzzle jingled the keys while he unlocked the inner door, then the cell door. Louisiana held his gun ready, angled to let Angie and Judd know he wasn't above shooting them.

Zestrum and Bodie provided backup with rifles as Claude exited the cell into the office. Puzzle secured the cell and the inner door.

Angie almost rushed to her father, then restrained herself. Claude gave her a reassuring look. Zestrum applied handcuffs and shackles.

"You see how the law treats an upstanding citizen," Claude said to his attorney.

"Indeed," said the stoic Judd.

"This is a disgrace," Angie said.

"Tell your friends," Claude told his daughter.

"I certainly will." She pulled out a camera and took a picture. Puzzle did likewise. "I'm gonna make a poster of this."

Zestrum pulled his charred hat off the hook as he headed toward the door.

Angie stared at him. "Nice hat."

"Your Pa owes me a new one," he said.

Zestrum and Louisiana flanked the rancher and escorted him out onto the street. Zestrum was not surprised to find Johnny hovering nearby, watching critically.

Everyone stopped their business to watch Etcheverry be escorted to the courthouse. Angie and Judd walked with stern expressions. Johnny trailed behind Zestrum.

At the courthouse, the bailiff opened the door. In the lobby, Judd gestured toward an office at the side.

"Judge Roberts has graciously allowed us to meet here." The attorney waited for Claude, Angie, and Johnny to enter the room, then turned to the deputies. "You may wait here." He unceremoniously slammed the door.

Zestrum and Louisiana shared a cynical look. *Humans!* And sat in chairs in the lobby. They heard footsteps on the sidewalk and a conversation with the bailiff.

Harris Black marched into the lobby. "Deputies, good morning. I wonder if I might ask a few questions about last night's events?"

Louisiana squinted at him. "And who are you?"

"Harris Black of *The Copperbank Sentinel.*" At their blank faces, he enunciated as if addressing infants. "The newspaper. Would you tell me what happened? The public has a right to know."

The deputies exchanged a look, then glared at him.

"We can't rightly say," Louisiana said. "It was dark."

"Really dark," Zestrum said.

Black draped his scowl with an unctuous smile. "According to my sources, you gentlemen were on the roof of the building, at a vantage point with a good view of the street and buildings across the way. What did you see last night that prompted you to open fire?"

"We saw the street and the buildings across the way," Louisiana said, feigning obtuseness.

Zestrum remained deadpan. "The street. Buildings."

Black's eyes narrowed as he tried to determine if they were mocking him. "You have over a dozen people locked up in the jail. What happened?"

"You'd have to ask the sheriff," Louisiana said.

"Or the mayor," Zestrum said.

"You're eyewitnesses. You're *participants*. You saw everything that happened out there."

"It was dark," Louisiana repeated.

"Really dark," Zestrum said.

Black's scowl deepened. "Listen, deputies, I can make you look good or I can make you look bad in my story. Which do you prefer?"

"Don't mention us at all," Louisiana said.

"You want me to rely on hearsay when you can provide facts?"

"Talk to Sheriff Bodie," Zestrum said.

The editor sniffed with dissatisfaction and trounced out of the lobby.

"He'll probably spell my name wrong," Louisiana said.

Zestrum snorted and settled in his chair. "That's a good thing! I 'spect the headline will be 'Mad borgs go on murderous rampage.'"

A half hour passed. Then the door opened and Judd appeared. "Deputies, you may take custody of my client."

Claude Etcheverry canted his head at an arrogant angle. Angie looked livid. Johnny looked perplexed. He glanced at Zestrum for guidance.

Zestrum gave the boy a steady look, then addressed his father. "Let's go, Mr. Etcheverry."

Zestrum and Louisiana returned Claude to the jail. Angie, Johnny, and Judd followed.

Out in the open like this, someone might take a potshot at the rancher. Or attempt to take him out of their hands.

Puzzle stood on the corner, rifle in hand, observing the crowd. On the jailhouse roof, Edwards had a bird's eye view through his rifle scope. On the porch, Bodie held a rifle.

Zestrum scanned the faces—curious, amazed, amused—and recognized folks he'd seen in the saloon, the bank, the hotel.

Farmers and shopkeepers crammed the sidewalks and spilled out onto the street, curious about the promenade through town.

This was most likely the first time citizens saw Claude Etcheverry in police custody.

On the stoop of the Dual Majesty, McConnell smoked a cigar while his employees craned for a look. Victoria Barkley, wearing a bright yellow day dress, met Zestrum's eyes, a hint of worry in her face.

Zestrum saw Jessica Colton among a group at the post office. She was looking toward him—at his hat. When their eyes met, she lowered her chin a fraction. He nodded slightly to her, then surveyed the vicinity.

In front of the Assessor's Office, Gerald Nowlin observed with a smug expression, delighted to see his rival in chains. Rachel watched with curiosity.

They ushered Etcheverry into the sheriff's office. Louisiana and Edwards put Claude back in his cell.

At the threshold, Zestrum blocked Judd, Angie, and Johnny. "You might want to wait with your lawyer at his office for the duration."

"I prefer to stay with my father," Angie said.

"It might be safer to wait with your lawyer at his office for the duration."

She bestowed a defiant look. "Are you saying you can't maintain the peace and keep my father safe while he's in your custody?"

"I'm saying you might want to wait with your lawyer at his office for the duration."

His unwillingness to say anything else angered her. "You keep repeating yourself, deputy."

"It's a bad habit, ma'am."

Bodie spoke up from behind Angie. "He's right, ma'am. The jail is no place for a lady and a boy."

Johnny glowered under that appellation.

Angie clenched her jaw, annoyed. "You're barring me from a public space?"

"It's a safety issue, ma'am," said Bodie.

Judd touched her arm, a signal to cease the argument.

"I see." She swept Bodie with disdainful eyes, then turned the disdain on Zestrum. "And to think my father considered hiring you. You're an ungrateful wretch." She turned. "Come on, Johnny." And she stormed off.

Johnny glanced at the deputies, then followed her.

"I shall return when the marshal arrives," Judd said, and he sauntered toward his office.

Louisiana and Edwards secured the inner door. Louisiana climbed up onto the roof with his rifle.

Puzzle joined Bodie and Zestrum on the porch. "She don't look happy."

"She ain't." Zestrum scanned the crowd. "It's stormy out here."

"They ain't never seen Etcheverry senior in jail before." Puzzle surveyed the folks. "They might be worried about who's next."

"They might think twice about breaking the law," Bodie said.

Puzzle cackled. "Wouldn't count on it."

Zestrum leaned in, whispering to Bodie. "I caught wind of some unfriendlies in the shadows.

Bodie nodded and went back to assessing the extensive damage to the building—and his scorched rocking chair. There were holes in the backrest slats. "They shot up my rocker."

"Charred it up real good, too," Puzzle said.

Bodie gave him a baleful look and shuffled into the office. Puzzle limped in after and shut the door.

Zestrum remained on the sidewalk with his rifle in hand.

* * *

At 11:30 Everett Slade and his two daughters delivered lunch in several large baskets.

"Set them right there," Zestrum said, supervising as they placed the baskets on the charred walkway. He knocked a signal on the front door.

Edwards inspected the baskets for contraband, then Puzzle hauled them inside. Puzzle sorted out bowls and cups for each prisoner. Edwards distributed the meal through the horizontal gaps in the barred walls.

"What the hell is this?" Claude Etcheverry bellowed.

"That's what public funds cover," Edwards said.

"What the hell is this?"

Puzzle stared at the goo. "I'm guessin' it's lunch. That's just a guess, mind you."

"I hear the food's better in federal prison." Edwards finished handing out bowls and returned to the outer office. He closed the door.

Puzzle peered into the bowl in his hand. "What do *you* think this is?"

Edwards looked at his bowl. "Don't recognize it."

Puzzle shivered with distaste. "Slade must really hate the Etcheverrys. I think I'll wait till the marshal claims his prize." He set the bowl in the nearest Slade basket.

"Gonna be a while yet," Bodie said. But when he looked inside his bowl, he pushed it away. "Maybe I'll wait, too."

Zestrum checked Jessica's basket and found two dozen oatmeal cookies wrapped in waxed paper. He handed them out to his companions. The nuts and raisins would provide protein and carbs to power through till one o'clock.

Louisiana climbed down from the roof to take a cookie. "You should probably know that Harris Black of *The Copperbank Sentinel* accosted us at the courthouse."

Bodie eyed him. "He was here, too. Vulture. I told him he'd get the story later."

"Maybe it'd be best to put the facts out there," Zestrum said. "So the locals don't get the idea we're persecuting an important citizen."

"I'm initiating a news blackout until these prisoners are in the marshal's custody. I'm formulating a statement right now." His voice dropped. "Seeing as the mayor is out of town and all, 'fishing.'" The sheriff tapped his pencil against the paper on his desk.

"Musta caught his limit by now," Puzzle said. "'Course, then he'll set to gutting and boning them. Maybe frying 'em up. Mounting the biggest one on a trophy."

"We might want to clear Main Street," Edwards said. "For the marshal's van."

"That's a good idea," said Bodie. "Puzzle, you and Edwards set up bollards and block off the whole street to the edge of town. A nice, clear straight shot to the jail."

"Pleasure to accommodate the order, Sheriff." Puzzle rooted around in the closet, picking up a roll of yellow Do Not Cross tape and dragging out a stack of neon orange bollards. He set the bollards in front of Edwards.

Edwards glared. "You expect me to carry those things?"

"You're the younger, stronger, meaner of us. I'll string the tape." Puzzle hobbled out the door.

Edwards looked askance at the sheriff. Bodie shrugged. With a grunt, Edwards lifted the stack and lumbered out the door. Louisiana chuckled.

"Go give him a hand," Bodie said.

Louisiana reacted as if ordered to latrine duty. "What?"

"They can't work and keep watch at the same time." The sheriff gave him a steady look.

Louisiana's face wrinkled in aversion as he marched out of the office.

Bodie returned his attention to his statement. "Don't rightly remember the order of all the little details." He glanced at Zestrum. "How about if you review it when I'm done?"

"Of course."

"I'm afraid you're getting a bad impression of Copperbank. Nothing but shooting and murder since you got here."

"Same as the place I left."

Bodie chuckled sardonically. "Humans demand heaven to live in and then do their best to turn it into hell."

"Fighting keeps us employed."

"Fighting makes us tired. Me, anyway."

"You'd get bored right quick without it."

A knock at the door. Zestrum opened the peephole cover.

"Deputy Doniphon?" said the narrow-nosed man dressed in black. He wore a tall black silk hat. "I'm Benjamin Rogers. Coroner."

Zestrum waited for Bodie's acknowledgment before opening the door.

Rogers offered the sheriff a folder. "Preliminary report on the man found in your house. Samuel Coleridge, 35, late of Indigenous Rock, employed by Claude Etcheverry six months ago to work the ranch and other assorted duties. Died of a blow to the head, administered by a blunt instrument."

"I left the truncheon on the bed beside him."

"A perfect fit for the dent in his skull. He died instantly." Rogers glanced at Bodie. "Effectively done, sheriff."

He grimaced. "Did you haul him out of there?"

"He's at my headquarters in a drawer. Is there next of kin to claim the body?"

"Haven't the faintest."

"Then we'll plant him in the pauper's section. With your permission."

Bodie nodded assent. "After the marshal leaves."

"As you say. Bobby is collecting the remains of the newly departed. Let me know if we miss any." Rogers touched his hat at the sheriff, at the deputy, and wafted out like a last wheeze of death.

Zestrum gazed out into the street where Puzzle was busy nailing the yellow tape to posts along the sidewalk, across the intersection to the next corner, and so on. Edwards and Louisiana set bollards at intervals to reinforce the boundary.

"You acquitted yourself damn well this morning," Bodie said, watching him.

Zestrum secured the door and looked at the sheriff. "Old skills."

"You could take the job permanent if you want."

He wasn't certain how to respond to the offer. Flattering, but lawmen had notoriously short lifespans in the Badlands. While he didn't mind helping out an old friend, he wasn't placing himself in permanent jeopardy for strangers.

"Just for your consideration." Bodie focused on the paperwork.

"You looking to retire?"

"Every damn day."

CHAPTER 27 – TUMBLEWEED WAGON

Edwards and Puzzle completed the barricades and stood on the opposite side of Main Street from the sheriff's office, rifles ready. Zestrum stood at the open door of the jail, cradling his rifle.

Perched on the roof, Louisiana called down through the closet. "I see the convoy coming in."

Bodie rose from the desk and stepped out front to greet the incoming convoy. Puzzle scanned the terrain and crossed the street to stand near him.

From the porch, they saw dust rising in the distance from the approaching caravan. Then they heard the thunder of hooves and rolling wheels as the entourage appeared at the far end of Main Street. Civilians filled the sidewalks, curious but keeping behind the yellow tape.

Harris Black of *The Copperbank Sentinel* tested the limits of the tape, chronicling the event in his little notepad for the evening edition.

The entourage resembled a circus parade arriving in town. Two deputies on horseback rode at the lead, then a cook's wagon, a prison wagon, and a remuda and wrangler followed. There were two prisoners in the tumbleweed wagon, their faces set in permanent glowers as folks jeered at them.

With the road cleared, they stopped in front of the sheriff's office. One marshal dismounted while the other remained on his horse, observing the surroundings. Puzzle waved to the man on horseback, who lifted a hand in response.

Bodie greeted the marshal with a handshake. "Reeves."

"Bodie." The marshal was a cyborg, blue-eyed, dark-skinned, tough as leather. He wore plenty of firepower in his holsters.

Bodie gestured toward Zestrum. "Zestrum, this here's Deputy Marshal Bass Reeves. Deputy Zestrum Doniphon."

Reeves and Zestrum shook hands. Neither thought the other looked like his reputation.

"Nice to meet you," Zestrum said.

"Likewise." Reeves indicated the other marshal. "Deputy Marshal Virge Madsen."

Madsen raised a hand in a brief greeting. Zestrum reciprocated.

Reeves addressed Bodie. "I hear you got a prisoner in need of a federal trial."

"I got twenty prisoners in need of a federal trial," said Bodie.

Reeves' eyebrows arched in conjecture. "Twenty?"

"Well twenty-four, but four can't be moved yet. It seems the other twenty-three were going to miss Etcheverry and did their best to persuade us to let him go before you got here."

"Looks like they did not succeed." The marshal regarded the singed sheriff's office, then glanced at the tumbleweed wagon parked in the middle of the road. "I'll have to lease a wagon and team to haul them."

"We got the livery fixing one up."

Reeves turned to Madsen. "Check out the vehicle."

Madsen set off toward the livery.

Reeves looked at Bodie. "Let's get started filling out those John Doe arrest warrants for Judge Apatow."

The two men went into the sheriff's office. Zestrum stayed on the sidewalk, monitoring the crowd that gathered to see the prisoners. Edwards and Puzzle ordered people back to a safe distance.

The wrangler drove the herd of horses into the corral at the livery for water and fodder. Once the animals were fed, the wrangler set to the task of changing out the horses on the two wagons.

The cook hopped down from the cook wagon and ambled to the General Store on the next block. Ten minutes later, he emerged carrying a sack. Two grocers loaded more sacks into his wagon.

The cook used the stopover to feed his crew. He folded down the hinged board at the rear of the wagon to make a tabletop and prepared lunch from the supplies in the chuck box.

The two prisoners in the tumbleweed wagon glared daggers at the gawking onlookers.

Deputy Marshal Madsen returned, followed by a sturdy freight wagon fashioned into a traveling jail on the fly, with a frame of bars secured onto the bed. Madsen proceeded to the chuck wagon for his ration.

Bodie called out. "Doniphon."

Zestrum went to the open door of the office and saw the sheriff and Deputy Marshal conferring over the papers. "Sheriff?"

"Cover for Louisiana. I need a word with him."

Zestrum went up the ladder where Louisiana was holding his rifle at the ready. "Sheriff wants a word."

Louisiana snapped to attention. "Me?"

"Yep."

Louisiana went down the ladder into office. Zestrum focused his mods on their voices and eavesdropped on the conversation.

"Deputy Marshal Reeves inquires if I might spare a deputy to accompany him to Steelreach with the load of prisoners." Bodie gave Louisiana the iron eye.

Louisiana seemed simultaneously pleased with and inconvenienced by the idea. "I only started work this week, Sheriff."

"And proved your worth. It's a week-long trip out and back. They're going direct to Steelreach now the two wagons are full."

Bodie and Reeves were waiting for an answer.

Louisiana tucked his chin and took on the challenge. "Well, sure. I'll go."

"Pay's $5 a day, six cents a mile, and $3 per prisoner delivered alive," said Reeves. "Since we got twenty from here, that's quite a payload."

"If they survive the trip," Bodie said.

Reeves laughed dryly without cracking a smile.

"I'll get my horse." Louisiana started toward the door.

Bodie glanced at the stack of John Doe warrants. "Louisiana." The red borg stopped at the doorway. Bodie looked at Reeves. "If you don't mind, we'll ride you escort to the county line."

Reeves inclined his head, then nodded agreement.

"Bring all our horses except Puzzle's."

"Sure thing." Louisiana hustled toward the stable.

Reeves studied the sheriff. "Expecting trouble?"

"Etcheverry's got a private army up at his place. A calculated show of force might discourage the rest of 'em."

Reeves agreed. "I value your advice, Sheriff."

Bodie handed the warrants to the Deputy Marshal. "Claude is the most commanding, but Chris is the most violent. The rest follow their lead."

"I'll keep the Etcheverrys separated."

"There's a third one at the doctor's office. He's a piece of work."

"Can he stand?"

"Gonna have to check with Doc Hartman on that." Bodie called up to Zestrum. "Zestrum. Would you be so kind as to fetch the doctor for consultation?"

"Sure." Zestrum headed down the ladder and hightailed it to the medical man's office. He caught the spindly assistant helping an elderly woman out of the main examination room into the waiting area.

Roy froze like a deer in torchlight. "You again."

"Doctor in?"

Roy nodded toward the inner office and proceeded to help the woman to the door.

Zestrum knocked on the open door and stepped into the sanctum.

Doc Hartman was writing notes in a chart. He closed the folder and looked at the deputy. "Are you here to collect Gabe?"

"Yep. Sheriff would like to consult with you on his condition."

"I'd be delighted."

The doctor accompanied Zestrum to the sheriff's office. Bodie and Reeves paused in exchanging papers to speak with the medical man.

"He's awake and there's no sign of infection, but he oughta be lying down for the next few days," said Doc Hartman.

"He can do that in the wagon," Reeves said. "Deputy Marshal Madsen is a trained medic, in case there's a problem."

Bodie handed Zestrum the applicable warrant. "Retrieve him."

At the doctor's office, Doc Hartman led the way to the surgery suite where Gabriel was recovering.

Gabriel was awake and angry. "You the one that chained me up?" He rattled his bound wrist against the bedpost.

Zestrum took out his key. "I'm here to take you to the marshal."

"I ain't going anywhere with you."

Zestrum held up the arrest warrant with Gabriel's name on it. "This here says you will."

"I don't recognize that document, borg."

"Your illiteracy doesn't factor into the matter." Zestrum unlocked the cuff. "Now, I can let you walk out there like a man or I can truss you up and cart you out like a side of beef."

"I'll walk." Gabriel sat up on the bed and swayed.

Laboriously the man got to his feet and stumble-staggered through the receiving area to the front door. On the sidewalk he leaned against a post, noticing the folks behind the yellow Do Not Cross tape. "What is this?"

"Apparently the arrival of the marshal is cause for public holiday." Zestrum motioned for him to move along.

Scowling, Gabriel trundled to the marshal's convoy. Doc Hartman hovered at his side, watchful of the patient. Zestrum escorted the prisoner, watchful of the citizens.

Madsen directed Gabriel to the second wagon. "You'll go here."

Doc Hartman assisted him into the improvised barred wagon.

"This ain't even a real transport," Gabriel complained.

"It's been conscripted all legal." Madsen shackled him to a hook bolted in the floor and locked the hatch.

Doc Hartman consulted with Madsen on the nature of the man's wounds and medicinal treatment.

The cook finished lunch cleanup, rinsing dishes, storing them in the chuck box, then lifting the board to clamp everything into place. An ingenious device, a chuck wagon.

Louisiana returned on horseback with a handful of other horses. Stable boy Charlie rode the tallest horse, leading three others by lead ropes. Louisiana signaled for Charlie to stay put and drew his rifle.

Bodie stepped outside with his rifle. "Time to move the prisoners," he told Puzzle and Zestrum. "Puzzle, you ain't going."

"Now see here, Mitch–"

"I got four prisoners that can't be moved. How much you wanna bet someone tries to move them before we get back?"

"Yeah, but–"

"Is Ethan up to the job?"

Puzzle sucked in a breath to speak, paused, and quieted. "All right, Sheriff."

The prisoners made the exodus from the sheriff's office in a single file, shackles or zip ties on ankles and wrists. Madsen and Reeves directed eight into the first barred coach and the other twelve into the second impromptu vehicle. Those men had to step around Gabriel to sit on the benches lining the interior. Gabriel was lying on a bedroll in the center, warning them to watch their feet. Madsen locked each prisoner to the floor at the ankle.

Doc Hartman monitored his patient until Madsen locked the cage door.

Ephraim Judd, Esquire spoke to Claude Etcheverry through the bars, assuring him he would meet them at Steelreach for arraignment. Angie reached toward the bars to touch her father's hand.

Reeves blocked her. "No contact, ma'am."

"Surely I can say goodbye to my father," she protested.

"No contact allowed, ma'am, it's the law." He stood in her way and she took a step back, clutching the small knife in her hand out of his sight.

Zestrum saw the knife. He suspected Reeves saw it as well but chose not to confront her. After all, she was having a very bad day. And he sure didn't want to have to add a woman to the group he was taking up to Steelreach.

Plus, Judge Roberts would release her if Bodie locked her up.

Zestrum spotted Johnny behind a barrel in front of the General Store. He'd have a word with him later. Witnessing one's father led away in chains was a hard blow to a young boy.

Harris Black had his little notepad and pencil in hand. "Mr. Etcheverry! You got any words for the press?"

Claude straightened himself as much as his shackles allowed. "I do have a statement for the press—and for the public in general. This is a massive miscarriage of justice formulated by those who seek to harm me and my family. Sheriff Bodie has arrested us on contrived charges due to his well-known prejudice against me. His grudges against my sons are longstanding and well documented in your very newspaper. I welcome my day in Federal Court to tell my truth and prove my innocence. I shall be absolved of these false claims and vindicated for this injustice foisted upon me and my kin. We shall be freed and exonerated."

Harris turned to Gabriel. "Gabe, you got anything to add?"

Gabriel propped himself up to show his face. "My father, my brother, my friends, and I are being victimized at the concerted effort of corrupt local law enforcement. These egregious charges are completely fabricated and constitute a violation of our civil rights as citizens of this country. My father has been victimized for defending his sons against these allegations."

Gabriel had remembered Judd's coaching well.

Harris turned to Chris. "Chris, you want to add to that?"

Chris scowled. "What they said."

Harris was busy scribbling his quotes.

Martha Anderson stood on the sidewalk observing. She stepped forward, causing people to move aside. Harris noticed her and eagerly flipped a page.

Ms. Anderson called out to Claude. "Now you look to be in your rightful place, Mr. Etcheverry. I hope the law sees fit to keep you there a long time."

Claude glared at her. "Ain't no law going to stop me from telling the truth."

"And I'll tell them everything I know about the truth concerning you and your kin." Murmurs of support rippled through the crowd.

Zestrum sensed impending violence.

So did the deputy marshal. Reeves spoke to the cook. "We got everybody fed?"

"Yes, sir. Everything's secured." The cook climbed onto the box of his wagon.

"Let's head out." Reeves mounted up.

At Louisiana's signal, Charlie slid out of the saddle and handed the reins to Edwards.

Puzzle hefted his rifle, surveying the crowd as the caravan prepared to depart.

Martha Anderson spoke quietly to Bodie. "Thank you, Sheriff Bodie."

"Just doing my job, ma'am." But the words helped heal the wound inside.

Edwards, Bodie, and Zestrum mounted their horses and joined the caravan. Madsen gave them the once-over, assessing their levels of assistance. Reeves appeared satisfied with their support.

Zestrum, Edwards, Louisiana, and Bodie rode with the caravan west out of town while Puzzle held down the fort. The wrangler brought the remuda to rejoin the troupe. The locals watched the grim parade.

Zestrum recalled riding the highway into Copperbank and encountering Johnny Etcheverry robbing folks. The kid had turned a corner—but would he stay around that corner now that his father and brothers were behind bars?

The column passed the church and the cemetery. Zestrum noticed Father Monaldi standing beside a fresh grave, his black robe fluttering in the hot breeze. Monaldi tipped his chin to acknowledge the entourage. Zestrum wondered what the man's sermon would encompass next Sunday.

The highway was a long straight road through the Badlands built by cyborgs. Those landscapers burrowed through the Continent and never stopped till they struck the East Seaboard. Then came the railroad, running parallel a hundred miles north. Zestrum figured eventually the engineers would connect these trunk lines with branches and spurs to facilitate civilization. Though the Consortium had no plans to develop the Interior, speculators did. There were enough emancipated cyborgs desperate for work to staff the formidable project.

Not me. I've got a farm. And a future here.

He pulled his mind to business.

The highway appeared clear, but there were those lines of mature eucalyptus trees on either side, and shadows wavered among the shade. All the deputies carried their rifles across their saddles at the ready. Staying vigilant and alert was wearing after a few hours, which made one vulnerable.

The prisoners were loud and obnoxious now that they were on their way to justice. Many complaints, curses, vows to exact vengeance on the law enforcement officers. No doubt Madsen and Reeves would recall each one for the magistrate to add to the charges. Threatening the lives of federal marshals was a felony.

Maybe these hired thugs didn't know that.

Louisiana and Reeves rode at the front while Madsen and Edwards rode at the back ahead of the remuda. Zestrum and Bodie moved alongside as extra eyes, pausing to fall back to the rear of the line, then trotting to the front.

They approached the fork in the road a few miles from the signpost indicating the county line. One road led north to Steelreach. The other led west to the coastline–the road Zestrum had taken to reach Copperbank.

Bodie and Zestrum came up beside Reeves.

"Thanks for the hand," said Reeves.

"See ya next time," said Bodie.

Louisiana waved to the sheriff. Bodie and Zestrum reined over to the side under one of those expanding trees, letting the caravan roll past. Madsen followed the improvised tumbleweed wagon ahead of the chuck wagon. Edwards stopped on the other side of the highway. The chuck wagon rolled by, then the remuda. The wrangler flicked his hand in farewell.

The sheriff and deputies gathered together in the middle of the highway and watched the dust rise in the wake of the caravan. The noise of angry men, rolling wheels, and hoofbeats faded in the afternoon heat.

Bodie visibly relaxed for the first time in days. "Well, it looks like—"

Blasts of gunfire echoed off the distant hills. The sheriff and deputies spurred their horses forward, keeping to the shade to obscure their approach.

The wrangler scattered the horses into the scrub brush at the left. The marshals used the stalled wagons as shields as bushwhackers fired on them from behind boulders and trees. Reeves was near the front wagon, Madsen at the chuck wagon. Louisiana skittered into the row of trees at the right.

Bodie and his deputies hopped off their horses to infiltrate on foot, carefully pinpointing the placement of the attackers. In the lead, Bodie held up five fingers, indicating he'd counted that many on the left side of the road. He signaled for Edwards and Zestrum to move forward.

Edwards and Zestrum used the thick trees as cover. They verified the attackers' placement and made their way toward the nearest one.

Reeves stepped beside the lead tumbleweed wagon and the gunfire stalled. Whoever was firing didn't want to hit the prisoners.

"Step away from the wagon, Marshal!" called one of the snipers.

"Stand down or pay the price," Reeves called back.

"Open the door and empty the wagon."

"Not within my purview."

A single bullet fired into the side of the wagon, splintering wood. The prisoners inside flinched to the ends of their shackles.

"We're not afraid to shoot you, Marshal!"

"You should be." Reeves aimed and fired into the brush. Somebody grunted in pain.

More gunshots. Reeves ducked down and returned fire.

Zestrum and Edwards came up behind a gunman and silently took him out. They proceeded toward the next shooter.

On the right side of the highway, Louisiana tracked the nearest gunman and shot him, then searched for the next.

Edwards stumbled over a tangle of deadwood on the ground. A gunman whirled around and pointed his gun at him. Zestrum shot the gunman and snatched up his weapon. Edwards thanked Zestrum with a nod.

Bodie zeroed in on the ringleader and moved through the brush to get behind him. The man popped up intermittently to take aim and fire at Reeves. When he popped up next, Bodie shot him dead.

Edwards spotted another man moving in the trees and fired his rifle. A gunshot ahead spooked him and he crept forward, rifle at his eye to fire. Louisiana appeared, holding his rifle at his eye. When they recognized each other, they lowered their weapons.

Edwards looked annoyed. "Damn near shot you."

"Damn near shot *you*."

Rustling in the brush between them made them both swing their weapons and shoot. The last gunman sprawled to the ground, dropping his pistols.

"All clear," Bodie called from the left.

"Clear," Louisiana called from the right.

The marshals and deputies dragged the bodies into a line at the edge of the road and assembled for debriefing beside the chuck wagon. The wrangler retrieved the scattered horses.

"Who are those guys?" said Edwards.

"I don't recognize any of them," said Bodie.

"I know 'em." Deputy Marshal Reeves looked at the tumbleweed wagon. "Relatives of the prisoners we picked up two days ago." He called to the prisoners. "Well, Clem, looks like your brothers got a little more than they asked for."

"You mean they was trying to get *them* out?" Edwards jabbed a thumb at the two original prisoners.

"Clem and Delroy there have a big family," Deputy Marshal Madsen said.

"Little smaller now," said Reeves.

Louisiana glanced at Claude. "Disappointed, Mr. Etcheverry?" The curses resumed.

Bodie smirked and turned to Reeves. "I'll send the undertaker out to collect them."

"Much obliged," said Reeves. "Wouldn't want to have to haul them three days."

Edwards grimaced. "Not in this heat."

Reeves faced Bodie. "And I thank you again, Sheriff." He stuck out a hand and Bodie shook it firmly. "We'll be on our way." He signaled and the entourage continued toward Steelreach.

Zestrum, Edwards, and Bodie watched the wagons roll into the distance. The sound of hoof beats and wheels gradually faded to quiet afternoon. The deputies stood a long moment, taking inventory of the past 24 hours. Then they rode to town. At the livery, they turned their horses over to the stableboys. Puzzle met them at the corner.

"Got a story for ya, Puzzle, but not this minute," Bodie said.

"I can wait a bit."

Bodie gazed in the direction they'd just come from. "It's good to have them on their way."

"How long before they're back?" Edwards said.

"At least a month. It'll take that long to process them before the judge."

"He's a hanging judge," Puzzle said.

"He's only hanged about 35 in the past five years," Bodie said. "The rest he's sent to federal prison or the work farm."

Puzzle giggled. "Can you picture Claude Etcheverry on a work farm?"

Edwards laughed. Zestrum smiled.

Bodie broke a smile for the first time today. "He'll be king of the dunghill in no time, I imagine."

They laughed a little easier, releasing days of tension.

"Well," Edwards said. "I am going to the Opal Café for some real chow. Who's with me?"

"I am," Puzzle chirped.

Edwards gave him a sidelong look. "You look done in, old borg. You need someone to carry you?"

He bristled. "I ain't done in yet, you little punk. I can still beat ya there."

"You with your gammy leg?" Edwards scoffed loudly.

"I'd get me a new one but I'm real attached to this one." Puzzle cackled and hobbled down the street with surprising swiftness.

The other three exchanged amazed looks.

Edwards hurried to catch up. "Hey! Don't want you eating all the ham before I get there."

"I'll leave you a few scraps."

"I don't want your scraps, old man."

"Then you better learn to run." A laugh.

Their banter faded.

Bodie looked at Zestrum. "You done good, Zestrum. I hereby relieve you of duty."

"Thanks, Mitch."

"I'll let the city pay for your lunch." He motioned toward the café.

"Thanks, but I think I'll go on home for a spell after I buy a cold drink."

"And a hat."

Zestrum tugged off his hat and regarded it with disdain. "And a hat."

Bodie's eyes grew amused. "See you around." The sheriff trailed after the other two.

Zestrum pulled a long breath, glanced toward the horizon, then headed for the hat shop.

CHAPTER 28 – A PLACE TO GO

He hadn't realized how exhausted he was till he climbed the steps to the porch of the boarding house. His boots felt unnaturally heavy and his hands clumsy on the doorknob. He gripped the banister to climb the staircase.

"Mr. Doniphon."

He turned to see Jessica Colton in the entry.

She was fixated on his hat. "New hat?"

He pulled his hat off so she could see his head was uninjured. "The old one got a little singed."

She breathed easier. "I hope you didn't eat any of that food that Everett Slade sent over to the jail."

He grinned a lopsided grin. "No, ma'am. I figured I'd clean up a bit and hike on down to the Opal Café."

"You'll do no such thing. You'll eat lunch right here."

"Lunch isn't included."

"You're entitled to two meals. This counts as a meal. You go to your room and I'll bring up a tray."

He was too tired to argue—and he enjoyed her bossy streak. "Yes, ma'am."

The hot meal was infinitely better than anything from Slade or the Opal Café. After eating his fill, Zestrum washed in the upstairs bathroom and flopped onto the single bed in his room for a necessary rest.

The next time he looked at the clock it was 6:30 and the sun was rising in the east.

He entered the dining room as the other tenants were finishing breakfast.

"Mr. Doniphon," said Bainbridge. "Been a while since we saw you at the table."

"It has." He sat in an empty chair.

"We heard you were involved in the gunfight yesterday," said Davis. "And the arrest of the insurgents."

"I was there at the invitation of Sheriff Bodie." He surveyed the platters of food.

"He deputized you, didn't he?" said Cole.

Zestrum glanced at the man, then scooped eggs, sausages, and biscuits onto his plate. "For the duration."

"The marshal had to hire a second wagon," said Davis. "Tandy at the livery said they had to jerry-rig a cage on the bed to handle the overflow."

"I hope it's sturdy enough to hold them all the way to Steelreach," said Bainbridge.

"I wonder who's going to run the ranch while the Etcheverrys are indisposed," said Davis.

Cole sniffled. "They'll be back within a week."

"I don't know," said Davis. "There are pretty serious charges."

"Claude Etcheverry has never been successfully prosecuted," said Cole.

"He's going before a *federal* judge," said Bainbridge.

Cole looked at Zestrum. "What do you think, Mr. Doniphon? Will the charges stick?"

Zestrum picked up his fork. "I have no idea."

The men looked disappointed at the lack of additional gossip.

"If you gentlemen will excuse me." Ms. Nolan left the room.

Jessica entered and her eyes brightened when she saw Zestrum. "Mr. Doniphon. Have you got enough here?"

"Plenty, ma'am," said Zestrum.

She nailed her tenants with a stern look. "Do you gentlemen need anything else?"

The three murmured negatives and departed, leaving the house for their workplaces.

Zestrum gave Jessica a grateful look. "Thank you, ma'am."

"You deserve a bit of quiet." She piled used plates and utensils. "Did you get adequate sleep last night?"

He speared a piece of sausage and smiled slyly. "Plenty, ma'am."

She gave him a long look. "That's good to hear. You take your time." She carried away dishes.

After he finished, he carried his plates into the kitchen.

Jessica was up to her elbows in sudsy water in the sink. "Mr. Doniphon." Her voice softened. "Zestrum."

"Where would you like these, ma'am?" His voice softened. "Jessica."

She pointed a soapy finger at the counter where other dishes awaited cleaning. "You shouldn't have bothered with that."

"It's no bother."

For a moment she studied him, her lips parted, her gray eyes locked on his. "Perhaps you would like to dry." She indicated a dish towel on a rack by the oversized refrigerator.

They worked in amiable silence. He dried and stacked dishes on the counter. She stored the dishes in the cupboards and wiped the counters.

She placed hands on hips, double-checking her domain, then untied the apron and tossed it in a hamper in the laundry room. She faced him. "Your clothes are finally dry."

"That's great to hear."

Her gaze flicked down his body and up to his eyes. "The laundry is in the back. If you'd care to come fetch them?"

"Yes, ma'am."

He followed her through the wide door to the private parlor in the back of the house. She shut the door and locked it.

CHAPTER 29 – GIVING COMFORT TO THE ENEMY

Zestrum walked from Colton House toward Main Street, passing citizens who offered polite greetings. Had his stint as deputy garnered esteem? He'd only been part of a team.

The appreciation was welcome, though.

At the sheriff's office Puzzle was sweeping the floor. Edwards was napping on the bedroll behind the desk. Bodie was writing on ever-present forms.

On the floor near Puzzle's chair stood a four-foot tall poster of a shackled Claude Etcheverry, waiting for mounting on the wall.

"Doniphon," Puzzle chirped, eyes merry. "I knew you'd miss us too much to stay away long." He grinned at his little joke. "I like your new hat."

Zestrum cocked his head a fraction. "I thought the old one was a little worn."

"You mean warm?" He cackled. "Your old hat told a story." He shuffled the broom along the baseboards.

Zestrum set the badge on the desk. "Forgot to give this back."

Bodie peered at him. "Sure you don't want to keep that in your back pocket?"

He wasn't sure Jessica would like that. And he had a contract with Nowlin.

Puzzle leaned on the broom. "Nothing better than being a deputy. You got land here so we know you ain't leaving."

Bodie waited for an answer.

"I'll be around if you need a hand in the future," said Zestrum.

"You got pay coming for your time on the job." Bodie's eyes twinkled.

Zestrum noted the man's incentive with a wry look. "I guess I should open an account at the bank."

"You bet you should," Puzzle said. "Rates ain't never been better. Copperbank Credit Union got a whopping 6.75% APY on the checking account balance. Compounded high-interest rates gonna maximize your savings and grow your money faster than you can make coffee."

Bodie and Zestrum looked at him.

"So I done heard." Puzzle snapped his broom into a corner as if extricating a stubborn stain.

"You'd better open that account soon as possible," Bodie said.

Zestrum nodded. "I guess so." He tilted his head toward the interior room. "Are the cells empty?"

"Strangely, yes." Bodie reclined in his chair. "But we do have the four at Doc Hartman's to deal with. Still, we may have entered a new age."

"The mayor even come back to town," Puzzle said, grinning. "Guess he finally caught his quota right after we caught ours."

"Townsfolk seem content, from what I saw," said Zestrum.

"Certain folks were happy to see three Etcheverrys leave." Bodie flipped aside one of the forms. "Others, less so. I can say the Dual Majesty was a lot calmer last night. Nobody got shot or stabbed."

"That's a start." Zestrum thought of Victoria, practically begging him to attend her performance at the saloon.

"Don't know if it'll hold." Worry crossed Bodie's face. "I'd like to see Claude and his kin pay for what they've done in this valley."

"Judge Apatow might hand down a life sentence," Puzzle said.

Bodie gave him a cynical look. "Let's not get our hopes up *that* high, Puzzle."

* * *

Halfway down the block Zestrum heard footsteps and saw Johnny running toward him. The kid abruptly slowed to a brisk walk, feigning nonchalance as if he'd happened upon the cyborg in his daily errands and not been hunting for him.

"Mr. Doniphon."

"Mr. Etcheverry."

"I thought maybe we could talk."

"Sure." He waited for the kid to lead the conversation but instead, Johnny found his boots fascinating and stood shuffling his feet. "Something particular or just general talk?"

Johnny thrust something toward Zestrum.

"What's this?"

"Ten dollars for your new hat. The Etcheverrys always pay their debts."

Zestrum thought about it, then took the money. If the kid wanted to assume his father's debt, he might be growing up.

"I thought maybe you could give me some, uh, advice. About the ranch. I . . ." His shoulders hunched, hands jammed in his pockets, while he struggled to explain the dilemma without sounding incompetent. "We lost a lot of hands when. . . with the . . . the thing the other night. I don't know where to, um, how to, um, replace them with. . ."

"How to hire on good capable wranglers?"

"Yeah. Chris and Gabe always did that." Then he admitted the truth. "I never paid attention."

"Has your sister sent out employment fliers?"

"She's preoccupied with the, uh, lawyer." He squinted, tilting his head. "She's going to Steelreach and told me to take care of it."

It wasn't surprising Angie Etcheverry wanted to attend the trial.

"First thing is advertise in the paper," said Zestrum. "That'll bring in applicants. You review their resumes, check their references, and interview them."

"That sounds, uh, good."

"You want to place the same ad in the local paper as the Coast paper."

"Coast paper?"

"It's a regional newspaper, covers the West Coast. There's lots of folks seeking jobs on the West Coast."

"Oh. Lots." He frowned as if troubled. "That's good."

Zestrum sensed the kid would hire the first thugs that came along just to fill the vacancies. "Would you like me to help you word the ad?"

"That'd be great."

"And maybe help you evaluate the curriculum vitae?"

He sighed in relief. "That'd be real great."

Zestrum contemplated his timeline for today. "Let's go on over and write that up."

The office of *The Copperbank Sentinel* was on Fifth Street. The humorless woman at the desk behind the high counter regarded them curiously as they walked into the reception area.

Johnny planted his palms on the counter. "I need to place an ad."

She set a form on the counter. "Ads cost per word, so keep that in mind." She glanced at Zestrum, then returned to the desk.

Johnny plucked a pencil from the cup on the counter, wrote his name and the ranch address—then looked at Zestrum.

Zestrum picked up a pencil and composed a succinct, precise want ad for a ranch hand on a spread in the Badlands. He knew the coded language cyborgs looked for in job descriptions and he employed those words. Claude's ads specified ranch work, security, and enforcement—which attracted hired guns. The new ad said herding, caring for cattle, and chores around the property.

He had Johnny review the ad.

"All those words?" the kid complained.

"The cost is worth it."

Johnny studied him a long moment before yielding. "Okay." He put the paper on the counter. "This is ready."

The woman calculated the price. "How many days you want this to run?"

Johnny's eyes crept to Zestrum for a hint. Zestrum held four fingers at his side, out of the woman's sight. "Four days," Johnny said.

The woman wrote a receipt. "Your total due."

Johnny pulled out his wallet and paid with crisp bills. Harris Black appeared from a back room. The editor wiped ink off his hands with a smudged cloth as he wandered toward the counter, scrutinizing the two of them.

The woman stamped "Paid" on the receipt and handed Johnny a copy. "This will go in tomorrow's morning edition."

"Thank you," said Johnny.

The woman's eyebrows shot up as if she'd never heard him utter those words. "You're welcome." She sat at her desk.

Harris glanced over her shoulder at the form. "Recruiting new ranch hands?"

"Yeah," said Johnny.

"Glad to see you're taking care of the place. Glad to see you're going to maintain your shipments of supplies to town. Glad to see you're going to continue to publicize your goods and services in the *Sentinel*."

Johnny and Zestrum heard the underlying message—the *Sentinel's* coverage of the events of last evening could go a different way without Claude Etcheverry's advertising dollars.

"We'll do that." Johnny opened the door to leave.

"Good, good." Harris' beady eyes latched onto Zestrum. "I'm still waiting for your exclusive story, deputy. Got a whole column open and ready."

"I ain't a deputy no more." Zestrum touched the brim of his new hat and sauntered outside behind Johnny

On the porch, Johnny spoke quietly. "You ain't gonna tell him more about the—thing, are ya? 'Bout my pa and my brothers' distress?"

"I ain't talked to him. Don't plan to." Zestrum proceeded with business. "Now. Over to the Telegraph Office."

They crossed the street and entered the Telegraph Office, a long nondescript building with a telegraph image burned into the wooden sign above the door.

The vestibule was adorned with photos of the building and employees. Behind the front counter, the space was ringed with workbenches stacked with coils of wire and cable and dozens of mechanical devices—a candlestick telephone, a rotary phone, a touchtone phone with answering machine, a Remington No. 2 typewriter circa 1880, a Rigol Digital Oscilloscope, a 1920s era Underwood typewriter, and an intriguing combination of typewriter and telegraph someone cobbled together.

A clerk was crouched behind the front counter, rummaging through shelves.

"Good morning," said Zestrum.

The clerk popped up—a girl wearing glasses, holding a thick loop of copper wire in one hand and a dongle in the other. She looked to be about fourteen years old.

"We need to send a message to the Coast paper," Zestrum said.

"Outgoing message." She slid a pad of lined paper across to him, then installed the dongle and wire into a calculator.

Johnny watched with fascination, uncertain what she was doing but too embarrassed to ask.

Zestrum wrote the same want ad.

The girl perused the words and calculated the price in her head. "Sixty dollars."

"Sixty dollars?" Johnny looked apoplectic. "That's more than the local paper."

She eyed him without flinching. "Instant communication is expensive."

He looked at Zestrum—got silent confirmation that was fair—and fumed. He laid three twenties on the counter.

The girl smoothed and examined the paper bills as if expecting to find them counterfeit. "Eight nine two seven four. Six zero zero four two. Three three six three six." She smiled. "Full house." She turned to the register.

Zestrum realized she'd interpreted the serial numbers as poker hands. When Johnny gave him a puzzled look, he raised a finger indicating he'd explain later.

"How soon you want this to go out?"

"As soon as you can manage, miss." Zestrum smiled to show there was no pressure.

She sidled to the quadruplex telegraph and donned headphones. She tapped her call sign on the iambic keyer, then keyed the message in rapid-fire Morse code.

Johnny gave Zestrum an amazed look. Zestrum was impressed but not amazed; he'd met telegraphers who could whip out messages at dumbfounding speed.

She listened for an acknowledgment from the other end of the line and signed off. She removed the headphones. "Message sent and received. Anything else?"

Johnny looked stunned. "You sent my message that fast?"

"That fast."

He sneered. "That wasn't worth sixty bucks."

Her eyebrows arched in warning. "Don't think so?"

"No, I don't. Ain't possible to do that that fast."

She smirked. "For you."

"Ain't possible to do that *competent* that fast. You didn't send nothing!"

A world of rage built in the girl's green eyes.

"She sent it," Zestrum said.

Johnny looked at him. "The hell she did. That was two minutes of tapping."

"She transmitted the message."

"How do you know?"

"I read it as she keyed."

Johnny blustered. "That's not possible, that many words that quick."

"Instant communication." She cocked her head and looked at Zestrum. "You read Morse code?"

"Learned it on the railway crew," said Zestrum.

"Consortium?"

"Yeah. Learned it from the telegrapher."

"I learned it from my ma."

Johnny held up a hand, closing his eyes to tether his temper, then glared at the girl with narrowed eyes. "What's your name?"

"Marconi."

Zestrum repressed a laugh.

Johnny obviously had no idea what the name meant in the history of telegraphy. "Marconi what?"

She smirked. "Adeleine."

He leaned ominously over the counter. "Do you know who I am?"

"Says right here John Etcheverry." She pointed at the pad.

"Do you know who my *family* is?"

"The Etcheverrys?" She seemed singularly indifferent to his clan.

His cheeks flushed red with indignation but before he could speak—

She turned her eyes on Zestrum. "What's your name?"

"Zestrum Doniphon. It's a pleasure to meet you, Ms. Adeleine." When she offered her hand, Zestrum shook firmly.

She flattened her palms against the counter and looked at Johnny, amused at his irritation. "You want a receipt or you satisfied I sent your message?"

Johnny glowered. "If Mr. Doniphon says you sent it, you sent it." He spun and headed for the door.

"John."

He stopped at Zestrum's commanding tone.

"You forgot to thank the lady."

He scoffed. "For doing her job?"

"For giving you superior service."

Johnny chafed—but he'd asked for advice on how to gain respect. He turned to Adeleine. "Thanks, miss. I appreciate your superior service."

"Sure thing, John." She winked, making him angrier.

He stormed out of the building.

Zestrum looked at her. "Thanks for your consideration, Ms. Adeleine."

"You're welcome, Mr. Doniphon. Let me know if you get responses. I like to know my work produces favorable results."

"I will do that." He touched his hat and stepped out onto the porch.

Johnny was pacing on the wooden sidewalk. His indignation wavered when he saw Zestrum's warning expression. "She had no call to talk to me like that."

"She was responding in kind. Something you ain't used to."

"She disrespected me."

"You disrespected *her*. Never disparage a professional doing their job."

"She ain't no professional."

"She sent your message for a fee. That makes her a professional. And you a fool."

He started to argue, then scowled, properly reprimanded. "I'm trying."

"Try harder."

He squirmed. "What do we do now?"

"You check your box at the post office for messages daily. When you get responses, we'll review the letters of interest. Then we'll schedule interviews and chat and see who's who."

Johnny's anger simmered down to gratitude. "Okay. Maybe you could. . . come visit tomorrow? There's some. . . things I ain't sure what to do with."

Ranch chores should have been the first things this kid learned. Was he that helpless without his father and siblings? Or did the ranch hands do everything for that family?

"I can ride out tomorrow morning."

"That'd be great. Thanks. Uh. Um." Again he inspected his boots as if he couldn't compose the proper words. "Do you think we could. . . practice more self-defense? I been practicing falling like you said, but I'm ready for the next lesson."

Zestrum saw how anxiously the kid wanted to learn. "Let's ride out aways to some grass."

"I'll get my horse and meet you at the livery." Johnny hustled off toward wherever he'd tied up his horse.

Zestrum headed toward the livery. He suspected Gerald Nowlin wouldn't be too happy he was assisting Johnny Etcheverry to hire help, but he was freelance and emancipated.

A landowner.

EPILOGUE – NO PLACE LIKE HOME

Zestrum angled the two rocking chairs to face the western sky. He'd repaired the flooring and the rail enclosing the wraparound porch, but there were holes in the roof and the place needed paint. Sunset was about to provide a spectacular show.

Footsteps approached from the house and Jessica joined him on the porch. "That's done."

"You spoil me, Jessica."

"I mean to." She sat in a rocker. "You have a wonderful view."

He sat in the other rocker. "That I do." He was looking at her.

She glanced at her hands folded in her lap. "Now Zestrum. I think you may be contemplating something else."

"I am indeed. And I believe you have similar contemplations."

"I believe I do."

The sun blazed red and orange against the clouds over a ridge of mountains in the distance. In the next quarter hour, the sun sank and the night sky appeared. From the porch, they had a wide view of the heavens.

"So many stars," she said.

"I hope you enjoy this place as much as I do." He contemplated the future. "Once I have steady water, I might take up gardening."

"You'll need help pulling weeds. Weeds are tenacious. Always crowding in where they don't belong."

"I've never been afraid of getting dirty."

"I know."

His face flushed at the memory of spending time in her bathtub. "You are my first houseguest."

"I am flattered."

"Most likely you will be my *only* houseguest." He smiled wryly. "I'm not much of a host. Got no ice box to keep the beer cold."

"There's more to life than cold beer."

They looked at each other.

"Warm brandy?" he said.

She laughed. "I was gonna say something else, but that is true."

"What were you gonna say?"

She rocked the chair, studying the view. "Friendship. Companionship." Her eyes returned to him. "Love."

"All precious."

She sighed. "I haven't felt that in a long time."

"Something else in common."

The silence stretched as crickets began their singsong melody and a wolf howled in the wilderness. More stars flickered to life in the darkening sky. Waves of green and yellow aurora borealis appeared.

"I meant to thank you for showing me the lake, where you plan to build that aqueduct. You were right about the water. It's *cold.*"

"It comes from up above." He gestured toward the purple mountains capped with snowpack.

She looked where he pointed, tilting her head. "So far away. And it took so long for us to *get* to the lake."

"I was going slow for you."

She smirked, then tugged at the knees of her skort and plopped her boots on the top rail as if planting a flag. "I can travel faster than that. I thought you were just slow."

"If you travel too fast, you miss the scenery." His eyes flicked to her calves.

She settled in the rocker, feet on the rail. "That was a winding road."

"Most old roads are winding. When they improve the highway, they'll straighten it."

"I don't reckon how, seeing as there's a river cutting through the canyon."

"We blasted our way through the Striker Range crooked, too. But they're improving the switchbacks. Smoothing the route. We were just the preliminary builders."

She studied him. "Do you miss them?"

He glanced at her. "The Strikers?"

"The comrades. Surely you made lifelong friendships."

"Well, I met a lot of characters, but I don't expect I'll see them again."

"You prefer being alone."

His eyes latched onto her. "Not today."

She smiled, glanced at her feet, busied herself with a wrinkle in her blouse. "I think your stake is quite nice. The house is a little rustic, but. . ."

"I'll renovate that."

"Once you have water, those trees will come right back. And you can plant fruit trees."

"What kind do you recommend?"

"Apricot, peach, apple. And fig."

"Fig?"

"I love figs. They're so hard to come by here. Not many folks like them."

"I'll order some trees from Steelreach."

"Only after you have water. They take a lot of water, fruit trees."

He gazed over the flat land before them. "I guess I'm just gonna have to work harder."

"Work harder?"

He glanced at her, then at the shimmering stars. "Getting that aqueduct completed as quick as possible. The sooner it's done, the sooner I have water, the sooner I can get those fruit trees, the sooner I can. . ."

"I didn't think I had that kind of influence."

He turned the full force of his gaze on her. "You influence everything I do."

"Me?"

"For the first time—in a very long time—I have someone to please besides myself." He leaned closer to her. "I want to please you, Jessica Colton. If it takes a grove of fig trees, I will be planting fig trees in the near future."

She placed her hand on his thigh. "Like I said. I love figs."

He leaned closer and they sealed the bargain with a kiss.

THE END

– GRATITUDE –

Dear Reader,

Although technically we don't truly know if you are a dear, you could be a telemarketer who calls during lunch.

We hope you enjoyed *Rio Cyborg* – Book 1 of *The Copperbank Trilogy* (if you have indeed read it). Your feedback is important to us as making you happy puts raisins in our pantry and we need raisins to make oatmeal cookies.

If you could take a few minutes to leave a review, we would greatly appreciate it. Your input may influence our next book and help our readers (well, our potential readers which actually are our nonreaders) to learn more about us.

A great way for you to learn more about us is to visit our website at **www.cinehunden.com** where you'll find exclusive content and even a free short story just for subscribing.

Our website has vignettes and illustrations for your entertainment. Join us!

~ Terry and Carol

PS: To make the process as frictionless as possible, if your phone is nearby, just grab it and hover over the QR code below.
You can even use the voice-to-text on your phone to speak your review (it points to cinehunden.com/review):

BUT WAIT... THERE'S MORE!

Limited time offer (as far as time can be limited).[1] If you subscribe right now, you will gain access to our short story, ***Puzzle Goes Home***, which takes place in the same universe as *Rio Cyborg*. Visit cinehunden.com/puzzle or capture the QR below on your mobile device.

Just think—you can be among the first to read this soon-to-be-classic companion to the novel. Subscribe now!

~ Terry and Carol

PS: Did you have fun with the last QR Code? If so, we've got one more for you (it will magically transport your phone to www.cinehunden.com/puzzle):

---

[1] We are required by our lawyers (of which we have none) to mention this limited time offer is only limited by the continued existence of humanity, the internet, and time itself.